LILAH

A Forbidden Love, A People's Destiny

LILAH

A Forbidden Love, A People's Destiny

A NOVEL

BOOK THREE OF THE CANAAN TRILOGY

MAREK HALTER

THREE RIVERS PRESS • NEW YORK

Translation copyright © 2006 by Howard Curtis

Sarah excerpt translation copyright © 2004 by Howard Curtis
Reader's Group Guide copyright © 2007 by Three Rivers Press, an imprint of the
Crown Publishing Group, a division of Random House, Inc., New York.
The Crown Reads colophon is a trademark of Random House, Inc.

Published in the United States by Three Rivers Press, an imprint of the
Crown Publishing Group, a division of Random House, Inc., New York.
www.crownpublishing.com

THREE RIVERS PRESS and the Tugboat design are registered trademarks
of Random House, Inc.

Originally published in France by Robert Laffont, Paris, in 2004.
Copyright © 2004 by Éditions Robert Laffont, S.A., Paris.
Originally published in hardcover in the United States by Crown Publishers,
an imprint of the Crown Publishing Group, a division of
Random House, Inc., New York, in 2006.

Library of Congress Cataloging-in-Publication Data
Halter, Marek.
[Lilah. English]
Lilah : a novel / Marek Halter.
I. Title.
PQ2668.A434L5513   2006
843'.914—dc22   2005024241

ISBN: 978-1-4000-5282-0

Printed in the United States of America

*Map by Richard Thompson, based on a series design by Sophie Kittredge
Design by Barbara Sturman*

10 9 8 7 6 5 4 3 2 1

First U.S. Paperback Edition

Then the Lord God said, "It is not good that the man should be alone; I will make him a helper as his partner."

—GENESIS 2:18

If he deserves it, she is a helper; if not, she is against him.

—MIDRASH RABBAH on Genesis 2:18

The fewer dogmas there are, the fewer quarrels;
and the fewer quarrels, the fewer calamities:
if that is not true, then I am wrong.

Religion is established to make us happy
in this world and the next.
What do we need to be happy in the next world?
To be just.

To be happy in this world,
insofar as the poverty of our nature allows it,
what do we need?
To be lenient.

—VOLTAIRE, Treatise on Tolerance, Chapter 21

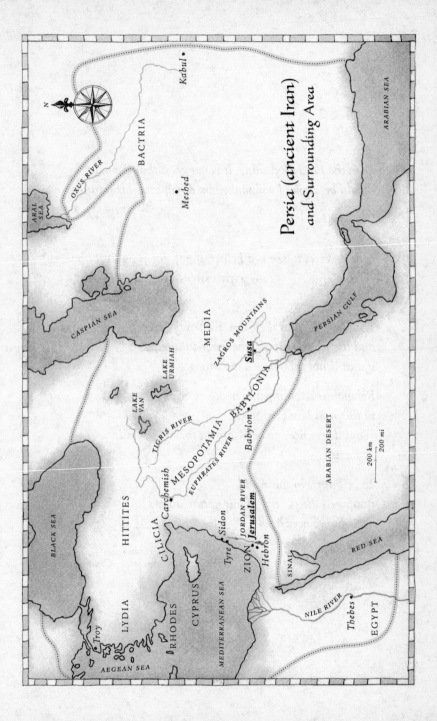

Persia (ancient Iran) and Surrounding Area

LILAH

A Forbidden Love, A People's Destiny

PROLOGUE

Antinoes is coming back.

My heart trembles.

My hand trembles. I hold the stylus tight between my fingers to make sure that the words the camphor ink is laying down on the papyrus are legible.

Antinoes, my beloved, is coming back!

Last night, a messenger in dusty tunic and sandals brought me a wax tablet.

I immediately recognized my beloved's writing.

A sleepless night followed. Tossing and turning on my bed, I pressed the tablet to my breast as if to stamp the words into my flesh.

Lilah, my sweet, my lover, in three days and three nights I shall be with you again. Count the shadows of the sun. I am returning nobler and more victorious! And yet, until I have you in my arms, until my lips have sated themselves on the scent of your skin, I will have achieved nothing in two years of separation.

My heart is beating faster than it does before a battle. Soon, by the will of your God of heaven and that of the mighty Ahura Mazda, god of the Persians, we will at last be man and wife.

All night long, my heart has been drinking in Antinoes' words.

If I close my eyes, I read them within me. If I try to forget them, I hear my beloved's voice whispering them in my ear.

That is my madness. And if I tremble, it is also with fear.

This ought to be the hour of peace. The darkness is receding. All is silent in the house. The handmaids have not yet risen, the fires are not yet lit. The light of dawn is as white as the milk that they say conceals deadly poison at banquets given by the King of Kings.

Man and wife, that was our promise. Antinoes and Lilah!

A children's promise, a lovers' promise!

I remember the time when we were like the fingers of one hand. Antinoes, Ezra, and Lilah. To see one was to see the others. Two boys and one girl, always together. The fact that one was the son of a lord who attended the meals of the Great King and the others the children of exiled Jews mattered little.

The roofs of the upper town of Susa echoed to our laughter. Whenever our mother called us, we heard a single cry: Antinoes, Ezra, and Lilah!

Then my mother's voice fell silent.

My father's voice fell silent.

A deadly disease spread through Susa. It spread through the fields along the River Shaour, it spread as far as Babylon, striking rich and poor alike, not only in Persia, but also in Zion, Lydia, and Media.

I remember the day when Ezra and I, our bodies drained of tears, stood before our mother and father, asleep in death.

We held hands with Antinoes. Our grief was also his. We stood shoulder to shoulder. The three of us had become one, like some strange animal whose limbs had become inextricably entwined.

I remember the scorching summer's day when Antinoes led us into his magnificent home and presented us to his father.

"Father, this is my sister, Lilah, and this is my brother, Ezra. Whatever they eat, I eat. Whatever they dream, I dream. Father, let them come to our house as often as they wish. If you refuse, then I will have no other roof over my head than that of their uncle Mordecai, who has taken them in now that they have neither father nor mother."

Antinoes' father laughed until he could laugh no more. He called the handmaids and told them to bring fruit and cow's milk. When our stomachs were full, we hurled ourselves into the great pools of the house to cool ourselves down. Children are greedy for happiness.

Our days were again carefree. "My brother, Antinoes!" Ezra would cry, and Antinoes would answer, "My brother, Ezra!" Together, they forged swords and bows and javelins in Uncle Mordecai's workshop.

Oh, Yahweh, why must we stop being children?

I remember the day when the games ceased and the laughter trembled at the touch of a caress.

Antinoes, Ezra, and Lilah. Two men and a woman. A new expression in their eyes, an unaccustomed silence on their lips.

The beauty of nights on the roofs of Susa, the beauty of embraces, the pleasure of bodies catching fire like lamp oil too long heated.

The three of us becoming one: that was over now. Now it was Lilah and Antinoes. Lilah and Ezra. Antinoes and Ezra. Lovers and siblings, rage and jealousy.

I remember it well; it churns in my memory like the dark waters of the Shaour in the rainy season.

The handmaids have arisen now. The fires are lit. Soon there will be cries and laughter. It may turn out a fine day, alive with hope and promise.

As I write, my face is reflected in the silver mirror above the writing desk. Antinoes says it is a beautiful face. That my youth is the scent of springtime.

Antinoes loves me and desires me, is generous with words that speak of his love and his desire.

But all I see in the mirror is a furrowed brow and anxious eyes. Is this the face—this sad, preoccupied beauty—that will welcome my beloved when he returns?

Oh, Yahweh, hear the plea of Lilah, daughter of Serayah and Achazya, I who have no other God than the God of my father.

Antinoes is not a child of Israel, but he is loyal to his promise. He wants me for himself alone, as a husband must want his bride.

Ezra will say to me, "Ah, so now you are abandoning me!"

Yahweh, is it not your will that our bodies should grow beyond childhood? That we should become men and women, each with our own breath, our own strength, the joy of our own senses? Is it not your will that a man's caress should delight a woman? Is it not your law that a sister should find other eyes to love than those of her brother, another voice to hear and admire other than that of her brother? Is it not your teaching that a woman should choose a husband according to her heart, as Sarah did, and Rachel and Zipporah, the wives of Abraham, Jacob, and Moses?

Whichever I am faithful to, the other's pain will be just as strong.

Why must I cause pain when my brother and my lover have an equal place in my heart?

Oh, Yahweh, God of heaven, God of my father, give me the strength to find the words to appease Ezra! Give him the strength to hear them.

PART ONE

Two Brothers and a Sister

The Roofs of Susa

I

n his message, Antinoes had not specified the place where they would meet. There was no need.

As she approached the summit of the tower, Lilah's heart began beating louder and louder. She stopped, closed her eyes, put her hand on her stomach, and tried to regain her breath.

It was not because of the dark, narrow staircase. She had found her way again easily enough. She had climbed these brick steps so often that it was no problem to find her footing. No, what made her breathless was the knowledge that Antinoes might be up there, on the terrace, waiting for her.

In a moment, she would see his face again, hear his voice, rediscover his gentle eyes and soft skin.

Had he changed? A little? A lot?

She had often heard women complain that when their husbands returned from the wars, they were like strangers. Even when their bodies were intact, they themselves had become colder, more aloof.

But she had nothing to fear. Antinoes' message was eloquent enough: The man who had written those words had not changed in any way.

She moved the gold and silver fibula that held her veil to her beautiful tunic, and adjusted her belt incrusted with mother-of-pearl. Her bracelets jangled, and the sound echoed like bells against the blind wall of the tower.

Lighthearted and smiling, Lilah climbed the last flight of stairs. The door to the terrace was open. The setting sun was blinding, and she shaded her eyes with her hand.

Nobody here.

She turned, looking all around the little terrace.

No voice uttered her name.

No cry of impatience greeted her.

Disappointment pierced her heart.

Then she smiled with relief. Beneath the canopy that covered most of the terrace was a low table heavily laden with goblets of fruit and cakes and pitchers of cold water and beer, and surrounded by thick cushions. A large red ceramic vase held an enormous bunch of pale roses and lilacs from the East, her favorite flowers.

Her disappointment faded away. No, Antinoes had not forgotten anything. Wars and battles had not changed him.

For their first night of love, he had covered their bed with rose petals from his father's garden.

◉

SLOWLY eating grapes, which were transparent in the twilight, Lilah rested her elbows on the parapet surrounding the top of the tower. At this hour, when night was approaching like a caress, there was nothing more splendid than the view from this terrace.

Some hundred cubits above the River Shaour rose the immense cliff walls of the Citadel. The royal courtyard known as the Apadana was lined with marble columns, carved in Egypt and transported by thousands of men and mules; these columns gleamed like bronze flames in the sun, and themselves were surrounded by marble terraces even more vast than the palace. Giant sculptures of bulls, lions, and winged monsters guarded the Apadana, which was reached by flights of steps so broad and so high they could have held the entire population of the city. Few, though, were entitled to climb them.

At the foot of the walls, enclosing the Citadel like a casket, were the palaces of the royal city, with their many gardens. In a last flash of brilliance, the rays of the setting sun, reflected in the lazy meandering of the Shaour, came to rest in the gardens, fading amid the dense cedars and eucalyptus trees.

The royal city was encircled by a brick wall, pierced with small square windows and flanked by tall crenellated towers, colored red, orange, and blue in places, which separated it from the busy streets of the upper town. These streets, squeezed between flat whitewashed roofs, ran as straight as if they had been cut with a double-edged sword. They stretched far to the east, the north, and the south—dark, crowded trenches that Lilah could barely make out from here. The hum of activity could still be heard: She imagined a mass of people in the streets, the awnings of the booths being lowered.

Antinoes' garden and house occupied a rectangular strip in the patricians' quarter, close to the royal palace. The garden was old and luxuriant. The elegant palms and cypresses lining the main alley leading from the outer wall to the house were as high as the tower itself.

A sudden sound made Lilah freeze.

The shadows were already lengthening in the twilight. She looked at the door leading to the staircase.

All she had heard was a slight rustling. But she knew he was there.

"Antinoes?" she called.

A face emerged from the shadows, a face she had so often evoked in her daydreams: the rather broad, hooked nose, the finely drawn nostrils, the tender, well-defined mouth, the arched eyebrows, the narrowed lids, the look in the eyes that made her tremble.

He uttered her name, very softly. "Lilah!"

He wore the dress of a Persian warrior: a short, close-fitting, long-sleeved tunic, purple with large fawn-colored circles, and equally close-fitting ankle-length trousers. The straps of his sandals were tied high up his calves. His belt was as wide as a hand, its gold buckle adorned with a lion's head. Three chains, of silver, gold, and bronze, linked it to a brooch in the shape of a bull's head pinned to his right shoulder. A felt ribbon embroidered with gold thread held his oiled and scented hair in place. A dazzling smile gleamed within his finely plaited beard.

He repeated her name, laughing now, almost shouting. "Lilah! Lilah!"

Lilah began to laugh, too. He held out his hands to her, palms upraised. She moved forward slowly and placed her palms on his. Antinoes' hands were hot. They closed over hers, and the mere touch was like an embrace. Antinoes' eyes gleamed in the setting sun.

"You're here!" she murmured, hardly aware that she had spoken.

He raised their entwined hands to his lips. He was still laughing, silently, as if he were out of breath. A caressing laugh, a laugh of pure joy, which enveloped them and carried them away.

They let go of each other's hands, the better to embrace. The laughter was swept away by their kisses. The kisses were swept away by their impatience.

For a long moment, the terrace around them seemed to contain the whole world. Susa had vanished. Time and troubles had evaporated. Only the deep, translucent sky of the dying twilight was still there.

They undressed, with all the clumsiness of long-separated lovers. Time, memory, impatience, and fear faded away in their turn.

Once again, they were Antinoes and Lilah.

THE silence of the star-studded night lay heavy on the city when, both out of breath, they untangled their limbs.

Here and there, torches glowed in the courtyards of the great houses. *Naphta* flames, held in wide dishes, danced on the walls of the Citadel, as they did every night, forming a royal diadem hanging in the darkness.

Antinoes freed himself from Lilah's arms and stood up from the cushions. He groped for a little chest of apple-tree wood containing a flint and a touchwood wick. A moment later, a torch crackled into flame.

Lilah now saw clearly the body she had held in the darkness. Antinoes' waist was slimmer, and his high buttocks made two dimples in his lower back. During the years in which the war against the Greeks and the King of Kings' brother had kept him far from her, he had grown harder.

He turned as he slotted the torch between the bricks on the parapet, not far from the table still piled high with food, and she discovered the scar.

"Your thigh!"

Antinoes smiled, with a touch of pride. "A Lydian sword at Carchemish. It was only the seventh time I'd been in close combat, so I wasn't very experienced. He was on the ground; I should have been more careful."

Lilah's fingers followed the twists and turns of the light-colored furrow in Antinoes' solid thigh.

He leaned down and seized her fingers, entwined them again with his own. "It's nothing. It took only a moon for the wound to close. Since then, I've only fought in a chariot. Where you're in a chariot, the enemy doesn't aim at the legs, but at the heart or the head. As you see, I still have both of those."

Lilah fell back, and stared up at the sky. "How many times," she murmured, "when the night and the stars arrived, I thought about that. Even though you were under the same stars, you were far from me, and I imagined you dying. Or you were seriously wounded, and you wanted to see me, but I had no way of knowing. A javelin went through you, and then the wax tablet informing me of your death went through me, too."

Antinoes laughed again. "It would never have happened. The Greeks and Cyrus the Younger's mercenaries learned to fear me." He kneeled, keeping a slight distance between them, and looked at Lilah in silence, serious now. "I know every inch of your face," he whispered, closing his eyes. "That was what I thought about. Your eyes, so black I can see myself reflected in them even by daylight, your lashes, your long straight eyebrows, as thin as a plume of smoke. Your high, stubborn brow, the brow of a young bull, your cheeks that blush both when you're angry and when I kiss them. I know every line of your mouth. I've drawn them a hundred times in the sand. The upper lip is longer and fuller than the other. A mouth so sweet, so alive, I can always tell what you're thinking."

His eyes still closed, he reached out his hand, trembling slightly. With his fingers, he traced the curve of a breast, glided over her belly, and stroked her hair, which hung loose down to her hips.

He opened his eyes. "In the last two years, I've seen many women," he went on. "The beauties of Cilicia or the northern Eu-

phrates, the wives of the great warriors of Lydia . . . The more
beautiful they were, the more they made me think of you. The
more foolish or provocative, the more I dreamed of you. And
whenever I happened to come across one who could compare
with you, I was angry at her for not being you."

He caressed her gently, as if reinventing her body with his fingers, imprinting every curve, every inch of skin, on his palm.

"When I fought, you were with me. Arrows and swords could
not touch me. The mere thought of your beauty protected me."

Lilah gave a throaty laugh, leaned forward, and embraced
him, ready to kiss him again. She pressed her hard nipples against
Antinoes' chest as if she wanted to be absorbed by him.

"I was never afraid when I fought," he murmured. "But every
day, I was afraid you would forget me. Every day I dreamed you
might forget Antinoes. The men of Susa would be mad not to see
your beauty."

"So, we both felt the same terror." She bit the back of his
neck, and he shivered. She laughed.

"Don't laugh!" he cried. "Now we're together forever."

For a brief moment Lilah froze at his words. But Antinoes'
kisses wiped out the cold. Her belly was soon on fire again, as Antinoes' member swelled against her thigh. She gripped his shoulders and pushed him down onto the cushions, her love's warrior
and her lover's enchantress.

THE moon was rising above the Zagros Mountains when she
whispered that it was time for her to return home.

"Stay the night!" Antinoes protested.

She smiled, and shook her head. "No, not tonight. We're not
yet man and wife, and I don't want Aunt Sarah to find my bedchamber empty in the morning."

"Oh, come on! Your aunt Sarah knows perfectly well that you're here, and she's delighted."

Lilah gave a little laugh and stroked her lover's eyelids, tracing his eyebrows with the tip of her index finger. "Then I'm the one who wants to get back to my bedchamber by dawn. Thinking about you, smelling the scent of you on my skin."

"You'll smell it all the better if you remain here. Lilah, why go? We've only just been reunited."

"Because I'm your lover," Lilah whispered, kissing his brow. "Your lover, but not your wife."

She started to move away, but Antinoes sat up and gripped her wrist. "When? When will you be my wife?"

She found it hard to meet his eyes. The darkness and the warm, flickering light of the torch made the shadows on his face seem harsher. She thought of how his face must look in battle.

"I'll go to see your uncle first thing tomorrow," Antinoes insisted. "We'll fix the day. As far as I'm concerned, everything is ready. I've made offerings to Ahura Mazda, I've left a tablet with your name on it for the royal eunuchs. You know that's the law for high-ranking officers. Now, the king and queen may oppose a marriage with . . . between a Persian officer and a non-Persian." He broke off with a grimace and shook his head. "Lilah, what is it? Don't you want to be my wife?"

"I want nothing else," she said with a smile.

"Then why delay?"

Lilah gathered her hair to cover her chest, and searched for her tunic among the cushions. Antinoes waited for a reply, but none came. He stood up abruptly and walked nervously to the parapet, barely illumined by the light of the torch. "I came back to be your husband," he said in a low voice. "I shan't leave Susa again until that house down there is your house." He pointed to the diadem of the Citadel, shining unperturbed in the night. "There, in a few days, I shall wear a helmet with red and white

plumes and a leather breastplate with the insignia of the heroes of
Artaxerxes. But without you, without your love and the thought
of you, even a Greek child could vanquish me."

He spoke without looking at her. Lilah covered herself with
her tunic. As she was about to hook the sides together, Antinoes
came back to her and seized her by the arms.

"It's Ezra, isn't it? It's Ezra who's holding you back."

"I have to talk to him."

"Hasn't he changed? Does he still hate me?"

Lilah did not reply. She freed herself from his grip and hooked
her tunic.

"Does he know I've come back?" Antinoes asked.

"No. I'm going tomorrow."

"To the lower town?"

Lilah merely nodded.

Antinoes grunted, and moved away from her angrily. "What a
fool!"

"No, Antinoes, he's no fool. He does what he thinks is right.
He studies and learns, and that's important."

An ironic look on his face, Antinoes was about to reply, but
Lilah raised her hand.

"No, don't mock, that would be unfair. Soon after you left, an
old man came to see him in the lower town. His name is Baruch
ben Neriah. He used to live in Babylon. That's where he found
out that our family possesses the scroll of the laws given by Yahweh to Moses. He's a gentle old man, and very learned. All his life
he's studied from copied and incomplete papyri. He invited Ezra
to join him in his studies. Since then, both of them have been im-
mersed in the texts. Ezra is becoming a sage, Antinoes, a sage of
our people, just like those who led the children of Israel before
the exile."

"That's fine. Let him study, let him become a sage. What do I
care, provided he leaves you free to marry me?"

"Antinoes! You used to love Ezra as much as I did."

"That was a long time ago."

"Not too long ago to remember. You know as well as I do that Ezra is not cut out for everyday life. One day, he will be a great man—"

"No. To be a great man, he'd have to stop being jealous. Jealousy lessens him, just as hate weakens a warrior before a battle."

Lilah fell silent, and tried to smile. She went to him, stroked his naked torso, put her head on his shoulder, and embraced him tenderly. "My one desire, my one joy, is to be the wife of Antinoes. Just be patient a while longer."

Antinoes buried his face in Lilah's hair. "No! I've had enough of being patient! I want you with me for the rest of our lives. I came back so that we could be together. And we will be. If Ezra can't accept that, we'll become man and wife in spite of him. All we need is your uncle Mordecai's approval!"

Trembling, Lilah took her arms away. "Antinoes . . ."

But Antinoes was not listening to her. He clasped her again to his naked body, indifferent to the growing coolness of the night. "And if we can't be man and wife," he went on, "we'll be lovers forever. If we have to leave Susa, we'll leave Susa, and I'll relinquish my chariot captain's breastplate and baldric. We'll go to Lydia, to Sardis. The sea is wonderful there, and I'll become a Greek hero . . ."

Lilah took his face in her hands and kissed him on the mouth to silence him. Passion again inflamed them. "I shall have no other husband but you, my beloved," Lilah said, holding him tight. "Give me time to convince Ezra. I don't want our joy to be his sorrow."

Bad News

The young slave pulled on the bridles, the mules munched their bits and snorted, and the chariot came to a halt in the shade of a medlar tree.

Lilah stepped down, and signaled to Axatria to help her.

The handmaid took the huge basket from between the benches, and arranged the leather straps so that her mistress could hoist them onto her shoulder. "It's too heavy!" she said, frowning. "It's not for you to carry such a load."

"It'll be all right," Lilah replied, propping the basket on her back. "No need to worry."

"Of course I worry! I'm ashamed, too. Your tunic will be a rag by the time you get to Ezra's house! God in heaven, what do you look like?"

Axatria tried to smooth the material, which was creased because of the straps, and without further ado pinned back the half-moon brooch that held the transparent shawl on Lilah's hair.

"I tell you, your hair will be out of place by the time you get to your brother's house. Just think how much he loves to see you looking beautiful! And what about your aunt? What would she say if she could see you laden like a mule, while your handmaid is sitting comfortably in the chariot . . ."

Lilah smiled. "Ezra will be pleased to see his sister even if she's a bit rumpled, and I won't tell Aunt Sarah, I promise."

Axatria seemed neither amused nor appeased by this answer.

Giving a little shake to make sure that the straps rested against her hands, Lilah walked away from the chariot, along the street that cut straight through the last gardens in the upper town. She stubbed her foot on the raised edge of a paving stone and, pulled by the weight of her load, swerved. Hardly had she had time to regain her balance than Axatria was gripping the basket.

"You see! It's much too heavy. Let me do it. It'll be much easier if the two of us carry it."

"Let go!"

But Axatria would not yield, and tried to take the straps from her hands. Lilah pushed her away so angrily that Axatria stumbled and almost knocked both of them backward.

"Axatria! Leave me be!"

"Why should I let you do something so stupid?"

Axatria's tanned, naturally dark complexion had turned purple in a flash. She was not pretty. She had a squat figure, her breasts were too heavy, and her hips too wide even though she had never given birth. She had the flat face typical of the women of the Zagros Mountains: a short nose, high cheekbones, thick, curly hair. But her vivacious eyes, her full lips, as frank as they were sensual, and her eager, mocking expressions were not without charm. Now, though, her eyes blazed with anger, her mouth like that of a bad-tempered mother dealing with an unruly child.

"Axatria," Lilah said, forcing herself to stay calm, "we've already agreed I'm to go alone. There's no point in arguing."

"You agreed with yourself, that's all," Axatria replied, sharply. "It's you who had this whim."

"It isn't a whim, and you know it."

They fell silent, glaring at each other. Lilah was the first to look away. The young slave was following the quarrel as he stroked the cheek of one of the mules.

"Am I in your way?" Axatria resumed, plaintively. "Why stop me from seeing him, Lilah? You know perfectly well . . . perfectly well . . ." Rage and distress prevented Axatria from finishing her sentence. There was no need. She was right. Lilah knew "perfectly well."

Lilah was embarrassed by the tears that glistened in her handmaid's eyes. "It's stupid, quarreling like this," she said, more harshly than she had intended. "Wait for me here. I shan't be long."

Axatria rose to her full height, her back arched and her eyes on fire. "Very well, mistress. Since you've made up your mind, and I'm nothing but a servant to you."

She turned away stiffly, lifted her tunic, and climbed into the chariot. Prudently, the young slave lowered his eyes.

Lilah hesitated. What was the point of protesting? There was only one thing she could say to appease Axatria, and she refused to say it.

She walked away with a heavy heart. It was a bad start to an already delicate mission. Behind her, she heard Axatria lecturing the slave in a sharp voice.

"Instead of eavesdropping, my boy, turn this chariot in the right direction!"

LILAH had only to walk some sixty cubits before the paved road became an uneven dirt path, which led to the labyrinth of the lower town. Prickly pear and acacia bushes, a few empty fields, and ponds overrun by frogs were all that separated wealth from poverty.

Lilah advanced, her eyes fixed on the ground, her shoulder already hurting from the straps of the basket. Axatria's words still rumbled in her head. She had never seen her like this.

Strong, intelligent, and conscientious, Axatria had entered Lilah's service the day Uncle Mordecai had taken in Ezra and Lilah, after the death of their parents. She was twenty at the time, not much older than her young masters, a young woman of insatiable energy. Within a few days she had fallen in love with Ezra.

At the time, he possessed all the incandescent beauty of adolescence. His charm struck Axatria like lightning burning up the driest soil. Lilah was not surprised. She, too, thought Ezra the handsomest of boys. As handsome as Antinoes, who was much admired by the young Persian girls, but wiser already, with a soul that went deeper.

Lilah had liked the fact that Axatria succumbed to Ezra's charms. It had amused her, but she had felt proud, too, and not at all afraid or jealous. Wasn't the tie that bound brother and sister an eternal one?

Axatria had been sensible enough never to display her feelings in words or gestures. However great her passion, she expressed herself entirely through the excellence of her service, the washing she did for Ezra, the meals she prepared. She was so discreet that Ezra had not become aware of her love until the day Aunt Sarah had gently mocked Axatria about it.

Axatria was content to receive Ezra's gratitude, his occasional fleeting kindness toward her, like wonderful gifts that were sufficient in themselves.

But it was their love for Ezra, the love of a sister and a handmaid, boundless but perfectly chaste, that had brought Lilah and Axatria together.

Then the terrible day had come when Ezra had left Uncle Mordecai's house and moved to the lower town.

His uncle and aunt had tried to stop him, but had been unable to, nor could they get anything out of him to justify his departure. Axatria, for her part, had stood in his way, her face bathed in tears.

"Why? Why leave this house?"

Ezra had tried to push her away, but she had quite shamelessly collapsed at his feet and stopped him, clinging to him like a human millstone. Ezra had been forced to answer her.

"I am going to a place where the children of Israel have not forgotten the pain of exile. I am going to study what should never have been forgotten. I am going to study what my father, Serayah, his father, Azaryah, his father, Hilqiyyah, and all their fathers for twelve generations learned from their father, Aaron, the brother of Moses."

What was Axatria, a daughter of Persia from the Zagros Mountains, to make of such words?

She was stunned into silence. Appearing to yield, she let go of Ezra's wrists. But as soon as he tried to take a step, she gripped his tunic.

"Take me with you, Ezra!" She begged, forgetting her dignity for the first and only time. "I'm your handmaid, wherever you go!"

"Where I'm going, I have no need of handmaids."

"Why?"

"Because it's impossible to study with a handmaid around."

"You don't know what you're saying! Who'll take care of you, give you food to eat, wash your clothes, keep your bedchamber clean?"

Ezra had pushed her away so roughly, there was no chance to reply. "Be quiet! I'm leaving this house to be closer to the will of God, not the will of a handmaid!"

For days, eaten away as much by shame as by sorrow, Axatria had been unable to stop weeping.

She was not the only one. The house of Mordecai and Sarah was full of tears and lamentations. For the first time, Lilah had seen her uncle brought low, incapable of going to work or even of feeding himself. Her aunt Sarah had closed her workshop for six days, as if in mourning. Axatria's tears had been swallowed up in the general sense of woe. She went about her daily tasks like a soul that had already passed into the other world. "Why? Why?" she would mutter from dawn to dusk, in a stunned whisper.

Then one day, Lilah had said, "I know where Ezra has found refuge. Get ready, and we'll go and take him food and clothing." That had been the first time.

Less than a moon later, they had again filled a basket and borrowed one of Uncle Mordecai's chariots, to which Mordecai had turned a blind eye.

Seasons had passed, rain, snow, days of stifling heat. Nothing, neither exhaustion nor sickness, had been able to force Lilah and Axatria to renounce their visits to the lower city.

Hardly had the sun risen than Axatria would fill a basket now set aside for this specific purpose. She would cram it as full as possible with small pitchers of milk, bread and cheese, bags of almonds, barley, and dates. The basket had become so bulky over time that it weighed more now than a dead ass, forcing Lilah to tense her muscles as she carried it.

Today she wanted to be alone with Ezra.

What she had to tell him was quite difficult enough without Axatria bustling around them.

CRIES jolted Lilah out of her thoughts when she was only half a *stadion* from the lower town. As if emerging from the earth, a group of about twenty boys, aged from four to eleven or twelve, wearing nothing but cloths around their waists, appeared between the first tumbledown houses and came running barefoot on the hard pebble-strewn earth, yelling loudly.

Two old men carrying tubs of asphalt on a hoist toward the upper town moved quickly to the side of the path.

Raising as much dust as a herd of young goats, the children reached Lilah and came to a sudden standstill, their screams ceasing just as abruptly as their run. Smiling sweetly, they lined up in two perfect rows, the little ones gripping the rags of the bigger ones.

"May the mighty Ahura Mazda and the God of heaven be with you, Lilah!" they cried in unison.

"May the Everlasting bless you!" Lilah replied, earnestly.

Surprised that Axatria was absent, the children looked from the basket to the chariot, which they could glimpse on the road to the upper town.

Lilah smiled. "Today, Axatria is waiting for you in the chariot. She has brought you honey bread."

No sooner had these words been spoken than the children leaped in the air like a flock of sparrows.

Lilah adjusted the basket on her shoulder. The two old men bowed respectfully before setting off again with their burden of asphalt. She responded to their greeting, and hurried on.

"Lilah!"

She heard the shout at the same time as the sound of running feet.

"Sogdiam!"

"Let me carry your basket!"

He was a well-built boy of thirteen or fourteen, strong enough to seem two or three years older than his age. When he was not yet one year old, a fall from a badly built brick wall on a stormy day had left him badly crippled. The bones of his legs had set again haphazardly, leaving him with shapeless limbs that he had learned to use through an effort of will. Today, despite a grotesque, lopsided gait, he was capable of running and walking for long distances without any pain.

His fine, kindly features easily made people forget his misfortune. His eyes burned with intelligence. Soon after settling in the lower town, Ezra had spotted him among the orphaned children who ran around the streets. Before long, he had found him to be a capable and devoted servant.

Lilah pointed to the piece of honey bread that Sogdiam was carrying in his hand. "Finish eating first."

"No need," Sogdiam said, as proud as a warrior. "I can do both at the same time!"

Glad to relieve the pressure on her shoulder, Lilah passed him the basket. The boy strained his young muscles and slid the handles onto his own shoulder.

"I think Axatria really filled it today . . ."

"It'll be all right," Sogdiam groaned, gallantly.

Lilah smiled at him tenderly. He set off at a walking pace, arching his back proudly, to hide the fact that the weight was pulling on his neck. They were being watched from the houses at the other end of the path. Sogdiam would not have missed for anything in the world the opportunity of showing everyone that he was privileged to help Lilah, the one and only lady from the upper town who dared enter the lower town.

"Axatria shouldn't have let you carry this load," he said severely, moving forward at a fair speed. "She's the handmaid, she should at least have done her share."

"I was the one who wanted it," Lilah said.

"Why? Because she's in a bad mood this morning? She was really shouting at us just now!"

Lilah could not help smiling. "It won't last," she said.

"What's the matter?" Sogdiam threw her a questioning glance. "Did the two of you have an argument?"

Lilah merely shook her head.

"It certainly looked like it," Sogdiam insisted. "She had tears in her eyes."

"There are days like that, when you feel sad," Lilah said, with a lump in her throat, then quickly changed the subject. "Tell me one thing. How do you know when we've arrived? Our chariot never comes near the lower town. You can't hear the wheels from here, and I don't see any of you in the fields. But no sooner do we get here than you all appear, screaming like Greeks!"

Sogdiam nodded proudly. "It's me who knows, not the others."

"You? And how do you know?"

"Easy. It's your day," Sogdiam said, as if stating the obvious.

"What are you talking about? I don't have a 'day.' I could have come yesterday or tomorrow."

Sogdiam laughed. "But you came today! You always come the day of your day."

"But it's not just the day, it's the exact moment . . ."

"It's the same," Sogdiam said. "You always come at the same time of the day. Didn't you know that?"

"Well . . . Perhaps not," Lilah said, surprised.

"But I know. In the morning I get up and I know. Sometimes at night, when I go to bed, I say to myself: 'Tomorrow, Lady Lilah will come.' And you come. Ezra knows it, too. He's like me."

"Are you sure?" Lilah asked, her voice betraying more emotion than she would have liked. "Did he tell you?"

The boy chuckled merrily. "No need, Lilah. The day of your day, he washes himself thoroughly, rubs his teeth with lime to make them whiter, and asks me to comb his hair. In all the time you've been coming, haven't you noticed how handsome he is

when you arrive?" Sogdiam was laughing so heartily, his limp became more pronounced.

Lilah laughed, too, to cover her emotion. "It seems I have no
eyes for anything, Sogdiam. Whenever I come here, I'm so busy
making sure you have all you need, I just don't pay attention."

Sogdiam admitted, with a pout, that this might be a valid
reason.

They walked for a moment in silence, along alleys, sometimes
past meager gardens.

The houses of the lower town were for the most part nothing
but huts of cane and mud. Some, known as *zorifes*, consisted
merely of roofs of roughly plaited palms supported by poles, with
no walls. Women were busy over their frugal hearths, while their
children tugged at their tunics.

Dirty as the streets were, and foul with stagnant water after
the rains, Lilah had always refused to venture in with her chariot.
The carved, cushioned benches, the axle heads inlaid with silver
and brass, were worth more in themselves than a hundred hovels
in this wretched slum.

From time to time, they were watched by inquisitive eyes.
Everyone knew who this beautiful young woman was, and where
she was going in the company of the boy with the heavy basket.
Men and women alike looked avidly at her splendid tunic, her elegant hairstyle, her leather clogs with their curved tips. Her very
way of walking was different from that of the lower town. She
moved forward with a light, lively gait, swaying her hips in a
manner reminiscent of dances, feasts, banquets, music, amorous
songs at twilight. In a word, she represented beauty; she was also
a reminder of what the world held for others.

As often as they had had the opportunity to marvel at Lilah,
the inhabitants of the lower city never tired of the spectacle. For
them, Lilah was a mirage, an image of something they would
never know.

Most had never entered the upper town, from where they were brutally driven away by the soldiers, let alone the Citadel. At most they could glimpse, above the roofs of the slums, beyond the gardens and the fine houses of the upper town, the outer wall and colonnades of the Apadana. Standing out against the morning sky, the Citadel seemed to touch the clouds, as suited the dwelling of the gods and the King of Kings.

Men and women alike had questioned Sogdiam, asking him if the lady of the "wise Jew," as Ezra was known here, lived in the Citadel. Sogdiam was so proud that people might think so that he answered yes. Yes, a woman as beautiful as Lilah could only live in the Citadel!

MUCH to his relief, Sogdiam put down the basket outside the house.

"Ezra is probably still studying," he whispered, pushing open the blue-painted gate cautiously to stop it from squeaking.

The house was a palace compared to the hovels that surrounded it. The rough brick walls supported a roof of palm leaves covered with asphalted earth, which afforded protection from both cold and extreme heat. Three square little rooms looked out on the courtyard. Against the outer wall was an arbor with a fragrant lemon tree.

"Wait," Sogdiam whispered, as Lilah headed straight for the study. "I have to warn them!"

Lilah did not have time to retort that she had no intention of waiting. A clear, distinct voice spoke her name.

"Lilah!"

Now that she had been alerted, Lilah noticed how well groomed Ezra was: the short glossy beard, the gleaming white teeth in a welcoming smile, the hair carefully parted high on the skull and tied at the back of the neck with an ivory ring from the East that Lilah had given him some time before. But his brightly colored tunic, held in at the waist by a brown linen belt, barely concealed how thin he had become.

"Lilah, my sister . . ." He came forward, his arms open. At the last moment, he froze in alarm. "May I clasp you to me?"

Lilah gave a mocking laugh. Ezra, faithful to every line of Moses' laws, wanted to know if she was burdened by what he called "the blood of womanhood."

She went up to him and placed her fingers on his lips. Her brother hesitated, torn between wanting to retreat and wanting to kiss her. Lilah laughed again. Taking him by the neck, she drew him to her and kissed his earlobe tenderly. "Have no fear," she whispered. "I'm completely pure. Would I have come if I weren't? Don't you trust your sister?"

Ezra gave a small grunt of satisfaction. Lilah closed her eyes. She felt happy, bound as she was to her beloved brother, forgetting the anxieties that had been tormenting her since the previous night. For a moment, they held each other, as if they had been apart, not for a few weeks, but for all the hours of eternity.

The same emotion overcame them each time they met. Brother and sister, born of the same flesh, sometimes so alike that they seemed to be of one body. But never of one mind.

Her lips pressed against Ezra's neck, Lilah lifted her eyes. Sogdiam was watching them. Swinging his hips so that he was almost bent in two, he turned away and hurried into the house with the basket.

Ezra took a step back, but kept Lilah's hand in his.

"Sogdiam tells me you make yourself handsome whenever I come to visit," she remarked in a serious tone, although there was a touch of merriment in her eyes. "But to me you seem thinner than ever. How is it possible? Axatria's baskets are full to bursting. Don't you eat?"

Ezra dismissed her questions with a wave of his hand. "I'm perfectly well. It's Master Baruch you ought to worry about. We had some bad news, and since then he hasn't slept well at night. This morning, we haven't studied because he felt too weak."

Lilah threw a worried glance at the room from which Ezra had emerged.

"Go in," Ezra said, with a nod. "He's waiting for you."

SIMPLY furnished as it was, the room gave an impression of warmth. The daylight came in through a wide opening in the west wall, and on either side of this window, which had a shutter of woven reed, were niches piled high with wax tablets. The northern wall was covered with a rug, a gift from Aunt Sarah. It had taken a great deal of effort on Lilah's part to persuade Ezra to hang it, but in winter it had proved effective in protecting the room from the wind and cold that filtered through the poorly laid bricks.

In the middle of the room, a cedar chest, blackened by the oil lamps that had burned on it, served as a writing desk. Around it were a number of wide-necked jars filled with papyrus scrolls, and two stools. A leather bag hanging from one of the beams on the ceiling contained styli and sticks of dry ink.

A low bed stood against the wall opposite the window. It had leather trestles on which was placed a woolen mattress wrapped in linen. An old man's head jutted out from the brown and green striped blanket, although his frail body barely showed beneath it.

Lilah kneeled.

"Lilah is here, master!" Ezra said in a loud voice, behind her.

The blanket was pushed back more briskly than Lilah had expected. Two pale, deep-set eyes peered at her, bright eyes that contrasted with the haggard face, the thousand lines on the brow and cheeks. Despite his great age, Master Baruch's hair was still dark. His curly beard, though, was as white as a lamb's fleece, and covered his chest. His thin, crumpled lips were barely visible, but revealed a few stumps of teeth when he smiled.

"Lilah, my dove! May the Everlasting bless you."

The voice was weak and hoarse, but cheerful.

Master Baruch pushed back the blanket a little more. His hands seemed to be nothing more than bones held together by the shiny, pockmarked skin that still covered them. He squeezed Lilah's hands with a strength and gentleness that amazed her every time. Leaning down, she kissed the old man's brow tenderly.

"Hello, Master Baruch. Ezra tells me you're ill."

There was a strange creaking sound. Master Baruch opened his mouth wide. Then he closed his eyes and his throat quivered. He was laughing.

"Ezra is young and very indulgent," he murmured, eyes still closed, once he had regained his breath. "He's so certain the Everlasting is going to make me a 'patriarch,' he thinks I'm ill! The truth, my dove, is that I'm not ill at all." He broke off, and again squeezed Lilah's hands. His eye opened again to reveal his piercing, ironic gaze. "It's simply my time to die, my dove. The Everlasting doesn't share Ezra's opinion! He doesn't want to make me a new Noah or Abraham. I shan't live three hundred years. Baruch ben Neriah I am, and Baruch ben Neriah I shall die. And soon!"

"The truth, master," Ezra said impatiently, behind Lilah's back, "is that you had a stomachache all last night."

"The stomachache is nothing," Master Baruch retorted, his voice firmer now. "A stomachache you're born with and you die with. I've had a stomachache for almost a hundred years. The sad thing, the thing that's turning my blood to water and shortening my life, is knowing that I shall never see Jerusalem rise again from her shame. I shall die while the city chosen by Yahweh is still de-

fenseless before her enemies. To know that the Ammonites and
Ashdodites are dancing on the ruins of the Temple, that's my ill-
ness, my dove. That's the punishment inflicted on me by the
Everlasting."

Lilah frowned. "Why do you say that, Master Baruch? Those
misfortunes are over. Nehemiah has long since rebuilt the Temple
and Jerusalem is living according to the laws of Yahweh. That's
what you yourself told Ezra and me when you first came here."

The old man raised his palms in vigorous protest, as if overcome by a wave of pain. "Forget those innocent words, my child!
Don't make my sin any worse than it is before the Everlasting."

Lilah turned to Ezra, uncomprehending.

"Clearly you haven't heard the news," Ezra said, giving her a
black look. "I'm not surprised. Nobody's likely to care about such
things in Mordecai's house."

With a shudder of anxiety, Lilah could not help thinking of
Antinoes' tablet. "What news?" she asked.

"Nehemiah, son of Hakalya, died at least five years ago. And
he failed."

"Oh!" Her relief did not escape Ezra. She felt her cheeks turning red.

Master Baruch's voice rose, now loud and clear. "'You will
come back to me,' Yahweh said to Moses. 'You will obey my orders, and act according to them. And even if you are banished to
the farthest borders under heaven, from there I will gather you
and I will lead you to the place I have chosen for my name to live.'
It was with these words in mind that Nehemiah, son of Hakalya,
left Susa. That is what we must carry in our hearts." He pointed
at Lilah, his pale eyes no longer smiling or ironic, but hard with
anger. "It is now fifty-four years since Nehemiah left for Jerusalem to reestablish the will of Yahweh there. And all he has re-
established is piles of bricks!"

"For four years Cyrus the Younger ruled over Judaea," Ezra interrupted. "We heard only rumors about Jerusalem and Nehemiah. The news that reached us was not good, but not bad either. Merchants who came to Susa assured us that Cyrus was showing as much affection for the Jews as his father and grandfather. The Temple and the walls of Jerusalem were as resplendent as in a dream, they asserted. The gossip of caravan drivers drunk on palm wine! Complete nonsense, but quite sweet to the ears of the exiled Jews, who were only too happy to shirk their bad consciences." He stretched out his arm, pointing to an invisible visitor in the courtyard. "Some of them came here, in a hurry to bow down to Master Baruch, claiming to be pious. 'Do you have news of Jerusalem?' we would ask. 'Do you know if Nehemiah is still fighting the Philistines, and the people of Manasseh, Ammon, and Gad?' 'Oh, no!' they'd reply, confident as could be, Nehemiah made the Law of Moses respected on the hills of Judaea and the banks of the Jordan! Jerusalem would shine as it had in Solomon's day! How did they know? They'd had a letter, or heard it from a relative who was visiting! It was all hearsay!"

Ezra slapped his thigh, gave a harsh, sharp laugh, and fell silent. But his eyes blazed with fury, his face suddenly magnificent.

A thrill went through Lilah. Yes, at such moments, no one, not even Antinoes, was as splendid as her brother. Lilah had long been familiar with Ezra's anger. And when it came, he was so fascinating that she always admired it as much as she dreaded it.

His throat was as delicate as a woman's, but when he was angry his voice would grow somber and curiously resonant. It was a voice that made the air tremble and everyone's heart beat faster. Ezra's whole body would appear to grow suddenly heavy, and he would have to move about and shake his limbs, as if he could not contain the strength of his muscles. Lilah was not surprised now to see him turn abruptly, walk to the window, then to the door, and come back at last to the bed in four long strides. He clapped his hands, as if scaring off a pack of stray dogs.

"Now we know the truth. In the month of Nisan, Artaxerxes waged battle on his brother Cyrus beneath the walls of Babylon. Cyrus was killed, and the lies and rumors died with him. Today the truth has crossed the desert! And the truth is that the Temple of the children of Israel has no doors or roof. And if it had, nobody guards them. Nobody knows the laws. Apparently all sorts of buying and selling go on there, loans, money changing. The walls of Jerusalem may have been rebuilt, but they're still wide open. The Philistines, the Ammonites, the Moabites, all the enemies of the children of Israel, whatever they call themselves, come and go as they please. The law taught to Moses by Yahweh no longer holds any sway there, any more than it did the day Nebuchadnezzar conquered Judaea, any more than it did during the sixty years when our fathers trampled the dust of exile, or during the hundred and fifty years that have passed since the decree of Cyrus the Great giving Jerusalem back to the children of Israel. The truth is that we might as well be back in the time when the Hebrews who had left Egypt danced before the Golden Calf at the foot of Mount Sinai! That's the news, sister. Nehemiah was ambitious and headstrong. But he failed."

Ezra sat down on one of the stools and slapped his thigh again.

"How can you be certain?" Lilah asked, after a moment's thought.

Her brother stared at her in surprise. Lilah smiled gently. She had not tried to oppose him, but had simply spoken what she was thinking. She had grown so accustomed to the fire and energy of Ezra's speeches that she no longer fell under their spell, as she had when they were both younger, and was able to think for herself. But Ezra's anger had now turned against her, like the desert wind abruptly changing direction.

That, too, was something to which she was accustomed. She leaned down and placed a hand on her brother's knee. "You may be worrying needlessly," she said tenderly. "If the rumors from Jerusalem after the battle of Cunaxa were false, why should these new ones be true?"

Ezra pushed away her hand brusquely, but before he could say a word, Master Baruch spoke up. "That's a good question, my daughter. If a bird flies in one direction, why shouldn't it fly in another?"

Rigid with anger, lips quivering, Ezra looked the two of them up and down.

Master Baruch pointed to one of the jars with a bony finger. "Show her the letter."

Ezra pulled a papyrus from the twenty or so in the container and threw it to Lilah unceremoniously. "It's a letter from Yaqquv, the guardian of the gates of the Temple, who was appointed to the post by Nehemiah himself before he died. The letter was written in Jerusalem two springs ago. It did not reach the Levites of Babylon until after the death of Cyrus the Younger. One of them brought it to Master Baruch, because the letter was addressed to him. Everything I just told you is here, written by Yaqquv, who saw it with his own eyes."

Even though it was rolled around a cedarwood stalk, the papyrus strip was in a bad state. Worn, yellowed, and torn, it looked as if it had been handled by hundreds of people. The ink was slightly ocher in color, different from that used in Susa. The writing was not Persian or Chaldean. Lilah recognized the tall, joined-up signs of the Hebrews, which Master Baruch was teaching Ezra. She herself could barely decipher them.

As if guessing her thoughts, Ezra took another papyrus from the jar. This one was shorter and newly written. "I translated the important points into the language of Babylon, made more than forty copies, and distributed them to the exiled families in the upper town. I was hoping to open their eyes to the wounds of Jerusalem. You might have had one in your hands. But perhaps it was madness to hope I could touch our uncle's heart, or even cross his threshold."

Lilah lowered her eyes. Her brother was right. This bad news had not entered Uncle Mordecai's house. She turned to the old man. "I'm ashamed, Master Baruch. Ezra's right. As you know, our uncle's house is closed to anything that comes from his nephew. But our uncle will come to regret it, I'm sure."

Master Baruch glanced at Ezra and sighed. "We're all ashamed. You, I, Ezra. All of us. Nehemiah was so confident when he set off. 'I confess the sins of the children of Israel! We have sinned against you, Yahweh! I am in sin, my father's house is in sin!' That's what he said as he left the Citadel. And we can say the same thing now. Time has passed, but nothing good has come."

He grimaced and fell silent. His soft fingers again sought Lilah's hand. Ezra also respected his silence. They remained like that for a moment. There was nothing to add. The words already spoken were enough of a burden.

Lilah heard noise coming from the adjoining room, which was used as a kitchen. Sogdiam was putting away the provisions. Ezra had regained his composure. Calmly, he replaced the papyri in the jar, then sat down again next to Lilah.

She did not need to turn to know that he was looking at her. She had no doubt of his affection for her. But she kept her head down and her eyes on Master Baruch's pockmarked hand squeezing her hand. She had come here to tell Ezra that Antinoes had come back and that she wanted to marry him. But how could she do that now?

How, after all she had heard, could she dare to say, "I, too, have news. Antinoes has returned from the wars to marry me. I spent the night with him. I love him. I can still feel his caresses. He wants to make me a great lady. One of those who enter the Citadel and bow down before the King of Kings!"

Suddenly Master Baruch's voice rose, drawing her from her thoughts. "Ezra has the anger of youth, and that's good," he said, smiling his half-wicked, half-serious smile. "All I have is the remorse of old age. I was not much older than the two of you when Nehemiah left Susa for Jerusalem with the consent of his King of Kings. At the time I was living in Babylon, among the exiles. I spent my days studying the teachings of Moses. A man named Azaryah came to me. 'Baruch,' he said, 'Nehemiah is forming a caravan for Jerusalem. He's going to rebuild the walls and the Temple. He needs hands and minds he can trust. He thought of you, because it's said you know a great deal about the Law that Moses received on Mount Sinai.' I looked at this Azaryah with the same look your brother might have given him. I stared at him with blazing dark eyes . . ." Master Baruch stopped. He gave a little laugh. "Although my eyes are light blue." He was always like this. Whatever the gravity of the situation, he could find amusement in the trials and tribulations of men, and especially his own.

"I thought about it for a while, and then answered Azaryah very seriously, 'I'm studying, and can't interrupt my studies.' 'Come,' he insisted, 'you can study in Jerusalem! Is there a better place to study?' I refused again. 'Going to Jerusalem will mean interrupting my studies, and I can't do it.' He lost his temper. He was breathing like an ox, this Azaryah, he was as red as a beetroot. 'Is that your answer to Nehemiah, Baruch ben Neriah?' he asked. 'That you'd rather study than rebuild the Temple of Yahweh?' 'Yes, that's exactly what you're going to tell him,' I replied, very proud of myself. 'Baruch ben Neriah obeys a higher will. When you're studying the laws taught by Yahweh, you don't interrupt them, even to rebuild the walls and the Temple of Jerusalem!'"

Master Baruch was laughing with his cracked mouth, but the tears that welled in his eyes were not tears of joy. "Oh, poor Nehemiah! Poor Nehemiah! May the Everlasting bless him for all time!" he exclaimed, beating his chest with his fists.

Lilah risked a glance at Ezra. He was listening impassively, with his head tilted. She waited a moment, then got up with a determined air. "I'm going to make an herb tea with honey," she said to Master Baruch. "I've brought some fresh herbs. And I'll bake some biscuits that you can dip in a little milk. It'll do you good and calm your stomach."

She went out before Master Baruch could protest. But his laughter pursued her even before she was through the door. She realized that though Ezra was a good pupil and had learned much from Master Baruch, he had not learned to laugh. That was a true gift, especially when your eyes were burning with the tears you were holding back.

THE kitchen was only six feet wide and twelve feet long, but it was simply and efficiently laid out. A long flat stone, worn smooth by daily use, protruded from the far wall, with a furrow cut into it to drain away the water through gaps in the bricks. Sogdiam was cleaning onion shoots and turnip roots. He had already carefully put away the sacks of vegetables and dried fruits in big cane baskets with lids, which were lined up on the side. Under a board of palm-tree wood that was used as a table for kneading, cutting, or crushing, there were other baskets, without lids, containing a few cucumbers and two small, white-veined melons.

Bunches of mint, sage, peppers, aniseed, cardamom, and oregano hung from the ceiling beams beside pieces of mutton and dried fish, which swayed in the heat from the stove. The brick stove itself, two feet high and shaped like a tank, stood in the middle of the room. Inside it, right at the bottom, a thick layer of embers glowed between big stones, on which stood a pitcher of already boiling water. A cleverly angled opening in the roof made it possible to let out the smoke without allowing rainwater into the room.

Lilah entered and asked abruptly if the dough for the biscuits was ready. Sogdiam turned and threw her a look. He wiped his wet hands on his tunic, then without a word lifted a cloth from the kneading board. Five very round balls rested on it.

Lilah pressed on one of them with her finger. The dough sank, soft but firm, and resumed its shape as soon as she took away her finger.

"I made them early this morning," Sogdiam said, resuming his task. "We had some flour left over from last week."

"So now we can bake them when the stove is hot enough."

Sogdiam thought of replying that he had been maintaining the fire since dawn for that very purpose. All Lilah had to do was place her hand against the bricks to be convinced of that, and to realize that he had not been lying when he claimed to know the day she would come. He judged it wiser to keep silent.

What was the point? Lilah paid him no heed. She did not even notice the trouble he took. With the back of his wrist, he rubbed his eyes, which were smarting more from the injustice than the heat of the stove.

Unafraid to soil her beautiful dress, Lilah picked up one of the balls of dough. Skillfully, she flattened it between her palms. Then, with a gentle, regular movement, she rolled the dough faster and faster between her hands until it was a very thin, soft disk.

Lilah leaned against the cylinder of the stove and, with the skill of habit, abruptly bent double and plunged her face into the burning heat. With a sharp blow, she stuck the disk of dough against the inner wall, where it made a sizzling sound.

Lilah stepped back, rose again to her full height, moved a lock of hair away from her brow, and seized another ball of dough. "While I'm making the biscuits, Sogdiam," she said, "heat a pitcher of water with mint leaves and the green part of fresh onions, the ones I brought earlier. Make sure you cut them very small first. And make a jug of milk for Master Baruch as well."

Sogdiam obeyed without a word. They busied themselves in silence. The space was so narrow that they constantly rubbed against each other, almost colliding as Sogdiam placed the herbs in the pitcher of hot water at the bottom of the stove. Lilah, her cheeks and brow reddened by the fire, stuck the last of the disks of dough in the stove and quickly wiped her hands. Then she lifted the lids from the baskets, and immediately made a face, surprised to find nothing there but the bags that Axatria had prepared that morning.

She stood up abruptly, and knocked Sogdiam's arm with her shoulder as he was carefully decanting goat's milk from a big gourd into a double-handled pitcher. The gourd fell from his hands, the pitcher overturned, and milk spattered the vegetables and the wall next to the draining table. Sogdiam caught the pot just as it was about to roll off the table and smash on the floor. With an angry gesture, he let out a torrent of oaths in the dialect of the lower town.

"I'm sorry, Sogdiam," Lilah cried. "It's my fault!"

"Yes, it is!" Sogdiam exploded, pushing the cork back in the gourd with his fist. "You said it—it's your fault! You've been walking all over me ever since you came into this kitchen, as if I wasn't even here. Your eyes are wide open, but you don't see me any more than if I were a spirit from the underworld!"

"Sogdiam!"

"Sogdiam do this, Sogdiam do that! Sogdiam got up at dawn to make everything ready; Sogdiam isn't lying when he says he waits for you. All you have to do is put the biscuits in the stove. Everything has been cleaned and put away. You can lift every lid in this room! Everything has been cleaned and put away! You don't have Axatria to help you today, so I'm helping you like a handmaid. But if Sogdiam wants you to say thank you, he's got a long wait!"

"So now Sogdiam is also losing his temper, is he?" Lilah took him by the shoulders, drew him to her, and pressing her lips to his brow. "Forgive me, Sogdiam," she whispered. "Don't take any notice, it's a bad day. Ezra's angry, Axatria's angry, you're angry, and I . . ." She fell silent, feeling sobs rising in her throat. She hugged Sogdiam tighter, not so much to comfort the boy as to reassure herself. "Of *course* I see you, my Sogdiam. Of course I thank you."

She gave him little kisses on his eyelids. Sogdiam did not reply, any more than he dared put his arm around her waist. He stood there stiffly, his body against hers, breathing in short gasps and shaking all over.

Lilah gently pushed him away. There was still so much mistrust in his eyes, she was reminded of a wild animal that could never be truly tamed. "Smile!"

Sogdiam's mouth quivered and stretched in a grimace that was not a smile but did acknowledge the depth of the affection he felt for her and his hunger for love.

Lilah took his chin and forced him to look at her. "You'll never be my husband, Sogdiam," she said, in a very low voice. "I'm much too old for you. But I know that I'll often regret it. And I also know that we'll always be friends!"

They remained like that for a few moments, long enough for Sogdiam, with a gleam in his eyes now, to be convinced that Lilah was not joking. Then, gallantly, he freed himself from her. "It's all right," he said. "There isn't too much spilled milk. I'll clean it up."

With a knot in her stomach, and surprised at the strength of her own feelings, Lilah watched him go about his work, cleaning and putting away the flat stone, the containers, and the dirty utensils. He was a serious and loyal young man, braver and more determined than most boys of his age in the upper town.

"I wasn't inspecting your work, Sogdiam," she said, in a neutral tone. "I'm well aware you do more work than Ezra asks of you. I was just surprised how empty these baskets are. Ezra eats nothing, and Master Baruch has the appetite of a bird, but there's almost nothing left of the barley and the dried vegetables Axatria and I brought you last time. There must have been at least four or five minas of each! I find it hard to believe you eat the rest of it. And there's no reason to throw it away . . ."

Sogdiam did not reply immediately. "We don't throw it away," he admitted at last. "We give it away."

"You give it away?"

"It was Ezra's idea."

"What do you mean?"

Once again, Sogdiam took his time replying. He looked down at the stove, where the crusts were getting darker. For some time now, the room had been filled with the sweet smell of barley, but neither had taken any notice.

"Your biscuits are turning red," he said.

"Lord Almighty!" Lilah hurriedly seized a long wooden spatula and a thick serge cloth. She bent over the stove, screwing her eyes up against the heat, skillfully prized the biscuits loose with the spatula, without breaking them, and collected them in the cloth. She stood up again, breathing hard, her face bathed in sweat. "One moment more and they'd have burned!"

"The herb tea must be ready, as well," Sogdiam said, and he, too, plunged his hand into the stove and took out the pitcher.

Lilah placed the steaming golden biscuits on a platter of woven palms, and added a few dates and the pot of milk. She looked at Sogdiam, who was filtering the herb tea into a large bowl. "What do you mean, you give away the food?"

Sogdiam looked at her. As reluctantly as if he were about to betray a secret, he pointed his chin at the courtyard. "Three or four moons ago, a woman from the *zorifes* came here. She was moaning so loudly you could have heard her in the upper town. We gave her a little barley." He stopped, and smiled. "Wait." Again he bent over the coping of the stove and took a small earthenware dish with a lid from beneath the ashes. "A surprise for Master Baruch," he announced, lifting the lid with the aid of a cloth and waiting for Lilah's reaction.

In a wreath of steam, a mouth-watering aroma reached Lilah's nostrils. "Mmm, it smells wonderful."

"Turnips, dates, and chopped fish mashed together, with a lot of cardamom, basil, and curdled milk. A recipe I invented."

"But Master Baruch has a bad stomach and says he won't eat anything."

"Oh, he has a bad stomach until he gets this under his nose! You'll see, as soon as he smells this, he'll shake with pleasure." Sogdiam shook, too, but with laughter.

Lilah laughed with him. "I didn't know you were so fond of cooking."

"I try this and that. I mix things, and taste them. If I like what I taste, I suggest it to Ezra and Master Baruch. They don't eat a lot, but they taste. They aren't hard to please. Sometimes, they really like it. Especially Master Baruch, to be honest. He always used to ask for the same barley gruel, because of his teeth. Or rather, his lack of teeth. And I was fed up with always smelling the same smells here in the kitchen . . ."

Lilah had dipped a wooden spoon in the dish. The delicacy of the taste surprised her. "It's excellent!"

Sogdiam glowed with pride.

"But you didn't use everything in the baskets, making this kind of food," Lilah went on. "So tell me—the woman who came here, what was she complaining about?"

"You won't let go, will you?" Sogdiam sighed. " 'No more flour,' she was bawling, 'no more flour, nothing more to eat!' She said she had three boys and no more food left to give them."

"What happened then?"

"She made such a racket, Ezra had to leave his study. 'Sogdiam, why do you let the courtyard get so noisy?' I explained to him. 'Why doesn't her husband give her enough to feed her children?' he asked. How was I supposed to know? I asked the woman. She told me she didn't have a husband. Ezra was angry about that. 'She has three sons and no husband?' I reminded him that my mother had also had a son and no husband. 'That's why you took me in.' I said. Ezra gave me one of those black looks of his. Like a moonless night, I always say. Master Baruch was laughing into his beard but, as usual, didn't say anything. The woman was still weeping in the middle of the courtyard, moaning loud enough to set your teeth on edge. Ezra came to a decision. 'Give her what she wants,' he said, 'as long as she stops crying. I need to study in peace.' And there you are."

"What do you mean, there you are? Did you give her all your reserves?"

"No. Just enough for four days."

Lilah shook her head, surprised. "How long ago was this?"

"The month of Kislev, to be precise."

"So you've been giving her grain since then? Is that why your baskets are so empty?"

Sogdiam lowered his eyes, trying to conceal a wicked little smile. "Her and others."

"Others?"

"The woman came back four days later. Not alone, but with

six other women. Younger than her, also from the *zorifes*. They weren't weeping, but they explained to me they were all in the same situation as the first one. One or two children, no husband. As summer and autumn were very dry, and the harvests poor, they weren't allowed to glean. They were starving. You could see it, I swear."

"So you gave them food, just like the first woman?"

"I asked Ezra first. He gave me another of those 'moonless night' looks. But not for long. He asked me if we had enough. I told him we did. 'So give it. I don't want them to cry. Give, but make sure you share fairly, because they don't have the same number of children.'"

Lilah was silent for a moment, an intent look on her face. "Is that what he said?" she asked, in a low voice.

"Yes." Sogdiam was staring at her anxiously now, and biting his lips. "Do you think I did wrong? They're women like my mother and—"

"Oh, Sogdiam," Lilah said, smiling to stop herself from crying. "Of course you did what you had to do."

⬤

AS Sogdiam had predicted, Master Baruch forgot the bitter taste in his stomach and his desire for an herb tea when he smelled the aroma of the dish the boy had prepared. For a moment, smiling thinly, he allowed himself to be overcome by the smell of the food. "Delicious," he murmured, a rapturous look on his face, while Lilah made sure he was comfortable. "Exquisite!"

Sogdiam had helped Lilah to bring in the bowls and place them on the writing chest. His eyes gleamed with pride.

"I was thinking of you as I cooked it, master. And your teeth," he added, bowing.

"May the Everlasting bless you, my boy, wild as you are!"

"Wild now, master," Sogdiam said, serious again. "But one day you may make a good Jew of me!"

Master Baruch roared with laughter. "It takes more than a dish of turnips and fish to become a child of Israel! But perhaps the Everlasting will make an exception for you."

Sogdiam laughed brightly and went out, dancing despite his limp.

"I didn't know Sogdiam was taking such good care of you," Lilah remarked, as she wrapped Master Baruch's frail shoulders in a blanket.

"For a barbarian," Master Baruch chuckled, "the boy certainly has many qualities. Perhaps the Everlasting has already made an exception for him."

Ezra had pushed his stool under the window, and sat there with a scroll across his knees. He had not looked up during this exchange.

"Master Baruch, can't you persuade Ezra that he, too, must eat from time to time? The news from Jerusalem won't be any better if he dies of hunger."

"You're right, my dove! You're absolutely right. His studies won't be any better either, I might add. An empty stomach does nothing for the eyes or the ears."

"I eat my fill," Ezra protested, without looking up.

"Increase your fill, then!" Lilah said, annoyed.

Apparently indifferent to the quarrel that seemed to be brewing, Master Baruch closed his eyes as Lilah filled his bowl. But after slowly eating a mouthful, he murmured, in that voice of his that was always obeyed even though it seemed never to give an order, "Such is the irony of the Everlasting. We're gloomy and sick because we received bad news from Jerusalem. Sogdiam does the cooking, and the shadow of Jerusalem no longer hurts our stomachs, only our hearts and minds. Is that why Nehemiah failed? Or because the people of Jerusalem no longer have the hearts or the minds to suffer what they've become? Lilah is right, my boy. Do honor to our Sogdiam and come and share my meal."

Reluctantly, Ezra resolved to try. After swallowing a few spoonfuls, he seemed to find the food pleasant, and emptied the bowl rapidly.

Lilah looked at him and smiled. Ezra was like that. Severe, serious, obstinate, deeply tormented by the desire to do the right thing, the correct thing. And sometimes too impatient, too impulsive and unyielding, unconcerned about the realities of life, as if the years of childhood were still with him. But perhaps that was only the result of his faith: According to Master Baruch, he was becoming wiser than any sage, purer than any zealot.

Ezra was aware of his sister's eyes on him. He smiled at her. It was a smile that had delighted Lilah for more than twenty years, a smile that spoke of the indestructible love linking brother and sister and, better than any caress, united them in the same tenderness, like two sounds in harmony on the same lyre, sweeping away all doubts and quarrels. Today, though, Lilah remained deaf to its call. With a pang in her heart, she looked at Ezra's beloved face and thought of her beloved Antinoes. God of heaven! How could she speak the words she had been repeating to herself all night? How could she say to Ezra the phrases she had written on the papyrus scroll now hidden under her bed?

She closed her eyes, and the prayer she had uttered during the night again filled her mind. "O Yahweh, God of heaven, God of my father," she implored, "give me the strength to find the words to convince Ezra! Give him the strength to hear them."

Ezra misunderstood her silence and her closed eyes. "Lilah, my sister, don't be sad, I'm eating! You were right to insist; it's very good. Who could have predicted that Sogdiam would like cooking so much? He was like a dog when he came here, all skin and bones."

Recovering her composure, Lilah smiled at him affectionately. "He told me about the women you give food to."

"Oh yes, we had to." Ezra drank his cup of milk in sips. "It's of no importance."

"What do you mean, it's of no importance? Of course it's important! These women are in need. Who can help them, here in the lower city, if not Master Baruch and you?"

Ezra threw a look at Master Baruch over his glass. The old man was wiping the bottom of his bowl with a piece of biscuit, which he then swallowed before looking up with an ironic glint in his eyes.

"In future," Lilah went on, "I'll bring a little more so that you don't have to scrimp for your own meals."

Master Baruch chuckled. "Lilah, my dove, it isn't Ezra who helps these poor women. Let alone me—as you've observed, I'm nothing but a stomach. It is written in the scroll of the laws taught to Moses. 'Do not gather the gleanings of your harvest, but leave them for the poor man and the immigrant!' Is it we who glean this grain and bring it here? Lilah, without you, the women who came into this courtyard would now be hearing their children screaming with hunger. And we, the sages of Zion, would have nothing in our stomachs, just the bitterness of bad news and remorse."

Blushing with embarrassment, Lilah rose hurriedly to clear the table. She was about to leave the room when Ezra asked, as if he had only just become aware of it, "Didn't Axatria come with you today?"

"She's waiting for me at the gate to the upper town."

Ezra laughed in surprise. "Why? Is she afraid of seeing me?"

"Oh no, all she thinks about is seeing you." She hesitated. "I was the one who asked her to let me come alone today."

"Why?"

Lilah hesitated again. Master Baruch had let his head roll back against the cushions supporting him and seemed to have dozed off.

"Antinoes is back," she said, in a very low voice.

Ezra's expression did not change, and he said nothing. Had he heard?

"He's back. I saw him yesterday. He fought Cyrus the Younger's Greeks and was awarded the breastplate of the heroes of the King of Kings."

Lilah fell silent. Her own words seemed to her out of place and offensive. She wanted to say, "I love him. I want him for my husband. He wants it, too, more than anything else. I love to be in his arms. And I also love you, with all the love in a sister's heart." But the words that emerged from her mouth were cold and fearful, devoid of color.

And Ezra's face remained as stony as before.

For a moment, they were both equally silent and motionless.

"Is that why you stopped Axatria from coming with you? So that you could tell me this?"

"No," Lilah breathed, hoping that Master Baruch was not about to wake up. "That wasn't why. It was so that you and I could talk. Antinoes hasn't changed his mind. He hasn't changed at all. Neither have I . . ."

Ezra rose abruptly and went and sat down on his stool.

"You loved Antinoes, Ezra. We—"

"Be quiet!" Ezra cut in. "I was a mere child, an ignorant young man. As ignorant as it was possible to be in our uncle's family. As ignorant as the children of Israel have become in exile. But not anymore."

"Ezra, I know that as well as anyone, and I'm proud of what you are, of what you've become. I would never—"

"A Persian warrior comes back to the royal city of Susa," Ezra interrupted. "What of it? It may be news to you, my sister, but not to me."

Lilah put her hands together to stop them shaking, but she sustained her brother's gaze. "Don't be so unyielding! Have you really forgotten that you used to call Antinoes 'brother'? Have you forgotten that he held your hand when you wept for our father and mother? Have you forgotten that when you kissed me, you kissed him, too?"

Ezra gave a curious smile, a beautiful, profound smile, which did nothing to soften his expression. "I haven't forgotten anything, Lilah. I'm working every day with Master Baruch so that we don't forget anything of what we are, we, the people who have a covenant with the Everlasting. I never forget anything that doesn't deserve to be forgotten. I haven't forgotten that you're my beloved sister, and that without you there would never be any life in this hovel, any beauty, any tenderness. I haven't forgotten who we are. I haven't forgotten that nothing, not even your Persian warrior, can tarnish the eternal love of Lilah for Ezra."

Master Baruch had woken up, and was looking intensely at Lilah. She stood up and walked to the door, intending to leave the room without a word. But she could not: She turned and said, with a knot in her stomach, "Nothing that comes from my Persian warrior can tarnish me, Ezra. It is he who gives me life and beauty and tenderness."

A Day for Anger

Mordecai's wife, Sarah, always supervised the women workers. She would go from one loom to the next, inspecting the work: the regularity of the stitches, the arrangement of the colors, the pressure of the weft, the texture of a line, the quality of a knot.

Today, though, she found it hard to take an interest. She was constantly going out into the empty courtyard, where the autumn sun cast long shadows erased occasionally by a passing cloud.

Her mouth, so perfectly shaped for the sweet things in life, would grimace in irritation, a frown would crease her brow, and her face would set hard as she returned to the workshop.

It was a long, vast gallery, with a series of arches along its length, allowing the daylight through all the way to the whitewashed wall at the far end, where seven weavers sat side by side.

Around the looms were reels of thread in piles, empty and full shuttles, reglets for keeping the lines taut, pails filled with needles of bone or wood. Bronze blades of different sizes, used for measurement, were carefully laid out on low trestles. At one end of the workshop, behind two large shuttles on pedals, some fifty carefully arranged baskets contained an assortment of woolen threads of every color in creation. At the other end of the workshop, the finished rugs hung from wooden racks.

A few of the workers walked to and fro, carrying baskets of shuttles. The weavers, though, sat beneath the looms. The tops of the frames hung from bronze rings sealed into the wall at a man's height. The bottoms of the looms rested on little trestle tables, beneath which there was space for the women's legs. Some sat on cushions, bending their legs with their calves under their buttocks. Others chose to put a pile of used pieces of wool between their buttocks and the rough brick floor.

Their hands moved with speed and precision, sliding, separating, pulling, counting. Weights that looked like tiny wheels were attached to the vertical threads. Every time the shuttles passed, the women would be hit in the stomach, or on the thighs or chest. The clank of the shuttles and the banging of the reglets could be heard out in the courtyard. Sometimes the noise was so loud that it was like the sound of some fabulous, insatiable animal chewing.

Not one of the workers looked up or turned away from her work. They sensed Sarah's approach, as if they had eyes in the backs of their heads, and their hands seemed to fly even faster and more skillfully between the threads.

It was nearly fifteen years since Sarah had opened her workshop, at the suggestion of her husband. Today, she knew every speck of dust. Simply from the noise of the shuttles, the reglets, or the needles, she could tell if the work was good or bad.

Although it was a great imposition, Sarah personally supervised the progress of the work, in the most meticulous fashion. Each day she would appear unexpectedly, sometimes in the morning, sometimes in the afternoon.

The sweetness of her appearance, the placid roundness of her body and her face, matched one part of her character. She rarely lost her temper, and only when the same worker repeated the same fault. Most often, she would gently touch a shoulder or a neck. Or stroke a cheek, especially if it was one of the young new workers, girls intimidated by the workshop, who were encouraged by a little kindness to forget the pain in their fingers and lower backs. Very occasionally, she would compliment someone. But compliments had value only if used sparingly; nothing was worse than an excellent worker who became too proud. That was a sad waste, like those wonderful peaches from the Zagros Mountains that came to the upper town in the month of Elul, ripe peaches that had to be eaten immediately because they were already on the point of becoming rotten.

Sarah did not hire older women as weavers. However experienced they were, they tended to be bad-tempered. And as it was for the mind, so it was for the body: If you wanted flexibility, nothing could equal youth. The girls who were chosen had to be willing to learn and obey. It was also useful to have a few among them who had brains in their skulls. But all of them had to be able to obey. A workshop of this reputation could not be run without strong leadership. For all her smiles, Sarah's tongue could be sharp and her eyes pitiless. And although the merchants who supplied her with wool or the many tools needed in the workshop were often seduced by her well-displayed curves, they soon learned to be on their guard when the time came for payment.

Many of the carpets and rugs produced by Sarah's workshop embellished the benches of the chariots built by her husband. But her girls were versatile, and could also make carpets and rugs in the styles of Judaea, Media or Parsumash, Lydia, or the Susa region. There was hardly a single noble family in the Citadel, or in Babylon or Ecbatana, that did not own something made in the workshop of Sarah, wife of Mordecai and daughter of Reka.

After a good dinner, washed down with palm beer, Sarah liked to say with a laugh, covering her mouth with her chubby fingers, that she had at least one thing in common with the King of Kings: Her workshop also reigned over all the regions of Greater Persia. She hoped the Everlasting would forgive her this vanity!

Today, though, her thoughts were elsewhere.

Her niece, Lilah, had still not returned from the lower town.

She did not need to keep her eyes on the courtyard to know that. She would have heard the noise of the chariot wheels on the flagstones. Forcing herself to concentrate on work, she turned to a tall, thin young woman who was following respectfully two or three paces behind her. "Helamsis, have you counted how many carpets have been finished today?" she asked.

"Yes, mistress. Five. They're on the trestle." Helamsis pointed to the far end of the workshop.

Sarah walked in that direction. "Have you checked they're the right size?" she asked, curtly.

Helamsis's answer was lost in the clatter of the shuttles and reglets. Sarah did not ask her to repeat. When she was in this kind of mood, Helamsis knew, it was best to obey her quietly and agree with her as often as possible. Even if Helamsis swore on the wrath of Ahura Mazda that every piece was exactly the right length and width, Sarah would still go and check for herself.

That was what she now set about doing. After a meticulous inspection, she put the shuttles back on the trestle with a sigh. There was nothing to criticize—they were perfect.

Sarah was about to ask Helamsis to take them to Mordecai's workshop on the other side of the courtyard when the long-awaited rumbling was heard.

"Ah!" Helamsis, who was well aware of the reason for her mistress's impatience, said with a sigh of relief. "Here's your niece Lilah's chariot!"

"WHAT a way to behave!" Sarah exclaimed.

As she had reached out her hand to help Lilah out of the chariot, Axatria had knocked into her.

"Can't you apologize, my girl?" Sarah roared.

The reproach had no effect. Axatria strode across the outer courtyard, dragging the empty basket behind her, and disappeared between the columns that led to the second courtyard, where the apartments and the kitchens were.

"What's the matter with her?" Sarah fumed, unable to ignore what had happened.

"Oh, today's the day for anger," Lilah replied, jumping nimbly from the chariot. "Everyone's angry: Axatria, Ezra, even Sogdiam."

"Angry? Why? Because of *him*?"

Lilah could not help smiling. *Him* could only be Antinoes. She just had time to adjust her shawl on her shoulders before her aunt took her by the elbow.

"Come, let's not stay here. I've had an herb tea of sage and rose brought to my bedchamber."

What Sarah called her bedchamber consisted, in fact, of two spacious rooms. One was a true bedchamber, while the other, furnished with low tables, chests, and a large number of cushions, was used as a reception room. From it, there was a view not only of the second courtyard but also of the gardens surrounding the house, a tranquil and delightful sight. Between the cypresses and the eucalyptus trees, the imposing walls and columns of the Citadel could be seen. Sarah was very proud of the room, and loved to receive her women friends there, as well as the wives of important customers.

"So, tell me, tell me everything!" she said, as she lay down on the cushions. "What did he say?"

Lilah knew that her aunt's gaiety would soon vanish. But she avoided replying to her impatient questions directly. "Ezra and Master Baruch have had bad news from Jersusalem," she said, as if that was what she had been asked. "The sage Nehemiah died without accomplishing his mission. The Temple may have been rebuilt, though Ezra has his doubts. But it is soiled with all kinds of bad practices, and the city itself is again lawless, with no protection for the Jews."

Sarah stopped as she was pouring the herb tea into silver goblets, and frowned. "Yes, I know that. Mordecai told us all about it a few days ago. It's sad, I know," she admitted, putting down the pot of herb tea. "But, well . . ."

"Ezra was black with rage. He thinks we exiles have been deceived. We've let ourselves be too easily taken advantage of. The laws of Yahweh are not respected, and the children of Israel are in danger."

Sarah gave an irritated sigh. "Ezra is always black with rage. He thinks we're guilty of everything."

"No, aunt. He only thinks that we don't pay enough attention to what's happening in Jerusalem . . ."

Sarah interrupted her, waving her hands as if brushing away flies. "Lilah, Lilah, my child! Leave these things to Ezra and Mordecai. They're not for us women. What I want to know is what he said about your marriage to Antinoes."

Avoiding her eyes, Lilah looked up at a flock of swallows circling above the garden. Was she also about to lose her temper?

Since she had left the lower town, she had been dreading this moment. She could guess in advance every one of the words that would be spoken: words of reproach she had heard so often, and which never had the slightest effect on her. If Ezra was frequently unfair to his uncle Mordecai and his aunt, they were no less unfair to him, obstinately refusing to judge his behavior with a modicum of good faith. Couldn't they at least respect his choices and admire his courage?

If only they would make an effort to understand him a little

instead of constantly reproaching him! Today was definitely a day
for anger.

Lilah tried to calm down by drinking a mouthful of the scald-
ing herb tea. It was a drink much loved by her aunt: Sharp and
sickly sweet at the same time, it seemed to have been conceived
in her image.

Sarah was leaning toward her. "I know you were with Antinoes last night," she said in a low voice, her face alive with
curiosity. "I heard you come home." She chuckled. "I'd have liked
to go and see you immediately, so that you could tell me everything. But Mordecai had decided to sleep with me, and that's
not something that happens often!" The questions came thick
and fast, and Lilah replied as briefly as she could. Yes, Antinoes
still loved her as passionately as ever. Yes, he had become a
hero of the King of Kings. Yes, he wanted her for his wife. Yes,
yes . . .

"And Ezra?"

Lilah bit her lip, then, seeing her aunt's big eyes shining with
impatience, she smiled. "Ezra is like Antinoes," she replied. "He
hasn't changed either."

"Hasn't changed? You mean . . ."

"You know what I mean, aunt."

There was no longer anything soft or tender in Sarah's face.
"You mean he won't hear of your marriage, is that it?"

"He's devoted to his studies, and nothing else interests him,"
Lilah replied patiently.

"All I know is, he's mad and he'll cause you a lot of unhappi-
ness." Sarah's voice was as harsh now as when she discovered a
defect in a carpet.

Lilah was on the point of standing up and leaving the room.
She, too, would have liked to speak her mind, to say loud and
clear that she was no longer a child, that all this was no one's

business but her own, and that she'd prefer to be left in peace. But that would not have been the truth. Whether she liked it or not, her marriage to Antinoes was everyone's business.

"No, I didn't tell him about the marriage," she forced herself to reply calmly. "There was no point."

"No point? No point in telling him about your marriage? What are you talking about?"

"There's no rush, Aunt Sarah. Give Ezra a little time. He knows Antinoes is back. He'll think about it."

"Think about it!" Sarah cried. "We know what he's going to think about it!"

Lilah said nothing.

"And what about you?" Sarah went on, frowning. "You want this marriage, don't you? You love each other! You're promised to each other . . ."

"What we've promised each other is no one's business but ours, aunt!"

Without intending to, Lilah had spoken curtly and had slammed her glass down on the tray.

Sarah gave a muffled moan, her chest trembling, and turned toward the garden. She was weeping. She had a very particular way of weeping: soundlessly, almost without tears. A violent shudder rippled through her throat and made her lips quiver.

"Aunt Sarah!"

"Don't you want to get married?"

"That's not what I said."

Her aunt looked at her for a moment in astonishment, then shook her head. "I don't understand you! I haven't understood your brother for years. But now you . . ."

"Ezra is doing what he thinks is right," Lilah said, remembering that she had used the same words in trying to calm Antinoes.

"Oh really? What does that mean—right? Doing everything he can to hurt his uncle and aunt?"

"Aunt Sarah! Ezra isn't a child, and hasn't been a child for a long time. Uncle Mordecai and you know what he's doing in the lower town and why. You should be proud and recognize his greatness."

"His greatness!" Sarah cried. "In the lower town? As if that wasn't enough to make us ashamed! He could just as easily pursue his studies here. Even with that old sage of his, who turned up out of nowhere like a beggar. There's no better man than Mordecai. Even after all this time, he would still welcome Ezra with open arms. But oh no!"

"Aunt Sarah, there are laws for the Hebrews," Lilah said, passionately, getting up from the cushions. "Laws for all of us, at every moment of our lives, laws that come from the God of heaven. We've forgotten them in our exile. They're written in Moses' scroll, which has been passed from father to son in our family for generations. Now the scroll of the law has come to Ezra. He wants to study it. Not only to study it—he wants to obey its teachings. Isn't that his right? Perhaps even his duty? Shouldn't we admire him for it as we're taught to admire the ancients, the patriarchs, the prophets?"

"What modesty! Ezra the equal of the ancients, the patriarchs, and the prophets! Is that all?" For a moment, they glared at each other. Then Sarah shrugged. "You sound more and more like him," she said, with disappointment in her voice.

"I don't sound like him. But I understand why he says what he does."

"You're lucky, then." Sarah rubbed her brow and eyes with her fingers, as if trying to extract an image from them. "You were there, in the house, in the garden," she sighed. "Always squabbling, but always adoring each other. 'My brother Ezra' here, 'my brother Antinoes' there! I can still hear you."

"Ezra is not the same as he was, Aunt Sarah," Lilah replied severely.

"Oh, I've noticed that! And you're not the same either." Sarah's voice broke, and her neck and chin started quivering again. "Antinoes is a chariot captain!" she sobbed. "He fights beside the great Tribazes. He can enter the Apadana whenever he likes and be invited to share a meal with the King of Kings . . ."

Lilah knew exactly what her aunt was feeling. Sarah had always loved Antinoes like a son. But she also loved the fact that his family was noble, and his name renowned. She was proud to be able to tell her customers that Antinoes, son of Artobasanez, the late satrap of Margiana, would soon be her niece's husband and Mordecai's heir.

Lilah walked away from the table and the cushions. Immediately, her aunt rose and rushed to her. "Lilah! Forgive me, my dear. I know how difficult this is for you. You love Ezra and . . . we all love him."

Lilah let Sarah take her hands.

Her aunt sighed, and mustered the strength for a little smile. "Perhaps you're right after all. You've always got on with him well. Perhaps it's better not to speak to him about Antinoes for the moment. His mood can be so changeable. In a few days . . ."

It sounded like a false hope, and Lilah turned away, embarrassed. But her aunt held her back, her face serious again, her voice low and firm.

"It's better not to say anything to your uncle either, my dear, until Ezra's made up his mind. Mordecai so much wants you to be happy. This marriage is really important to him! To all of us. To the workshops. Do you understand?"

The Queen's Friends

ow could she sleep?

Antinoes' voice said, "We are together forever. Without your love, I would be so weak, even a Greek child could vanquish me."

Ezra's voice said, "Do not soil the walls of this room with his name."

Aunt Sarah's voice said, "This marriage is really important to all of us!"

With a furious gesture, Lilah threw back the blanket, which had got tangled between her legs. A bad dream had awoken her, and she had tried in vain to get back to sleep. The darkness of her bedchamber seemed to weigh on her, the air as stifling as if someone had been burning sticks of cedar.

She groped for her shawl and put it on over her night tunic. Pushing back the shutter noiselessly, she stepped out, barefoot, onto the narrow terrace that ran alongside the women's rooms, its crenellated wall overlooking the inner courtyard.

She took a deep breath, and at last her throat felt less tight.

Veiled by clouds, the sky was heavy and opaque, moonless and starless. The west wind blew in from the desert in gusts. Soon it would die down, and the *zarhmat,* bringing the autumn rains and winter ice from the north, would chase it away. The diadem of the Apadana shone above the sleeping city, as it did every night. Lilah could not help thinking again of Antinoes.

Her eyes searched for the tower that had welcomed their lovemaking. It was hidden in the darkness, but Lilah saw it all the same, just as she still felt Antinoes' breath on her skin, the thrill of his caresses. She placed her hands on the wall, searching for a support she would have liked to find on her lover's shoulders and solid chest. For that was what Antinoes represented for her: not only the heat of desire, but a peace and a calm that no one else could give her—certainly not Ezra.

The remorse that had woken her came back, more pitiless than ever. Aunt Sarah was right. She had lacked courage when she had spoken to Ezra. At the first sign of his anger against Antinoes, she had fallen silent. She had not kept her promise.

What would she say to her lover when they met again? "Be patient. Be patient awhile longer . . ."

"I've been patient for such a long time," he would reply.

Was he asleep at the moment, or was he awake, like her, his mind in turmoil? Was he up there on the tower, trying to glimpse her through the darkness?

She smiled at her own childishness.

"Lilah . . ."

The whisper made her jump. She turned, her heart pounding. There was nothing around her but the blackness of night.

"Don't be afraid, Lilah. It's only me."

She recognized Axatria's voice. A shadowy figure took shape beside her.

"Axatria! What are you doing here?"

"I didn't want to frighten you."

"Why aren't you asleep?"

Axatria gave a tender little laugh and took her hand. "For the same reason as you."

She lifted their two joined hands and pressed them to her cheek, which Lilah realized was damp with tears. "Are you crying?"

"I've been telling myself I was silly and that I ought to ask you for forgiveness."

"What have I to forgive you?"

"My stupidity. My bad humor. Squabbling with you this morning. I assumed you weren't asleep either, and I thought of joining you in your bedchamber, but . . ."

Lilah embraced her and held her tight. "I forgive you, Axatria. Of course I forgive you."

Axatria pushed her away gently, sighed, and wiped her tears with a corner of her tunic. "I'm afraid."

"Afraid of what?"

"If you quarrel with Ezra, what's to become of me?"

"Axatria . . ."

"Lilah, Antinoes came back to marry you. And because of that, you're going to quarrel with Ezra."

Lilah looked out at the darkness and said nothing.

"Ezra will never agree to your becoming Antinoes' wife. If you go ahead, he'll never want to see you again. You won't be his sister anymore."

"How can you be so sure? Did he tell you that?"

"There's no need. You know very well that's how it'll be."

Far away in the royal city, dogs barked. The sound of a horn or a flute rose in the darkness. Then the wind carried away the echo. There were houses where the night was a celebration . . .

"Ezra can't do without you," Axatria sighed. "But all the same he'd rather give up seeing you than share you with Antinoes."

Lilah knew Axatria was right: The threat Axatria was describing was precisely the one she dreaded. "Antinoes can't do without me either," she replied in a low voice. "He tells me I protect him in battle."

Axatria nodded. "Yes, I believe him."

Axatria squeezed Lilah's hand until it hurt. They were so close, Lilah could feel Axatria's body shaking with sobs, even though Axatria was trying to control them as best she could.

"You'll have to choose Antinoes. You're too beautiful and proud to remain in your brother's shadow. But if Ezra doesn't want to see you again, he won't want to see me either."

Lilah braced herself not to yield to Axatria's contagious emotion. "Nothing has been decided."

"I'll lose the little he gives me," Axatria continued, as if she hadn't heard. "I'll lose everything. But who could blame Ezra? He's doing what he thinks is right. That's all he thinks about— doing what is right. He studies to be a just man, he listens to Master Baruch, everything he says and does is in a spirit of justice. If he's jealous of Antinoes, he thinks that's the right thing, too. In the laws he studies, a Persian cannot marry a daughter of the land of Judaea."

"Nothing has been decided," Lilah repeated, more firmly. "We must trust in the Everlasting."

"You can! He's your God. But what about me? Shall I make offerings to Ahura Mazda, Anahita, or Mithras? I love it when Ezra talks about the God of heaven. But I'm not Jewish. I have no god and no country. I'm just a handmaid from the Zagros Mountains who loves her master. Even if he hardly looks at her, which your aunt finds so amusing . . ."

"Axatria!" Lilah took the handmaid's face in her hands to silence her. "Axatria, nothing has been said or done. You, too, must be patient."

THE sun was already high when a loud knocking was heard at the gate of Mordecai's house. Two servants ran to it, grumbling, ready to reject an impatient customer. No sooner had they raised the beam that kept the two leaves of the gate closed than the gate was thrust open from the outside, and a dozen soldiers rushed into the courtyard. They carried javelins and wore felt helmets with red plumes, leather breastplates, and baldrics decorated with black tassels, holding straight daggers. From the workshop, Sarah let out a cry of terror.

The weavers broke off their work and crowded behind their mistress. The soldiers lined up in double file. A chariot came noisily through the gate and stopped in front of them in the middle of the courtyard. A wagon followed behind.

Pulled from his own workshop by the noise, Uncle Mordecai came running. Despite himself, he was wide-eyed with admiration for the elegance of the horses, the high body of the chariot, its serpentine golden handrail, and the lining of the interior with its blue and yellow geometric pattern. The spokes of the wheels were carved in the shape of leaves and the hubs lined with silver. It was an expensive piece of work, and not from his workshop. The customer had strange tastes, but clearly also had the means to indulge them. Mordecai walked forward to welcome the visitors, but, before he could even bow, he froze.

The gold carving on the front of the chariot was instantly recognizable: the head of a winged man resting on a sun wheel and surrounded on both sides by winged lions.

The emblem of the King of Kings!

God of heaven!

The man who was standing behind the driver noticed his astonishment. He made a gesture, and two of the soldiers moved aside to let Mordecai pass.

"Come closer."

The man had a curt voice, a round body, and the smooth cheeks of a eunuch. He wore a plaited and oiled shoulder-length wig. He was neither tall nor fat, and had a surprisingly withered face and a small mouth framed, like his eyes, by deep lines. His splendid ochre tunic was itself full of folds and pleats.

Mordecai hesitated. Sarah was coming toward him, her face as white as a sheet. The women had retreated into the workshop, clinging to one another.

The eunuch grunted with impatience and waved his hand again. Mordecai walked toward the chariot with as much dignity as he could muster. When he stopped again, the eunuch's eyes were on him, looking him up and down as if not sure which breed of animal he was dealing with.

"Are you Mordecai the Jew, son of Azariah, son of Hilqiyyah, Mordecai the chariot maker?"

It was less a question than an assertion.

Mordecai was normally an imposing figure: tall, with a narrow, angular face, lively eyes, and coal-black eyebrows. There was hardly any situation he was unable to face. But now, there was an unpleasant quiver of fear in his voice as he replied, "Yes, I am Mordecai, son of Azaryah."

Should he bow? Treat him as if he were a lord of the Citadel?

The soldiers around the chariot waited impassively, and the driver was as still as a statue. Out of the corner of his eye, Mordecai noticed more soldiers, standing at the entrance to the house, beside a wagon drawn by two mules.

The eunuch gave a half smile, which seemed to transform his face into a pool of water shivering in the wind. "My name is Cohapanikes. I am the third cupbearer to the Great Queen, mother of the King of Kings, first master of the world. I have come for your niece, Lilah, daughter of Serayah."

Behind Mordecai, Sarah let out a cry. Other cries could be

heard from the workshop. Mordecai opened his mouth, gasping for breath.

The eunuch seemed pleased with the effect he had created. He raised his arm, which was as smooth and pale as his face, and brandished a cane of Egyptian ebony with an ivory and coral tip. "It is the queen's wish! Obey!"

Mordecai found it hard to take this in. "The queen wants Lilah?" he said in astonishment.

"Are you deaf? It is an order from Queen Parysatis. Your niece, Lilah, must follow where I lead." He laughed again. "Don't make that face. The queen is doing you a great honor, chariot maker. Come on! Hurry up! The queen is waiting, and the queen does not like to be kept waiting."

⬤

SITTING in the wagon, Lilah needed the whole journey across the city to recover her composure.

It had been Axatria and Aunt Sarah who had come running and told her, with much rolling of eyes, about the incredible thing that was happening.

"But why?" Lilah had asked. "What does she want with me?"

There had been a gleam of pride in Sarah's eyes, chasing away the terror they had held a short while earlier. "She must have heard tell of your beauty," she had suggested. "Perhaps she wants you in her service?"

The suggestion had seemed so preposterous to Lilah that she had stood rooted to the spot.

Panic had seized the whole household. Axatria had made an effort to dress Lilah appropriately. Sarah had pushed her away: Nothing was suitable, nothing was beautiful enough, and they did not even have time to rearrange her hair!

"It's because of Antinoes," Lilah had said at last.

Axatria and Sarah had looked at each other, all pride or excitement gone from their faces. Axatria had grimaced and shrugged her shoulders. "That may be so, but *he* won't tell you that," she had muttered, pointing to the outer courtyard, where the queen's eunuch could be heard shouting.

The third cupbearer had impolitely refused the wine Uncle Mordecai had offered him while he was waiting, then had stormed and threatened until Lilah was finally ready to come out.

Then he had fallen silent. He had screwed up his eyes, and had looked her up and down with the same arrogant expression he had previously used for Mordecai. At last, a smile of satisfaction had creased his face. It was not a reassuring smile.

When Lilah had sat down on the bench in the wagon, Uncle Mordecai had looked at her out of his pale face, and had begged her with his eyes to be careful. Sarah had lifted a trembling hand, the tears already down to her chin. Axatria and the handmaids and the workers who had gathered by the gate had looked at her as if they would never see her again.

The third cupbearer had given the order to depart. The wagon had set off, and Lilah had closed her eyes, trying to reassure herself and not to think of what might await her.

THEIR cortege attracted attention as it passed through the streets. Two soldiers ran in front of the cupbearer's chariot. The wagon followed, surrounded by the other soldiers.

They had turned onto the royal road, which was so broad that twenty horse-drawn chariots could pass side by side. It started at the southern ramparts of the upper town, crossed into the royal city through a gate surmounted by two huge towers, and ended at the foot of the Citadel. It was straight, lined with trees and rose-bushes, and the middle part was paved with pink and white ornamental marble tiles as perfect as a woven carpet. Only royal chariots and soldiers during processions, on feast days, or when the King of Kings was moving from one place to another were allowed to use it.

The raucous sound of a horn rang out as they approached the towers of blue glazed bricks decorated with hundreds of winged lions. Without slowing down, the cortege passed through the wall into the royal city. As they did so, Lilah glimpsed rows of guards stationed in front of the two huge leaves of the gate with their bronze carvings.

The cloudy gray light returned as they came out on the other side. The soldiers who were running by the sides of the chariot and the wagon stopped, and were replaced by four horsemen in long tunics who took up position beside the chariot.

The royal way continued, as straight as ever. It was now lined with colored walls—ocher, yellow, and blue—surmounted by square, crenellated towers. There were no people walking here, no signs of everyday life. Lilah soon lost her bearings. The walls were so high that they even concealed the cliffs of the Citadel.

The cortege abruptly veered right, turning from the royal road into a narrower street with lower walls, and Lilah gave a start. The flights of steps and gigantic walls of the Citadel rose before them, barely half a *stadion* away, closer than she had ever seen them.

She pulled her shawl across her chest. She felt a knot in her throat. Her astonishment and curiosity turned to fear. There were more gates, arches, and courtyards. At last, they entered a huge garden. From here, Lilah could see the festoons of the ceramic friezes and the multitude of characters decorating the steps leading up to the Citadel.

To her surprise, their escort turned left, away from the Citadel walls. They entered a copse of pines, palms, and cedars. The east bank of the Shaour appeared between the trunks. The wheels of the vehicles and the hooves of the horses again echoed on flagstones. In front of them rose a huge palace, built on a terrace at a lower level than the river. The windowless outside wall of white-tinted bricks stretched as far as the river's east bank. It had only one gate, which was scarlet in color. The gate opened as the cortege approached, leaving them just enough time to pass before it closed again with a muffled sound.

The horsemen, the chariot, and the wagon came to a halt in a long, narrow courtyard, lined with cowsheds and water tanks. Beyond a porch and a metal gate, Lilah made out a series of smaller courtyards, arches, colonnades, and patios. Servants approached, all dressed in green and purple striped tunics. Their smooth cheeks and short hair indicated that they were eunuchs.

The third cupbearer got down from his chariot.

"Take her to the cleaning room," he ordered, without looking at Lilah. "She needs to be ready as soon as the queen has finished her meal."

LILAH knew of the rumors that circulated about Queen Parysatis. They were the kind that, once heard, could not easily be forgotten, the kind that people whispered to each other, fearing the very words they were speaking.

The queen was surrounded by a host of servants—handmaids and eunuchs—over whom she held the power of life and death, which she exercised according to her mood. Some had to apply her ointments and scents to themselves before she used them, others had to taste her food and drink. The queen had a fear of being poisoned, although she herself was an expert in the use of poisonous plants. She would sometimes have a eunuch's tongue cut out if he had accepted a less-than-perfect dish, or a hand-maid's hands cut off for not rejecting an ointment she thought was too lumpy.

Parysatis, it was said, had only two loves: her sons and the power she enjoyed as a queen and the mother of the King of Kings. It was whispered that her pleasures were as refined as they were cruel, her whims infinite, her desires unusual and never sated. The lords of the Apadana would break out in a cold sweat whenever they had to share her meal. Two of the wives of her eldest son, Artaxerxes II, had died because they had opposed her will. And Lilah had heard Antinoes himself express surprise that the most powerful of generals were more afraid of the queen mother's hatred than of the massed armies of the Greeks.

And now Parysatis had brought her here from Mordecai's house! A young Jewish woman from the upper town—not much more than an insect in the eyes of the queen.

But an insect whom Antinoes, son of Artobasanez, the late satrap of Margiana, wanted to marry . . .

What did Parysatis want? Merely to satisfy her curiosity?

The voice of a eunuch drew Lilah from her reflections. He presented her with a basket filled with fine bracelets and necklaces.

"Take these jewels and put them on. You will soon be taken to our queen."

Rather than obey, Lilah looked out through the wide window. A low sky, swollen with clouds, hung over the plains and hills to the west of the Shaour. It was not easy to tell what time of day it was. Lilah felt as though she had been in the palace for a long time, but that might be the effect of waiting and the long process of washing and dressing to which she had been subjected.

How pointless it had been for Aunt Sarah and Axatria to fuss over her clothes and hair before she left Mordecai's house! Saying little, treating her with neither formality nor familiarity, a number of handmaids and young eunuchs had led her to a small room where her clothes had been removed before she could even protest.

The handmaids had pushed her, naked, into a narrow pool, into which the eunuchs had then poured the warm, scented contents of two big jars. To her shame, they had washed her as if she stank as much as a girl from the lower town. Then they had taken her into an adjoining room, where laurel and eucalyptus leaves burned in braziers, dried her, and scented her with a thick, oily golden cream. After this, she had had to wait for her skin to absorb this liniment.

Shocked as she was to be stripped, prodded, and smeared in such an unrestrained way, Lilah had soon realized that both the handmaids and the eunuchs performed their tasks with unmistakable coldness. She could not even look them in the eyes. Their expressions remained distant and indifferent. As they worked, they spoke no more than was strictly necessary. They seemed to be thinking about nothing and seeing nothing. In their hands, Lilah was not a person, merely a duty to be fulfilled.

Ill at ease and fearful at first, Lilah finally became angry when they brought a white linen tunic that was so thin as to be transparent. The unusually shaped tunic left her right breast and most of her back bare, and stopped at mid-thigh. Her cheeks scarlet with shame, she had demanded the dress in which she had arrived. Her anger had barely raised notice from the handmaids.

"No woman appears before the queen in her own clothes unless she is the wife of a lord of the Apadana. That is the law. Queen Parysatis has ordered you to wear this tunic, and you must obey. Have no fear, you will get your clothes and your jewels back when it has been decided that you can go home."

Then they had given her a shawl to cover what her tunic revealed, and had made her wait again. The wait had been so long that she had had plenty of time to think of the moment when she would be displayed to Parysatis in this shameful attire.

Now the eunuch was pressing her to put on the bracelets of silver and ivory.

"Do not look at the queen before you bow," he advised. "And do not speak except to answer the questions you are asked."

THE handmaids led her into a small square courtyard that was like a well. Leading off from it were a number of corridors, in front of which stood eunuchs in guards' costumes. Four of them came and took up position around Lilah. Together, they plunged back into the vast labyrinth of the palace.

Lilah had the curious impression that the dark corridor along which they were walking was going around in a circle. Suddenly, she was blinded by the white light of day. A few more steps, and they were on the threshold of an extremely strange room. The high ceiling was supported by thin cedar columns covered with brass, and between the capitals of these columns brightly colored ropes were stretched. From the ropes there hung, parallel to one another across the room, a dozen immense transparent veils.

Although each of the veils, a light purplish blue in color, was very thin, all of them together obscured the far end of the room from view. They swayed gently in the breeze, iridescent in the light of day, which shimmered on their surface as if on the quivering fur of an animal.

Lilah was aware of the sound of voices, and a few tenuous notes played on a harp. Then there was a banging sound, and the eunuchs stepped aside to let her pass. One of them took hold of the shawl in which she had draped herself. Without a word, he ordered her to walk toward the veils.

Holding her arms tight across her half-naked chest, Lilah stopped before the first of the veils, uncertain what to do. With the tip of his spear, the guard lifted the veil and signaled her to continue.

She had to go through the remaining veils herself. They brushed against her, enveloped her, blinded her. Soon, she was so lost, she no longer knew in which direction she was moving.

Again, she was startled by the banging. She came to a standstill, as if caught doing something wrong, and at that moment a voice rang out imperiously.

"What is the name of the one who approaches?"

Stunned, Lilah breathed her name in what was hardly more than a whisper, and the voice repeated the question.

"Lilah," she said again, as loudly as she could. "Lilah, daughter of Serayah."

"Come two veils closer."

She obeyed, looking up at the beams on the ceiling to orientate herself. The veils still separating her from the rest of the room were less opaque now, and she could make out a colonnade leading to a garden.

"What are you doing here, Lilah?" the voice asked.

She could not reply. A shiver of fear went down her spine, insidious and clinging. Her hands were shaking. She forced herself to close her eyes, in order to regain her composure and not let emotion overcome her. The strangeness of this situation was only meant to impress her, to make her imagination run riot, to show her how weak she was. The veils were only veils, not monsters or wild beasts! Lilah rose to her full height.

"I have been summoned by the queen," she declared.

"Come closer."

Her heart pounding, Lilah lifted the veil directly in front of her. There were only two left now. She made out a dais between the columns. On it were a few figures, and in the middle a long bed beneath a canopy.

The notes of the harp were now distinct and clear. Lilah

caught a glimpse of the musician—a woman—beside one of the columns. Armed guards stood around the outside of the room, the gray daylight reflected in their metal breastplates.

"Come closer, girl, come closer," a woman's voice, different from the one that Lilah had previously heard, ordered.

Lilah realized that the queen had spoken.

Breathless now, she lifted the last veils. Still trying to hide her breast with her free hand, she took a few steps. The floor here was of marble. The cool air from the garden made her shiver. She remembered the eunuch's injunction and bowed briefly, bending one knee. She held her right hand in front of her, palm upward, and raised it to her lips as she rose again.

A deep laugh came from the bed. "Well, well. Come closer."

Parysatis, her chest supported by pillows, was half lying on the bed, which was covered with a green and purple silk rug. She was amazingly small, her body almost hidden beneath a cape embroidered with gold threads and precious stones. A silver band with strips of colored silk attached to it held her hair in place. Her face was like that of a prematurely aged child. Her skin, as clear and fine as a highly polished piece of ceramic, was furrowed with deep lines on the brow, cheeks, and neck. She was smiling, but her large sky-blue eyes, flecked with gold, were fixed and expressionless.

In a clatter of bracelets, her hand appeared, as white as milk. She waved her ringed fingers impatiently. "Come closer! Let me see you in the light."

Lilah obeyed. Two very young handmaids were kneeling on the bed, staring at her impassively. Beside the bed, on a wide stool, the third cupbearer sat, smiling the same ironic, self-satisfied smile he had had when he had first seen Lilah in Uncle Mordecai's house. Behind him, other handmaids and a few eunuchs, all very young, knelt on the dais, waiting. One of the eunuchs held on his knees the cedar planks whose banging had punctuated Lilah's progress through the veils.

"Come on, show yourself!" Parysatis cried.

Lilah hesitated. She could not be any closer to the queen's bed. What more did she want?

"Turn her," the third cupbearer commanded.

The two young handmaids glided to the foot of the bed and each seized one of Lilah's wrists. Holding her arms apart, they began spinning her around like a top.

Now Lilah understood why she had been forced to wear this tunic that left her half-naked. The handmaids continued turning her around. She closed her eyes, as dizzy with shame and anger as with the spinning. She had no need to see the queen's eyes, or the cupbearer's. It seemed to her as though every inch of her skin were being flayed to satisfy their curiosity.

"Well, Cohapanikes, what do you think?"

"She's beautiful, my queen. A beautiful girl, that much is obvious."

Parysatis nodded. They watched her as she whirled faster and faster, the short tunic lifting to reveal her thighs. Then, with a click of her fingers, the queen ordered the handmaids to let go of Lilah's arms.

Lilah had to make an effort to keep her balance. Mustering all the courage she could, she raised her eyes and looked at the queen.

The fine network of lines around Parysatis's eyes creased. The blue eyes narrowed, cold and calm, as impassive as the eyes of a snake waiting to strike. "Beautiful, but full of pride, that's obvious, too," she observed, without raising her voice.

"You have to admit Antinoes has good taste," the eunuch said, amused. "They say also that Jewish women are prudes in lovemaking, but not without skill."

"Quiet, cupbearer!" Parysatis cried. "Keep your tongue for my wine!"

Cohapanikes stopped smiling, and the folds of his face froze.

The notes of the harp vibrated like threats in the silence. For a few moments longer, Parysatis continued looking Lilah over.

Suddenly, the queen pushed back the cape and reached out her hands. The young handmaids rushed to support her as she got out of bed.

Standing, Parysatis was not much taller than the young girls serving her. Her thin tunic, visible now through the open cape, revealed a body that was younger and firmer than Lilah had imagined, which made the marks of age on her face seem all the stranger. Parysatis became aware of her surprise and looked at her mockingly.

"You thought me older than I am, didn't you, Lilah, my girl? Typical of the young! They see lines on a woman's neck and think she's old."

"My queen—".

Parysatis silenced her with a gesture. "Be quiet. If you aren't, you'll lie. And you must never lie to me."

Her face relaxed. She came closer still, lifted her ringed hand, and touched Lilah's bare arm lightly. Her fingers were soft and warm. She moved them from Lilah's shoulder to the back of her neck. Lilah gave a start, and had to make an effort not to retreat. The queen's fingers left little impressions as they glided over Lilah's chest, pressing harder as if she were searching for the bones beneath the skin. It was not so much a caress as an inspection. Lilah felt as though she were being examined like an animal.

"You have beautiful skin," the queen said. "How old are you?"

"Twenty-one."

"And you have no children yet?"

"No, my queen."

Parysatis chuckled, and her mouth opened to reveal small teeth, many of them as black as coal. She turned to the third cupbearer, who had joined her and seemed huge beside her.

"Do you hear that, Cohapanikes? Twenty-one! Not much

younger than this palace! She should long since have been married! When I was your age, my girl, the great Darius sought the
gold of his throne between my thighs every night, and I had already given birth to the King of Kings, who is your master today."

She gave a high-pitched laugh that shook her chest. In a gesture, which this time seemed surprisingly friendly, she took hold
of Lilah's hand. "Come, follow me."

She drew her in between the columns. The handmaids, the
eunuchs, the cupbearer, the musician, and the guards followed at
a distance of a few cubits.

"Your father and mother are dead," Parysatis said.

"Yes, my queen."

Still holding her hand tight, Parysatis descended the steps
leading to the garden. Lilah had the impression that she could tell
lies from truth merely by the touch of her hand.

"And you have known Antinoes a long time," the queen said.

It was not really a question. Parysatis was simply demonstrat-
ing the strength of her curiosity, as well as her royal power. There
was, unfortunately, no longer any room for doubt in Lilah's mind:
Antinoes was indeed the reason for this strange encounter.

"I've known him since we were children, my queen," she replied.

Without slowing down, Parysatis chuckled again. "Since you
were children! And you have no child yourself? You're surely not a
virgin?"

"My queen . . . ," Lilah hesitated, her voice muffled by shame.

Parysatis waved their joined hands brusquely. "Don't lie, I
told you! And don't be a prude! Of course you're not a virgin.
Parysatis can tell if a girl is a virgin as soon as she looks at her."

For a while, they advanced in silence. Lilah made an effort to
conceal her fear, as well as the humiliation of being almost naked
in front of everyone.

Letting go of Lilah's hand as abruptly as she had seized it,

Parysatis turned into a path lined with bamboo. The garden, enclosed by the outer walls of the palace, was extremely dense in
the middle, a tangled undergrowth of many species. As they
passed, thick clouds of butterflies flew up from the clusters of
amaranth and buddleia and whirled above their heads.

Carefully adapting her pace to that of the queen, Lilah wondered what mad questions Parysatis would ask next. Would she
get out of this palace alive? What should she answer and not answer? What did the queen want? Was Antinoes also in danger?

The path sloped gently toward the center of the copse. A
strong smell, pungent and feral, came from the undergrowth. It
grew stronger and more unpleasant as they advanced. It was a
smell such as Lilah had never known, but it did not seem to
bother Parysatis greatly.

The undergrowth suddenly thinned out, and a clearing appeared. Here, the bamboo trunks were merely a low hedge bor-
dering a pit a dozen cubits deep and with sides as sheer as if they
had been cut with an ax. At the bottom of the pit, Lilah was surprised to discover thick bushes, ponds, stunted trees with torn
trunks, and the ground furrowed with well trodden paths of soft
earth.

Not much more than twelve or so feet from the path where
Parysatis was advancing, a platform of logs jutted out over this
anarchic vegetation. Black carrion birds were sitting on the platform. As the two women approached, they flew off, screeching,
on heavy wings.

"Come closer, Lilah," Parysatis ordered, without turning. "Let
me introduce you to my friends."

As if in response to her command, a roar split the air. It was
answered by another, then another. Down in the pit, the bushes
moved. Lilah glimpsed flashes of fur, and let out a cry. Simultane-
ously, two lions with full manes leaped onto the platform, and

stood there with their mouths open, revealing shiny yellow fangs. With their huge paws, they stamped on the logs as if about to launch themselves. Lilah was unable to hold back another cry, certain they were about to leap in her direction.

But it did not happen.

One of them tipped its head back and raised its muzzle toward the sky. Its flowing mane spread over its breast like a corolla of fire. It gave another terrible, ear-splitting roar, while the other, whipping with its tail, growled and turned in a circle.

Lilah was terrified. Her teeth chattered and her bare skin was covered in gooseflesh. The lion roared again, less loudly this time, as if already becoming bored. Its mouth open threateningly, its ink-black pupils fixed on these newcomers, whose smell excited his nostrils, then it lay down. Behind it, with the humility of a less powerful male, the other lion followed suit.

For a moment, silence fell on the pit. The birds had stopped flying above the copse. Lilah could sense Parysatis's eyes on her, the humiliating smile, the greed and the cruelty.

So the rumors were true: Parysatis's greatest pleasure was to have people at her mercy, to observe their fear.

Lilah's pride sustained her: She struggled to dismiss the terror that froze her lower back and would have stopped her from fleeing a moment earlier. She rose to her full height, holding her shoulders tightly and clenching her jaws, aware of the hate growing in her heart.

"Up until now," Parysatis said, "my lions have never jumped as far as this path. Have no fear, Lilah, my girl. Come closer."

Lilah lowered her arms and obeyed without hesitation. Behind her, the handmaids, the eunuchs, the third cupbearer, and the guards stood a fair distance away and showed no desire to move any closer unless Parysatis ordered them to do so.

"Forgive me for crying out, my queen," Lilah said softly.

"It took me by surprise. I've never seen a lion before. They're beautiful."

The queen half closed her eyes and laughed. "Don't try to be proud, Lilah. I know you're afraid. Everyone is afraid of Parysatis. Haven't you heard that in the upper town? I'm sure you have. I know people tell tales about me. And they're right to fear me, because it's true: I'm cruel and pitiless. These creatures you see before you are my friends. My only friends. They rid me of anyone I find troublesome. That's what it means to be a queen, the wife of one King of Kings and the mother of another. Even my sons may one day put poison in my bread. But they're the only ones who have nothing to fear from my friends."

She laughed, walked up to Lilah, and again took one of her hands in what appeared to be a gentle, affectionate gesture, but was in fact quite terrifying, because it drew Lilah so close to the bamboo at the edge of the pit that she could feel it rubbing against her bare legs.

"You're beautiful, but that's neither here nor there. My palace is full of beautiful handmaids, and up there, in the Citadel, my son has hundreds of concubines, each more beautiful than the next. Beauty bores me, Lilah. They think I envy it, but they're wrong: It simply bores me. You have a little courage and a lot of pride. Perhaps some intelligence, too. That's a lot of qualities for a girl. That fool Cohapanikes is right: Your Antinoes has made a good choice. That's a point in his favor. It's braver and more difficult for a man to choose an intelligent woman than a beautiful woman."

For a moment, she was lost in thought. Below, the bushes moved. A black panther with a magnificent coat appeared on one of the paths and raised its golden eyes toward her indifferently.

It occurred to Lilah that the queen had only to move her hand to throw her headlong into the pit. She had no doubt that Parysatis, small as she was, was strong enough to do it.

"You've known Antinoes since you were children, but do you know the man you take between your thighs when he comes back from the wars?"

Lilah shuddered. She had barely heard the question. Down in the pit, more animals had appeared in the bushes. Four impatient she-lions took up position beneath the platform and growled.

"A warrior is like a young lion," Parysatis continued, without waiting for a reply. "He kills, he tears the flesh, he thirsts for blood. He rapes, he forgets. He's not meant for a young girl like you. Antinoes is a good boy, though. His father was useful to me once. He behaved well. I may be cruel, but I'm not disloyal. Your Antinoes is like his father, honest and upright. There are not many people in this palace you could say that about. He's fought for my son Artaxerxes, but hasn't raised his hand against Cyrus the Younger." Parysatis grinned and looked at Lilah. "Did you know that my friends have rid me of all those who raised their hands against Cyrus the Younger at the battle of Cunaxa? What a banquet that was!"

She laughed, and held out her hand, still joined to Lilah's, toward the two lions, which seemed now to be dozing on the platform.

"Look at them, they've eaten their fill!" She laughed again. "You're Jewish, Lilah. What will you do if the King of Kings names Antinoes satrap of Bactria? Will you follow him to Meshed, Bactra, or Kabul? Will your god follow you that far? To a place where you won't have your uncle or your brother with you, or any of your people?"

"I shall follow him," Lilah replied, unhesitatingly. "We made a promise to each other a long time ago. I shall keep my promise as he will keep his."

Parysatis gave Lilah a sideways glance and let go of her hand. She seemed pleased with herself, as if she had enjoyed a good piece of entertainment.

"I like you, Lilah. You're innocent, but I like you. What I don't like is the thought of your becoming Antinoes' wife. I don't know what I'm going to do with you."

The Sage of the Lower Town

hrough the beaten earth of the kitchen, then rising through his feet into his bad legs, Sogdiam felt a heavy vibration. He listened carefully, and heard a kind of rumbling that was too rare in the lower town not to attract attention.

He went out into the courtyard. A chariot and horses; he was sure of it. It was the stamping of hooves, the rumbling of a chariot's wheels, that was making the ground vibrate. He heard people shouting, children yelling, still quite far away.

He saw dust rising above the wall of the house and the surrounding roofs. As incredible as it might seem, someone was venturing into the streets of the lower town with a chariot and horses!

The dust came nearer. He had a premonition that they weren't just coming through the lower town—they were on their way here, to Ezra's house.

Through the open door of the study, he glimpsed Master Baruch, hunched on a stool, waving a scroll of papyrus in his hands and speaking. On the other stool, his back almost turned, staring at the wall in front of him as if gazing upon the most fascinating of landscapes, Ezra was listening. From time to time, he bowed his head slightly. Sogdiam had seen them like this so many times that for him it was the most normal, most reassuring sight in the world.

He crossed the courtyard with his lame but rapid gait, and opened the gate that led to the street. Some of the neighbors, drawn like him by the noise of the horses, were already there.

Sogdiam thought about Lilah. Could it be her chariot? But it wasn't her "day."

This might be a special occasion, though.

No, it was impossible! Lilah would never come in a chariot, as special as her visit might be. She would be too embarrassed to flaunt such luxury in a slum like this.

He frowned, anxiously. If it wasn't Lilah, who was it? Who, if not a lord of the Citadel? A lord, or else guards, soldiers: the kind of people who never brought anything good with them when they came into the lower town.

Suddenly, at the end of the street, men and women stood aside. Some climbed on the walls, others jumped into the gardens. Two black horses appeared, their coats as shiny as silk, their manes woven with tassels of red wool, drawing a light chariot with ironclad wheels, its body strengthened by a strip of brass. The handrail at the side was lined with leather sheathes and pouches—room enough for javelins, arrows, and a long-bladed sword. The kind of chariot Sogdiam had never seen before: a war chariot!

Too stunned to move aside from the middle of the street, Sogdiam stared openmouthed as the chariot and horses came straight toward him. The officer who held the reins was wearing a pointed felt helmet decorated with woven ribbons and a long cape of blue wool with yellow flecks. Behind the chariot was an

escort of about ten soldiers carrying spears. Children yelled with
excitement.

Nimbly shifting his weight, Sogdiam leaped to the gate to let
the chariot pass through into the courtyard. But as the horses
with their quivering nostrils passed so close to him that he could
feel their breath on his cheek, the warrior brought the chariot to a
halt with a mere flick of his wrist on the reins.

The soldiers ran to take their places against the wall of the
house, on either side of the gate. The children stopped yelling.
The warrior got down from the chariot. Against his thigh was a
plain sheath containing a broad knife with a steel hilt. The gold
brooches holding his cape were decorated with the heads of bulls
and lions. A dazzling smile shone between the fine locks of his
beard. The smile was addressed to Sogdiam: The officer was staring straight at him.

Brave and proud as he was, Sogdiam retreated into the courtyard. The officer followed him through the gate and held out his
hand. Everyone in the street, neighbors and children, then heard
these incredible words:

"Don't be afraid, Sogdiam. I'm your friend."

Sogdiam blushed, as if caught doing something wrong, and
threw an anxious glance toward the study. Master Baruch and
Ezra had not yet noticed anything.

Leaving the soldiers, the chariot, and the crowd of onlookers
in the street, the warrior closed the gate behind him. He took off
his helmet, and his oiled hair fell to his shoulders. Sogdiam felt
his chest turn hot and cold. He already knew who this officer was.

The man Ezra hated. The man Lilah loved.

He swayed slightly on his deformed legs. Anger, envy, vexa-
tion, and pleasure danced in his heart. The warrior frowned. There
was nothing threatening in his expression; quite the contrary. He
uttered the words Sogdiam was waiting for.

"I'm Antinoes, and I've come to see Ezra."

"Ezra is studying," Sogdiam replied, in a voice that seemed to him weak and ridiculous. "He's with Master Baruch, and can't be disturbed."

Still smiling, Antinoes looked at him in surprise. He turned his face toward the study, and saw that Sogdiam was telling the truth. Antinoes nodded, pulled the end of his cape up onto his shoulder, and made as if to walk even closer to the house. Sogdiam, quite unafraid, considered barring his way, but his bad legs refused to move. Antinoes also remained where he was, for now, Ezra had stopped studying, and was staring out at the warrior with his dark eyes. Beside him, Master Baruch was silent. Antinoes raised his hand in greeting. Ezra moved abruptly on his stool, and by way of response, turned his back. He unrolled a scroll on the table and said something to Master Baruch. The old man nodded, and the two of them resumed their muffled murmur.

"You see," Sogdiam said, with all the confidence he could muster. "They haven't finished. You'll have to leave."

As if he had not heard, Antinoes stood for a moment facing the study. Then, to Sogdiam's surprise, he burst out laughing: a good-humored laugh, without a trace of irony. "That's all right. I'll wait. Bring me a cup of water, will you?"

Relieved, Sogdiam hurried to the kitchen. When he came out again, Antinoes was standing in the middle of the courtyard, as if keeping guard on the wall of a citadel. His cape fluttered in the sharp north wind. The stormy light filtering through the low, dark clouds glinted on his knife as well as in his eyes. He showed no impatience, and made a friendly gesture to Sogdiam when the boy handed him the cup.

To Sogdiam, the thought of Lilah snuggling in this man's arms was as painful as a burn. It was one good reason to hate him. Ezra was another. Yet Sogdiam could not bring himself to do it. He could not help blushing with pleasure when Antinoes gave him back the cup and said in a soft voice, "Lilah loves you a lot, young Sogdiam. She told me so. She told me you were very brave and not at all like other boys."

Sogdiam bowed his head, and thought about what to reply. He did not have time: Antinoes had started walking toward the study. When he reached the doorway, he bowed politely.

"Forgive me, Master Baruch, if I interrupt your teaching. I have come to talk to my brother, Ezra. I haven't seen him for a long time."

There was a strange silence. Master Baruch looked up at Antinoes, his eyes glittering with curiosity; he did not seem the least bit offended. Ezra, though, stood up, pushing away his stool noisily. He walked up to Antinoes, going so close to him that Sogdiam thought they were either going to embrace or fight. His face was ice-cold, and his voice made the boy lower his eyes.

"You're disturbing me in my studies, stranger. I don't think that's very polite."

"Ezra!"

"You come here dressed and armed as if for war, flaunting your gold to the people of this town, who are dressed in rags, and you claim that I'm your brother, which is a lie. You can leave the way you came. We have nothing to say to each other."

Antinoes clutched his cape. Sogdiam sensed the shudder of anger that went through him. Yet when he spoke, his voice remained low and calm.

"You know as well as I do how one of Artaxerxes' officers has to move around. He travels by chariot and is always escorted. It doesn't matter if he's in the Citadel or the lower town; for him there's only one law and one kingdom. And you're wrong. I have something to say to you, something you need to hear. I came back to Susa to make Lilah my wife. I'm sure you know that already. But I've come here to ask you, as someone who was once my brother, not to condemn Lilah if she makes that choice."

There was a silence so heavy that Sogdiam felt it weighing on his shoulders. He was embarrassed that he was still in the courtyard, hearing this conversation. But it was too late, now, to hide in the kitchen.

His face closed, Ezra hesitated. Sogdiam feared he would throw Antinoes out into the street.

"My sister is free to choose her husband," he said, his voice whistling like the north wind.

Antinoes raised an eyebrow. "You won't oppose her decision, then?" he asked.

Ezra smiled, although the smile did nothing to soften his expression. He turned to Master Baruch, as if calling on him as a witness. But the old man sat bent over a papyrus, clearly indicating that he wanted no part in this quarrel.

"My sister is free to make her own decisions," Ezra said. "But there are laws for us, the children of Israel and the people of the covenant. They are not the same as your laws, son of Persia, just as our God is not the same as your gods."

"What do you mean, Ezra?"

"'Do not give your children to Molek,' the Law of Moses commands. 'Do not profane the name of your God. A woman who goes with an unclean man is herself unclean.' And if a woman is unclean, her brother can no longer go near her. He can no longer be her brother. Lilah will choose."

"Oh, I understand!" Antinoes laughed bitterly, anger getting the better of him. "If Lilah becomes my wife, you'll never see her again."

"It's not my decision. I'm obeying the Law and the Word that Yahweh taught Moses. The Law says that the women of Israel must find husbands among the men of Israel. And you are not part of that people. That's all."

"You have a short memory, Ezra. There was a time when you

put your arm around my neck and made me swear we'd never be separated. A time when you said, 'Lilah is the heart and the blood that unites us.'"

Ezra half opened his mouth. His brow and cheeks had turned scarlet. Sogdiam saw him clench his fists until they were white, and thought he was about to hit Antinoes. Then everything relaxed suddenly. Ezra's chest swelled and he gave a small, harsh laugh.

"Yes, there was a time when I wasn't yet Ezra. But that's over. And you're wrong. I have a long memory, much longer than you could ever imagine. It goes back to the first days of the people of Israel. To the day when Yahweh called to Abraham on the mountain of Harran."

"You talk about your God, Ezra, but all I hear is your jealousy," Antinoes retorted. "You know I've always respected your God. You know that even if Lilah is with me, she will always be with you!"

"I think you should leave now."

"Ezra!" Antinoes roared, this time raising his hand to underline his words. "Ezra, don't force Lilah to choose between us. Don't make her unhappy!"

Ezra did not reply. He turned, went back inside the study, and closed the door—something that Sogdiam had never seen him do before.

Antinoes stood for a moment in front of the closed door. At last he turned, his eyes apparently unseeing. In the street, the horses were snorting impatiently. The soldiers could be heard scolding the children, and the children laughing in reply.

Antinoes turned abruptly and walked away. His face was pale. Sogdiam saw him walking like a blind man. But as he reached his side, he raised his hand. Sogdiam jumped when Antinoes' hot palm came to rest on his neck.

Antinoes stroked his neck lightly, then, without a word, quickly left the courtyard, climbed into his chariot, and started the horses off at a trot, forcing the soldiers and the children to run.

THE workshop was fragrant with the fine powder of cedarwood and plane wood, the shavings of juniper and oak. The aroma of peas and roast pork fat mingled with the smell of almond gum and freshly tanned leather. To Mordecai's sense of smell, it was like music, a deep, haunting song against which the noise of saws, planes, gimlets, chisels, and mallets stood out. The well-ventilated workshop, as vast as a house, and cluttered with shafts, hobbles, benches, towers of ropes, and newly mounted wheels, was more than just a good place to work. It was a world in which he was king. A world of infinite possibilities in which every kind of chariot needed in the Susa region was made. Chariots with two or three benches, drawn by mules, horses, or sometimes asses and oxen, although that was hardly ever done anymore; war chariots and traveling chariots; chariots for royal parades or for transport.

Today, however, perhaps for the only time in his life, Mordecai was unable to savor the pleasure of it.

He came and went without seeing the workers, without seeing the work in progress. The truth was, he had lost interest in it. He stood at the side of the street, his ears on the alert, trying to detect the sound of a chariot. Not one of his own chariots, or a customer's, but the chariot of the queen's third cupbearer, which had carried Lilah off to Parysatis's palace that very morning.

With a heavy sensation in his stomach, he had been awaiting her return for hours. It was almost dusk, and there was still no sign of her. The north wind, as keen as an old man's breath, made the light hazy. It would soon rain. And Lilah had still not returned.

Mordecai knew that on the other side of the courtyard, bustling among her weavers, Sarah was equally worried. She had come and pestered him a hundred times. Did he have any news? How could he have had any? The 101st time, Mordecai had ordered the door leading from her workshop to the courtyard to be barred.

But that had not brought him any peace.

He continued listening for the rumble of a chariot. The street was a busy one, and many chariots came and went. But Mordecai had a sharp ear. He would recognize the third cupbearer's chariot anywhere. No other chariot made the same sound, because none were so heavy or had such big wheels.

Perhaps he was wrong, though. He heard a commotion in the street, soldiers shouting orders to the crowd to step aside, the points of spears moving above the heads of the onlookers. But the sound of this chariot was different—too light. He saw two magnificent black half-breeds, an officer with a felt helmet standing in the chariot. A war chariot . . . Despite himself, he looked behind the escort, hoping to see the little mule-drawn wagon that had carried Lilah off. There was nothing.

But the Persian officer was driving his horses straight toward the workshop. Mordecai's heart leaped, and he let out a cry. "God of heaven! Antinoes!"

Anxious as he was, Mordecai welcomed Antinoes warmly. He was proud that the lively, curious boy who, a few years earlier, had run between his feet in the workshop and called him Uncle Mordecai, just like Ezra, was now a Persian warrior. Moved, Antinoes opened his arms wide. Both overcame their embarrassment in an embrace that filled them with nostalgia.

Mordecai laughed. "I'm not used to embracing one of Artaxerxes' officers in full dress uniform!"

"Under the uniform, I'm still me!" Antinoes protested, taking off his helmet and cape. "I haven't changed all that much, and I'd still like to call you Uncle Mordecai."

Mordecai felt tears welling in his eyes.

With sheer delight, Antinoes breathed in the smells of the workshop. Here, too, nothing had changed. "During the last campaign," he said, passing his hand over the smooth surface of a shaft, "I saw many beautiful places. You can't imagine how vast and wonderful the world is. But I always missed this workshop."

His eyes shining with emotion, Mordecai could not resist showing him a few new inventions, from which his latest work had benefited.

Meanwhile, rain had started to fall in great drops on the dusty street. Soon, it was pouring down on the city. A few lightning flashes streaked the sky. Mordecai hustled his workers to put the fragile pieces of wood in a safe place. Antinoes parked his chariot inside the workshop. The soldiers in his escort took refuge in a neighboring inn, where they were served bowls of fermented milk and bread stuffed with lamb's offal and herbs.

In the blinking of an eye, the crowd vanished as if by magic, and the street was deserted. Mordecai glanced at it anxiously. "I hope this rain doesn't last long . . ."

Antinoes looked at him. Mordecai forced a smile and drew him to the other side of the workshop.

"I've been forgetting my duties. Come into the house and quench your thirst."

"I ought to say hello to Aunt Sarah first . . . and Lilah, if that's all right with you."

"Later," Mordecai said. "For now, we have to talk."

They sat down on long cushions in the dining room. As the handmaids bustled about them, Mordecai declared in a somber tone, "Lilah is not at home."

Antinoes put down his cup of palm beer and looked him straight in the eyes.

Mordecai sighed as if a stone were weighing on his chest. "One of the queen's cupbearers came to fetch her."

"Parysatis? Lilah is with Parysatis?"

"Since this morning."

"May Ahura Mazda protect her!"

"And our God Yahweh! Yes, my boy."

They were silent for a moment. The rain was still falling as heavily as ever on the flagstones of the courtyard, filling the air with a smell of wet dust.

"I was hoping she'd be back before nightfall," Mordecai resumed in a low voice. "But with this rain, the cupbearer won't want to get wet bringing her back. I'm getting worried. She's been too long in Parysatis's hands. What if the things they say about her are true?"

"I should have guessed," Antinoes said, without answering Mordecai's agonized question. "In a few days' time, I'll receive the arms of Artaxerxes' heroes. I'll be given a new command. That was what attracted Parysatis's attention to me, especially as I also deposited the tablets announcing my marriage to Lilah."

"But what does she want with you? Why summon Lilah?"

"Parysatis likes nothing better than to interfere in the marriages and careers of the officers loyal to her elder son. That way, she can keep an eye on everything our King of Kings does."

"Lord Almighty."

"It works. She's so powerful now, Artaxerxes himself fears her. They say her lions ate some of our king's favorite generals because they'd fought Cyrus the Younger, sword to sword."

"But Cyrus led an uprising against Artaxerxes!" Mordecai said indignantly. "He was marching on Babylon and Susa in an attempt to usurp his brother's place!"

"Cyrus was Parysatis's favorite son, that's all that matters. Artaxerxes didn't dare oppose his mother. But now Parysatis can't hatch any more plots against him, so she has to be content with manipulating the lives of his officers."

"Do you think—" Mordecai's voice broke, and he passed a

weary hand over his face. Then he asked, more firmly, "Do you think we need to fear for Lilah?"

Antinoes paused for a moment. "We can fear anything from a mad queen with a lot of power. Perhaps she only wants to see her and persuade her not to marry me. Or perhaps she wants her as her handmaid. Who knows?"

"You have friends in the Citadel, they could—"

Antinoes interrupted him with a gesture. "Tonight, I'll be refused entry to the White Palace. If I insist, I'll upset Parysatis. But if Lilah isn't back by tomorrow, I'll go to the queen, whatever the cost."

"God of heaven!" Mordecai muttered. "We were so happy that you'd come back and were going to marry Lilah! Now I don't even dare talk to Sarah for fear she'll start moaning!"

THE rain had eased off, but the daylight was rapidly fading. Neither Mordecai nor Antinoes had asked for a lamp. The sky was perfectly suited to their mood.

"And to think I went and quarreled with Ezra!" Antinoes suddenly groaned.

"Oh?" Mordecai said, lifting his eyebrows. "How is our sage of the lower town?"

"I thought it would be a good idea to talk to him about Lilah and me," Antinoes said. He shrugged his shoulders and fell silent, looking out again at the wet, shadowy courtyard. He jumped when he thought he heard the rumble of a chariot. But it was only a noise from the workshop.

"Don't tell me, Antinoes!" Mordecai said, the anxiety that had been tormenting him replaced by his usual anger against Ezra. "Don't say anything! I can guess what happened. Our sage Ezra treated you as if he didn't know you. He threw back at you a few phrases from those scrolls he reads all day long and told you that you couldn't make Lilah your wife because the Everlasting was against it."

Antinoes could not help smiling bitterly. "Yes," he said. "He's threatening never to see Lilah again if she marries me."

Mordecai raised his eyes to the streaming sky. "Oh, Ezra!" he moaned. "I loved that boy like a son. You were there, Antinoes; you know I'm not lying. I still love him. He's the finest, most intelligent young man the Everlasting has ever given life to. But I admit it: Sometimes Sarah has to hold me back, I get such a strong desire to run to the lower town and teach him a good lesson. May Yahweh forgive me!"

He moaned again, sweeping the air with his powerful arms, and his long face, usually so full of life, seemed to drain of all energy, as if washed by the rain. "Ezra isn't Parysatis," he said at last. "If we have to celebrate the marriage without Ezra, we'll celebrate it without Ezra. Lilah will have to be content with my approval. Provided—"

He broke off and leaped to his feet. Axatria was crossing the waterlogged courtyard, waving a lamp. The sound of the rain covered her cries until she was near.

"Lilah is back, Master Mordecai! Lilah is back!"

She stopped when she saw Antinoes. She caught her breath, and a radiant smile lit up her rain-drenched face.

"She's here, she's fine. The cupbearer brought her back, in his gilded chariot. He was soaking wet and shivering, and nowhere near as proud as he was this morning!"

NIGHT had fallen and the lamps had been lit in the long communal room by the time Lilah, in a weary voice, finished telling the story of her encounter with Parysatis. She sat bolt upright, despite the exhaustion in her face, which was accentuated by the shadows from the lamps. But only Antinoes noticed a grave, hard gleam in her eyes.

Overjoyed that she was back, Mordecai and Sarah plied her with questions. Sarah and Axatria wanted to hear again how she had been bathed and scented, and how she had passed through the veils in the reception room, while Mordecai was anxious to understand better what it was that the queen had told her.

Lilah replied calmly, carefully avoiding describing the tunic she had been forced to wear, as well as some of the things Parysatis had said at the edge of the lion pit.

Antinoes watched her in silence, reining in the desire to take her in his arms, caress her gently, and reassure both her and himself as he breathed in the scent of her skin. Lilah's composure, the curious assurance she showed after such a day, intimidated him, he had to admit, made her seem slightly strange to him, for the very first time since they had become Antinoes and Lilah.

"So Parysatis didn't forbid anything, didn't demand anything?" he asked at last, concealing his surprise.

"No," Lilah replied, looking him straight in the eyes and smiling tenderly, even with a touch of amusement. "The queen has a high opinion of Antinoes, hero of the King of Kings. She intends to make him a lord of the Citadel."

"May Ahura Mazda protect me!" Antinoes cried. "That's an admirer I could do without!"

"Why?" Sarah cried. "You ought to be pleased." She turned a casket upside down in front of them. The necklaces and bracelets that Lilah had worn in the palace fell onto the table with a jingling noise. "Look: gold, silver, even lapis lazuli! Would the queen have offered these jewels to Lilah if she had something bad in mind?"

Antinoes whistled through his teeth. "Less than a year ago, Parysatis gave the wife of one of her nephews some rings. One

ring for each finger. Then she commanded her eunuchs to cut off
the poor woman's hands and feed them, with the rings on, to her
lions. The woman was screaming with pain, so Parysatis made her
drink a potion that burned her throat to a cinder. That way, she
was able to watch her die slowly as her blood drained away, without being disturbed by her screams."

"God in heaven!"

A shiver passed through them, and it had nothing to do with
the coolness of the storm. They did not dare look at each other,
let alone at Lilah.

Lilah leaned down and placed her hand on Antinoes' thigh.
"Come now," she said, with a soft, warm laugh. "Don't scare us
any more than you have to. We all know what the queen is like.
But she didn't cut anything off me, and her lions seemed to have
eaten their fill. She was curious to see a young Jewish woman.
There's nothing extraordinary about that."

Antinoes met her eyes and nodded, a trifle hesitantly.

"A young Jewish woman who'll soon be the wife of a great
Persian," Mordecai said. "In my opinion, we mustn't delay your
wedding any longer. Antinoes already went to see Ezra. Too bad
for Ezra!"

Lilah stiffened, and her mouth grew hard. She took her hand
off Antinoes' thigh.

"I thought it was my duty to speak to him," Antinoes said
softly.

"And you can imagine how it turned out," Mordecai sighed.
"He treated Antinoes like a stranger. The shame of it!"

Antinoes smiled to tone down Mordecai's criticism. "Ezra is
famous in the lower town. The children showed me the way
to his house. Everyone was impressed with the chariot and the
escort."

"Oh, of course!" Lilah said in an icy tone. "A war chariot with
an escort, an armed officer. I'm sure that was very impressive."

"Lilah!" Sarah protested.

"It was pointless to set Ezra against you any more than he already is," Lilah went on, to Antinoes.

"Lilah," Mordecai cut in, impatiently, "it doesn't really matter what Ezra thinks. You don't need his approval to marry Antinoes. You have mine, that's all that matters."

"Oh yes!" Lilah said. "That's all that matters. I'm certain it's the law. Ezra can't complain about that."

"The important thing is to hurry up before the queen changes her mind. Ezra will come round."

Neither Lilah nor Antinoes seemed to be listening to Sarah and Mordecai. They were looking at each other. Antinoes would have liked to explain why he had needed to see Ezra, and that he had been careful to make his visit as straightforward as possible. But Lilah's face reduced him to silence. Her beauty was intact, despite the fatigue that showed in her taut cheeks and temples and her pursed lips. But there was still that curious flame in her eyes, which had been there ever since her return from the queen's palace. An icy flame, calm and intense at the same time, which she had never had before.

Then she closed her eyes. Antinoes had the impression that Lilah was going a long way away from him. That, too, was a new sensation.

While Mordecai was still speaking, Lilah stood up. Antinoes immediately did likewise, without daring to touch her.

"No, uncle," Lilah said calmly. "I know you're only thinking of my good, but things can't happen like that. Parysatis doesn't truly care whether Antinoes is my husband or not. And whatever we do, she can undo with a word. As for Ezra . . ."

She turned to Antinoes and placed her hand on his chest. He had the feeling she was leaning on him for support. He seized her wrist and held it.

"Antinoes has known it since the first day we loved each other," Lilah went on. "We need Ezra's approval before we can marry."

"Lilah!" Sarah cried, standing up.

Mordecai seized Sarah by the shoulders and clasped her to him.

"What I'm saying is true, Aunt Sarah. What would our marriage be like if I were never to see Ezra again?"

Again there was silence.

Without a word, without even attempting to touch her, Antinoes walked away from Lilah. A few moments later, he rode off in his chariot. The rain had only just stopped, and the soldiers of the escort, their bellies heavy with beer, torches in their hands, had to wade through the now-muddy streets.

IT took several more days before everyone was able to breathe more easily. So many things had happened in such a short time that everyday life seemed to have smashed against these events like a boat against a reef.

The wedding of Lilah and Antinoes had not been forgotten, but no one spoke about it. At Mordecai's vigorous urging, Sarah—making an effort to which she was unaccustomed—managed to hold her tongue and even to avoid meaningful glances.

Meanwhile, as the autumn sun returned to the transparent sky over Susa, the thought of the queen was on everyone's mind, as threatening as a cloud of ash. It would wake Mordecai at night, and during the day he would often stop in the middle of his work, his ears on the alert, thinking he could hear the third cupbearer's chariot.

As for Lilah, she would wake with Parysatis's smile before her eyes. In her dreams, the queen's ambiguous caresses became reality again. She saw herself standing naked on the platform above the lion pit. And the lions all had the queen's face, that strange face like an aged child's.

Her anger against Antinoes, for stupidly strutting about the lower town in his warrior's uniform, had faded. She was sorely tempted to run to him and melt in his arms, to find again the same peace and trust she had once known. Who else could she tell about the resolution she had made during her humiliating visit to Parysatis?

She resisted the temptation. Deep inside her, a decision was being born, a decision that went beyond love and affection, but which she would eventually share with her beloved just as she had shared the breath of desire.

But it was not yet time.

In any case, Antinoes was quite busy.

Every day, he had to go to the Citadel. Like all officers of his rank, he had to appear in the great royal courtyard of the Apadana while the King of Kings was taking his meal, either alone or enjoying the charms of a few concubines.

Then, if he so wished, Artaxerxes would summon some of his officers to keep him company behind a screen. He would question his generals and heroes, and make them tell him about their battles and the customs of the countries they had passed through or conquered.

A quarter of a moon passed in this way. Then finally, one morning, Axatria prepared the basket of provisions to take to the lower town.

When Lilah saw her, she smiled in approval.

It was "the day of her day," as Sogdiam called it. She was ready to go and see Ezra. She was ready at last to say to him the words she had uttered a hundred times in the silence of the night.

LILAH and Axatria were each carrying one strap of the basket. As usual, the children walked with them, yelling. But this time they got quite close to the house before Sogdiam ran to meet them, hopping on his deformed legs.

His eyes bright as much with annoyance as excitement, he explained without pausing for breath that he had been perfectly well aware that Lilah would come today and that he hadn't forgotten her, far from it.

"But just as I was leaving the house, Ezra wanted me to make some herb tea and bake a few little loaves of bread. He and Master Baruch have a visitor. Someone important!"

He took hold of the leather handle of the basket, which Lilah was holding in order to take some of the weight off Axatria.

"Someone important, and someone he hasn't quarreled with," he added, stealing a glance at Lilah.

"Antinoes should never have come in a chariot."

"Yes, he should!" Sogdiam protested. "Everyone was really pleased to see such a fine chariot in our streets. It doesn't happen often." Sogdiam paused for a moment, lost in thought. "He's handsome, too," he resumed, his voice filled with admiration. "And kind, for a Persian. Ezra lost his temper, but he stayed calm. As if the enemy were firing arrows at him on a battlefield and every one of them missed."

Lilah blushed, and looked away.

Axatria had the presence of mind to change the subject. "What makes you say the visitor is important?" she asked.

"It's sure he is," Sogdiam said, rolling his eyes. "Ezra and Master Baruch stopped studying as soon as he entered the courtyard. Master Baruch stood up to greet him. His name is—Zacharias, son of Pareosh. They ordered me to bring him food and drink. It's obvious he's important, Axatria."

As they crossed the courtyard toward the kitchen, Lilah and Axatria glanced at the study, the door of which was open as usual.

Master Baruch, Ezra, and the visitor were sitting on stools and conversing animatedly.

Lilah had no idea who the man was, but she immediately identified him as one of those Jews from Susa or Babylon who, unlike her uncle Mordecai, still dressed in the manner of the old days before the exile. He wore a long tunic with dark blue and gray stripes and a cylindrical hat. His hair was short and thick, and his beard long and sparse, with none of the refinement of which the Persians were fond. He seemed taller than Ezra and at least forty years old. His mouth was small, his eyes mobile, his voice insistent. He underlined his words with his short, chubby hands as if he were writing them in the air.

Axatria and Lilah were careful to empty the basket in the kitchen without making too much noise. They could hear the voices from the study, but muffled by the walls, so that only the odd word reached them. Lilah's curiosity soon got the better of her. She placed a finger on her lips to silence Axatria and Sogdiam, slipped out of the kitchen, and slid along the corridor with her shoulder against the wall, until she was close to the door of the study.

"Ezra, what I say, I think," the stranger was saying, "and everyone in my family thinks it, too. I have a hundred and fifty sons and nephews. Your letter planted an arrow in our hearts. We knew nothing about the disaster. We were happy with the work Nehemiah was doing in Jerusalem—"

"You were happy because you were here, living a life of luxury!" Master Baruch interrupted him, sarcastically. "You weren't with Nehemiah. You didn't care about what was happening there in Jerusalem, where happiness still has no place! You forgot all about the wrath of the Everlasting, who chased us from the land of Judaea for being deaf to his Word."

"You're right, Master Baruch! You're only too right!"

"Of course I'm right, Zacharias! The things I reproach you for,

I reproach myself a hundredfold. We are here, under the protection of the king of the Persians, while the Everlasting is waiting for us there."

"That is the way things are," Ezra interrupted, in a firm, calm voice. "Some of the children of Israel are here, and some are there. In other words, they are nowhere. They have been a people, from father to son. But they are no longer a nation living on the land to which Yahweh led Abraham."

"So why did Nehemiah fail?" Zacharias cried. "He left at the will of the King of Kings. He left with gold and soldiers. He left with the hand of Yahweh on him!"

"Are you sure?" Ezra replied, still just as calm.

"What do you mean by that?"

"If Yahweh's hand had been on him, he would not have failed," Master Baruch sighed. "Since when has the will of Yahweh not been done? Do you think, Zacharias my friend, that the walls of Jerusalem and the Temple would not have been rebuilt if Yahweh had wanted it?"

"That's where the error lies," Ezra said, in the same even tone. "Nehemiah went to rebuild the walls, but Yahweh did not support him. Why? Because it is not only the walls of Jerusalem that need to be rebuilt, Zacharias."

"I know," Zacharias said. "The Temple, too, and—"

"It was hearts and minds that broke the walls of the Temple," Ezra said, in a stronger voice. "It was hearts and minds that allowed Babylon to reduce the land of Judaea to dust. It is hearts and minds that need to be rebuilt before we can put the stones back on the walls."

There was a silence.

"You're right, Ezra," Zacharias said in a low voice. "As the proverb says: 'The fathers eat sour grapes and the sons' teeth are set on edge!'"

Ezra's laugh was almost a cry, sharp and harsh. "No, Zacharias!

You're wrong. You and your people and all the exiles who go around moaning about the past. You're letting your ignorance guide you! Have you forgotten Ezekiel's words in Babylon? 'All lives belong to Yahweh! The father's life belongs to him as does the son's life, for Yahweh is just. He does not condemn the son for the sin of the father. On the contrary, if the son is without sin, he makes him fruitful. He who lives in the Law of Yahweh lives without fear. The blood of the father does not fall on the son, the sin of the father does not flow in the son's veins.' That is the justice that Yahweh taught Moses, Zacharias. And the reason that Yahweh has not allowed Jerusalem to rise again is because we are not living according to his decrees. None of us, Zacharias. You, me, your people, the exiled Jews, as well as those living there in Jerusalem claiming to be children of Israel."

Lilah heard what sounded like a moan. The three men remained silent for a long moment. Lilah was about to move away from the wall and show herself at the door of the room when Zacharias spoke again.

"You speak the truth, Ezra," he said, in a voice full of emotion. That's why I and my people turn to you. That's why I've come to see you to say, 'Lead us, and we will follow.'"

Ezra grunted in irritation. "It isn't to me you should turn, but to the Word of Yahweh. That is what will lead you. You don't need me for that!"

"Oh, yes, we do! No one knows the scrolls of Moses better than you. Master Baruch says so himself. Question us, Ezra! You will hear only stammering. You explain one thing to me, I understand something else. You must have realized that by now."

"Do as I do. Do as Master Baruch does. Take the scrolls, read and learn. That's all you can do."

"How can the ignorant man learn what he doesn't know, if you won't guide his spirit and his heart?" Zacharias objected, forcefully. "How can he turn to the words of the Almighty if you and Master Baruch don't make their meaning clear through your studies?"

"Zacharias!" Master Baruch chuckled, mockingly. "Your words are flattering to me. But I don't advise anyone to undertake such a long journey with me as their light. As you can see, I'm nothing now but a lamp without oil." He gave his strange laugh, and shouted, "Lilah, my dove, when have you ever feared to disturb us? Stop hiding behind the door and come in."

Lilah's entrance into the room put Ezra and his visitor in an awkward position. Zacharias hardly dared look up at her, but Master Baruch greeted her so effusively and with such good humor that it was impossible to maintain the serious tone of their discussion.

Zacharias soon left. They promised him that he would be welcome as often as he liked.

When the outer gate closed again, Master Baruch gave a half-severe, half-mocking sigh. "You heard for yourself, my dove: that Zacharias has a bad conscience! It's clear he doesn't know much, and it's also clear that he'd be more useful in Jerusalem than stuck here moaning! There are dozens like him, and they all admire your brother. But although admiration may be sweet to the ears, it doesn't lead to knowledge, let alone to courage."

Lilah turned to Ezra, certain he was going to reply. But he said nothing, merely looked at her. Perhaps he had not even heard Master Baruch's provocative remarks. She knew that look so well that there was no need for words. She read fear in his eyes, and questions, and expectations. "Are you going to talk to me about Antinoes?" the eyes whispered. "Have you come here, my beloved sister, to tell me what I don't want to hear?"

With a loud sigh, Master Baruch sat down on the bed.

Lilah smiled. "Why mock their admiration, Master Baruch?" she said softly. "Perhaps it's merely the truth."

"What do you mean?" Ezra asked, with a frown.

"That it's time for you to be what everyone expects you to be."

Ezra smiled, disdainfully. "Oh, people expect something of me, do they? I only care about what Yahweh expects of me. And I answer him by staying here and completing my studies, reading his Word until it's as natural as breathing."

"Do you think that's always the right answer?"

"Lilah! Are you trying to teach me wisdom?"

Master Baruch had half sat up, and was moving his hands above his snowy white beard. "Let her speak, my boy, let her speak!"

"Zacharias says to you, 'We need you. Explain it all to us, lead us.' Why refuse?"

Ezra laughed nervously. "And where should I lead them?"

"To Jerusalem."

Ezra leaped to his feet. "You're mad!"

"Do you think so? Do wisdom and courage mean anything anymore if we don't continue the work begun by Nehemiah? As Master Baruch says, what's the point of moaning if it doesn't lead us to take action?"

Ezra glanced at Master Baruch. The old man had stopped laughing. His eyes were bright and alert, although his breathing was almost inaudible. Sogdiam and Axatria appeared in the doorway, carrying platters. Ezra did not take the slightest notice of them.

"As I told Zacharias, the reason Nehemiah failed is because Yahweh has judged it isn't yet time to rebuild Jerusalem."

"That's an easy excuse for someone who lacks the courage to confront his destiny."

Ezra blushed to the roots of his hair. Lilah went to him and seized his hands. She felt a tremor go through his body. "Didn't Moses, Aaron, and all the people of Israel discover that the hand of God was on them when they confronted Pharaoh's spells?" she said softly. "Isn't that what you yourself taught me, Ezra?"

Master Baruch chuckled. "That's good, my girl, that's good!"

"Moses often asked Yahweh, 'Why me?'" Ezra replied harshly.

"And the Everlasting replied, 'Because I have decided it!'" Master Baruch flung back at him.

Ezra shook his head and took his hands away from Lilah's. The blush remained on his cheeks, but now his black eyes shone not with anger but with a new emotion. "Come, now!" he said, after a moment's reflection. "You're forgetting that Nehemiah was able to leave Susa and lead the exiles to Judaea because the King of Kings had decided it was in his own interest."

"Yahweh planted a sensible policy in Cyrus the Great's brain," Master Baruch said.

"Yes, master. But I don't hear anything like that coming from the Citadel."

"What if it did come?" Lilah said. "What if Artaxerxes summoned you and said, 'Go, Ezra, lead your people back to Jerusalem! Rebuild the walls of your Temple!'"

"Lilah, you're mad."

"Answer me, Ezra. If he asked, would you accept?"

Ezra stood still for a moment, looking at her.

Master Baruch's eyes were nothing but two slits, the pupils barely visible.

Ezra began to laugh, a sharp, nervous laugh. "Come on, Lilah! You know it's not possible. Look at me. Look at this room, look at our surroundings! Why would the King of Kings even spare me a glance?"

"Because Yahweh wants it."

Ezra's face clouded over, and he raised his hand. "Lilah, don't talk like that. It's not—"

"Let her have her say, my boy," Master Baruch interrupted, without smiling.

"I've been thinking about it for days now, Ezra. And now I know I'm right. I know it, just like that Zacharias, just like all the people who call you 'the sage of the lower town.' Do you think they admire you because you spend your days with your nose stuck in papyrus scrolls? Because you've become as wise as, if not wiser than, Master Baruch?"

She glanced at the old man. He encouraged her with a nod.

"No, what they admire, Ezra, is the stubbornness that made you come here and stay here. And we need that stubbornness in order to hope, to stop being a people scattered like crumbs in the dust of Artaxerxes' kingdoms."

Axatria and Sogdiam were listening in the doorway. Ezra made a move to chase them away, then changed his mind. He smiled, and stroked Lilah's cheek lightly.

"I love your words, my sister. They prove your affection for me. But what you're saying is false. The exiles don't expect anything like that. If they did, they would have crossed the desert with Nehemiah, and Yahweh would have stretched his hand over them. No, they're perfectly happy here, just like our uncle Mordecai, I can assure you."

"Because no one has stood up and shown them where their duty lies," Lilah insisted. "Because no one has taken the first step into the desert. Because no one has gone to the King of Kings and said, 'Let me go to Jerusalem and rebuild the Temple of the God of Heaven.'"

Ezra laughed. He took Lilah by the shoulders and clasped her to him, a joyful expression on his face. Axatria, Sogdiam, and Master Baruch had not seen him as happy as this for a long time.

"Lilah! We aren't children anymore! We're too old to play with dreams. But when you say such things, I realize how much you love me—"

"No, Ezra!" Lilah pushed her brother away with a gesture as firm as her voice. "Don't treat me like a child. I'm not blinded by my love for you. I *know* who you are. Now it's up to you to find out how much your words and your courage are really worth."

Ezra's joy had already vanished. Now he looked helpless and

confused. "I have no desire to be what you describe," he said. "I'm studying with Master Baruch. My studies can't be interrupted, even to rebuild the walls of Jerusalem!"

"Ah, now he's saying what I said to Nehemiah!" Master Baruch cried in a shrill voice. "Oh, yes, that's precisely the kind of stupid remark I expected of you, my boy!"

"But isn't it what you taught me?"

"Oh yes, I said it, I said it!" Master Baruch's small, frail body shook with laughter. He winked at Lilah. "And now I say this: Studying has no end, but the master of studies has an end."

There was a strange silence.

Lilah walked to the door and out into the courtyard.

"Lilah, you cannot say what the will of God is!" Ezra cried behind her. "That would be blasphemy."

Lilah turned and nodded, smiling. "That isn't my intention. But if Artaxerxes commands you to appear before him, remember how Moses urged Aaron to appear before Pharaoh."

FOR a long time, as the chariot took them back toward the upper town, they were silent, lost in thought. But at last Axatria spoke.

"Once again, you saw Ezra and you didn't speak to him about your marriage. Your uncle and aunt will be worried."

"Ezra knows everything he needs to know about my marriage," Lilah replied.

"But he still doesn't want it."

"That doesn't matter."

Axatria opened her eyes wide in surprise. "Don't you want to get married anymore?"

"Did I say that? I made a promise: I will marry, Axatria. Afterward."

"Afterward?"

Lilah did not reply.

Axatria was silent for the whole length of one street, her eyes fixed on the nodding head of the young slave driving their chariot.

"Do you really believe what you told Ezra?" she said at last. "That the King of Kings will summon him to the palace?"

"Yes."

"But Ezra's right. It's impossible. How could the King of Kings know who Ezra is, and that he—" She broke off, and looked intensely at Lilah. "Oh!" she breathed. "Parysatis didn't send for you just to give you a few jewels, did she?"

Lilah smiled, but said nothing.

The Promise

The bathhouse was long and narrow. The walls and ceiling formed one vault of glazed bricks, decorated with sea monsters, men who were half fish, and birds that no man had ever seen with his eyes. Wreaths of fragrant vapor muffled the lapping of the water, the whispers and laughter.

The eunuchs had led Antinoes up to a canvas screen at one end, which blocked the view of the long pool that occupied almost the whole space. Servants were boiling eucalyptus and benzoin oil and amber resin, which they then poured in the water. The air was so heavy and fragrant that Antinoes had to become accustomed to it before he could breathe freely.

His baldric had been removed, as had his weapons and even his sandals; potential assassins had been known to hide their blades in them. He sat down on a low bed, and a swarm of handmaids brought him brass trays laden with brightly colored drinks and little cakes powdered with almond and cardamom-scented honey.

He was already starting to sweat. He had prepared himself to be patient, and not to let fear undermine his reason. Yet when the voice rose from behind the screen, he jumped as if swords had suddenly been unsheathed around him.

"Antinoes! Handsome Antinoes! Discreet Antinoes! It seems the only way I could get you to greet me was to send for you, even though you've been back in Susa for some time now!"

"My queen . . . ," Antinoes stammered, unsettled as much by the ironic sensuality in Parysatis's voice as by the reproach itself. "My queen," he went on, trying to make his voice sound firmer, "how could I have dared appear before you without being summoned?"

There was a raucous laugh on the other side of the screen. "Yes, how indeed? How could you have dared?" Parysatis laughed again. Antinoes relaxed: It had been the right answer.

He heard the sounds of water, but no more words for a long time. Antinoes did not dare eat or drink. The bed where they had put him was soft and welcoming. But he sat upright and stiff, as motionless as the eunuchs and handmaids around him.

"It would seem you are not lacking in courage, young Antinoes," Parysatis said suddenly. "Our King of Kings has set his eyes on you; I had to do the same." Her voice was coming from farther away now, and echoing against the vault. "Carchemish, Gordium, Sardis, Arbil, and Opis . . . Can you hear how much I love you? I know the names of all your battles by heart. Does this Jewish woman of yours, this Lilah, know as much?"

At Lilah's name, Antinoes felt the bite of fear in his lower back. Even in the battles Parysatis had just mentioned, he had rarely felt it with such intensity.

"Well, Antinoes?" Parysatis said, impatiently. "Must I wait for your answer?"

"No, my queen. I was simply thinking that you are right. Lilah does not know the names of my battles."

"Modest Antinoes!" Parysatis chuckled.

Again there were sounds of water, and women's laughter. Antinoes heard the queen giving orders, demanding clothes and drink. Her voice came closer. He could hear the rustling of cloth. She must be standing quite close to him behind the screen.

"So you want to marry her?"

"Yes, my queen."

"She tells me you made her a promise."

"Yes, my queen. We were children, but we haven't changed."

"How can that be? You, the son of my beloved Artobasanez! Your father let you run around with that Jewish girl?"

"He loved her like a daughter, and I like a sister."

Parysatis laughed. "Don't lie, soldier. You don't love her like a sister. Is it true that Jewish women are quite inventive when they make love? That's what I've heard."

"I don't know, my queen. I've never known any other woman."

"Oh, Antinoes!" Her laughter echoed against the brick vault. "Antinoes! No Greek woman, no Assyrian woman, not even a girl from the mountains?"

Antinoes sensed that the eunuchs who were watching him were smiling. He did not move a single muscle of his face, sure that whatever expression he had—fear, composure, or anger— would immediately be reported to Parysatis and would be circulating throughout the Citadel by evening.

"No, my queen," he admitted after a pause.

"So," Parysatis whispered, "you love her."

Antinoes heard a sound like the cooing of a pigeon, then realized it was a laugh . . . Parysatis was laughing again.

"A hero of the King of Kings in love with a Jewish woman. That's a rare occurrence in these parts! But you're not a child anymore, Antinoes. Childhood promises are doomed to die with childhood."

There was nothing he could say to that, so he said nothing.

"It's true, then," Parysatis said, amused. "You *are* brave. You don't dare say, 'Yes, my queen.'"

Again, he said nothing.

"Do you know that if you marry this Jewish woman, you'll become the son of a chariot maker?"

"Yes, my queen."

"Don't be stupid! Don't answer, 'Yes, my queen.' Answer, 'No, my queen, it's impossible. I, a future satrap, cannot marry a Jewish woman!' If you can't do without her, make her your concubine. A hero of the King of Kings, a future satrap, can have as many concubines as he can have whims."

"My queen, you speak the truth. I love Lilah. She is my lover, and the woman I have promised to marry."

"Oh, how stupid you are!"

There was no laughter in Parysatis's voice now; it was cold and hard.

Proud as he was, Antinoes could not stop his breathing becoming faster and more irregular. He could not stop sweat pouring down his brow, and not only because of the stifling air.

"What have you to say to me, Antinoes?"

He closed his eyes. "My queen, I obey my king in everything. I have deposited the tablet announcing my wedding, as an officer is supposed to do."

On the other side of the screen, there was a long silence. Then a loud handclap. The eunuchs rushed forward and, in the twinkling of an eye, moved aside one of the canvas panels.

Stunned, Antinoes now saw the pool of warm, transparent water, in which half a dozen young girls were swimming. And very close to him, on a bed, a pale-faced eunuch massaging the small, oiled body of Parysatis.

She was lying on her stomach, naked, with her eyes closed. Pressed against the bed, her face seemed more strangely crumpled and aged than ever. Antinoes bowed low and remained in that position.

"Not many people, Antinoes," Parysatis said, in a caressing voice, "have seen Parysatis in her bath and lived to tell the tale. Stand up, and let me look at you."

He did as he was told, pressing his hands to his thighs to stop them shaking. Parysatis opened her eyes and looked closely at the young warrior's face, while the eunuch continued his massage. Then, with a sudden gesture, she pushed him away and sat up, revealing her youthful breasts.

She clapped her hands. The young girls hastened out of the pool, and came and lined up next to her. The oldest was not yet fifteen, while some were still only children. Their smiles concealed neither their embarrassment nor their fear.

"Parysatis's nieces," the queen said, her mouth smiling but her eyes still icy. "You can choose. Antinoes, Parysatis's nephew! I'd like that!"

Antinoes said nothing. Parysatis grunted and clicked her fingers at the girls, who quickly got back in the pool.

"Since when have warriors talked about love, hero of the King of Kings? You'll be the laughing stock of the Apadana if this gets out!"

She stood up, no longer concealing anything of her nakedness, and ordered her handmaids to rub her body with scented oils. Antinoes lowered his eyes.

"You're a child, Antinoes. You have no idea what's serious and what isn't. Fortunately, this Jewish girl of yours has more brains than you do. She knows what it means to be sensible."

Resuming their games, the girls started laughing and splashing each other. Parysatis frowned angrily and screamed at them to get out. Her command echoed against the vault of the bathhouse. The armed eunuchs ran alongside the pool, driving back the queen's nieces with the tips of their spears. With squeals of terror, the girls disappeared into a narrow tunnel at the other end of the room.

"I could feed your Lilah to my lions," Parysatis said in a low voice, when calm had been restored. "Then you would be released from your promise. But something strange is happening, Antinoes. I'm like you. I've started to like this Jewish girl. She pleases me. And she's sensible enough not to have any desire to keep her promise."

Parysatis's cooing laughter mingled with the thick steam of the pool. She pushed away her handmaids, walked right up to Antinoes, and lifted his head. "Don't you want to know why?"

Sustaining the queen's gaze, Antinoes said nothing.

"Place your lips on mine, hero of the King of Kings," she ordered, with a sorrowful pout, "that I may know what your Jewish girl tastes."

SARAH carefully opened the door of Lilah's bedchamber. Axatria, who was changing the sheets, jumped.

"You scared me, mistress."

"Isn't Lilah here?"

Axatria's face lit up. "She ran to Antinoes' house," she said, in a low, conspiratorial tone. "She couldn't contain her impatience. They haven't seen each other for days. She has many things to tell him."

Excited, Sarah closed the door of the chamber behind her. "Is that it? Has she spoken to Ezra?"

Axatria stuffed the dirty linen into a basket, and shook her head. "She spoke to him, yes, but not in the way you think."

"Don't be so mysterious!" Sarah said in annoyance. "Tell me."

"Lilah says Ezra must go to Jerusalem."

"To Jerusalem?"

"Yes, with men from Susa and Babylon, to finish the work of the sage Nehemiah. She says he's the only one who can do it."

"What are you talking about, girl?"

Axatria had to start the whole story from the beginning. She told Sarah about Lilah's visit to the lower town, the encounter with the man named Zacharias, and, word for word, or as near as made no difference, what Lilah had said to Ezra.

Sarah had to sit on the bed in order to listen to the end without fainting. When Axatria finished, she remained as still as a log.

Axatria had no intention of allowing anything to spoil her joy. "I always knew Ezra would become a great man," she said, proudly. "Lilah says the God of heaven will convince the king to send Ezra to Jerusalem. She knows it. And I believe her."

Sarah looked at Axatria with a gloomy expression. But then words broke through the wave of desolation submerging her. "You aren't even Jewish," she said, "but you're going to teach me what Ezra is worth and what the Everlasting expects of him?" And with that she left the bedchamber.

When night fell, Mordecai sent for Axatria. She had been weeping, and her red-rimmed eyes were ready to pick a quarrel. But Mordecai was gentle with her, and Sarah was silent, so she repeated what she had told Sarah earlier. Mordecai listened carefully. Then he, too, fell silent, puzzled by what he heard.

"Are you sure about what you're saying?" he asked at last. "Lilah said that in spite of everything she was going to marry Antinoes?"

With a sigh of exasperation, Axatria repeated Lilah's words. "'I shall marry him, Axatria. I promise.' That's what she said."

"Lilah's mad. We're worried sick about her marriage, and all she can find to do is proclaim Ezra the savior of Jerusalem?"

"If she says Ezra can do it, it's because she's right!" Axatria protested, her voice trembling with resentment. "She knows it better than you do."

Mordecai raised his hand to demand silence. He was smiling. "Our Lilah has more than one trick up her sleeve. She's thought this out carefully. Once he's in Jerusalem, Ezra won't be too bothered about who she marries."

Axatria and Sarah looked at each other, pensively.

Sarah was not very convinced, but she nodded. "May the Everlasting hear you," she sighed.

ANTINOES' mouth was sweet and warm. Lilah lost herself in it, abandoned herself fully. His palms lifted her and swept her up in his caresses. The anxieties of the last few days at last fell away from her like scales.

Through her kisses, she herself led him and accompanied him on the waves of desire. They breathed as one, although he was impatient while she lingered from embrace to embrace, stretching the time as if it would never end.

At last they rolled apart, and lay side by side, regaining their breath, hair tangled, hips still touching, lips bruised, hands incapable of ceasing their caresses.

Antinoes' bedchamber was heated by braziers, and lit by a single oil lamp.

Lilah listened to the rain hammering the leaves in the garden. She heard a door slam, and, in the distance, fragments of conversation, a handmaid's voice. She was not accustomed to the sounds of Antinoes' house.

"The other day, at your uncle's house," he murmured, "you didn't tell the truth. Parysatis is refusing to let us marry."

A shudder went through Lilah, as if the cold air from outside had entered the room. It was over; the truth was out, as clear as daylight. She closed her eyes, as if that could protect her a few moments more.

"She sent for me this morning," Antinoes said. "I was in her bathhouse!"

He could see Parysatis's mocking face behind his closed eyelids.

Lilah turned on her side, kissed his mouth, then placed her fingers on his lips. "No," she whispered, "I didn't tell the truth. But how could I tell you? I still felt too ashamed. The way she looked at me! Not only that. She touched me! I was wearing a tunic that left me almost naked before her. I had to listen to her telling me who I could and couldn't love! I was afraid of the lions, but there was at least a moment when I thought it would be better to be eaten by them than humiliated by Parysatis."

Lilah stopped. Antinoes tried to speak, but again she pressed on his lips to silence him.

"Then the idea came to me."

She sat up, leaning against Antinoes' hips. She stroked his neck, his powerful shoulder muscles. She was smiling, but gravely, joylessly.

"There I was, before Parysatis. 'What am I going to do with you?' she said. 'What can I do with a Jewish girl?' She started threatening me. 'I could do anything I like with you. Make you my handmaid. Or feed you to the lions. I could make you my slave. That's something we don't have in this palace: a beautiful Jewish girl who's a slave to our every whim! I could give you to my monkeys if I felt like it. There's only one person I wouldn't give you to, my girl, and that's the man you chose—that Antinoes you like so much!'"

Lilah was still trying to smile through her tears. Antinoes held her close to stop her shaking. But she continued speaking, forcing the words out as if extracting them from stony ground.

"It wasn't only cruel and odious. It was unjust. I stopped

listening to her. We can't listen to such things. Hatred closes our ears. We become deaf. 'What is this kingdom where a mad queen has the power of life and death?' I thought. 'She soils the air we breathe. She soils the very thing that makes us man and woman. She besmirches the love of husbands and wives! What is more unjust than the power of the strong when it's unchecked?' "

She shivered, and clenched her teeth. Antinoes sat up, drew her to him, and placed his head between her breasts. Listening to the beating of her heart, he waited for her to continue.

Lilah took a deep breath and went on. "It was then that I thought of Ezra. Not precisely of him, but of what he's been saying since he started living in the lower town: that the Everlasting has given us laws so that his people can live without humiliation, so that the sons and daughters of Israel can hold their heads up high and not have to submit to the insults and whims of the kings of Babylon and the Pharaohs with their false gods. But we have stopped following Yahweh's decrees. We have broken our vow, broken the covenant that protected us from the madness of the powerful, their oppression and their idols. Because of that, we no longer have Yawheh's hand over us, but Parysatis's hand."

She stopped and dug her nails into Antinoes' skin.

"Parysatis is mad," he said softly, "but she's the only one. The Jews are respected in Artaxerxes' kingdoms. You live among us just like any other people. I'm a Persian and you're in my arms."

She kissed him and caressed him. No, her words were not directed against him. There was no greater love than theirs. But he had to understand. "Antinoes, Parysatis's power has *no limits*. It will corrupt everything. You saw her today. Don't tell me of it, I don't want to hear! I can imagine, and what I can't imagine I sensed earlier in the taste of your first kiss. You, the son of a lord of Susa, who tomorrow will be one of those before whom the peoples of Persia and all Artaxerxes' kingdoms will bow down, were humiliated by her just as I was. I know."

Antinoes did not object.

"As I was saying, the idea came to me," Lilah went on. "Ezra must go to Jerusalem while there is still time. He must complete Nehemiah's work, and give us back a land where no one will humiliate us. He must accomplish what he was born for. And we must help him. Nehemiah left with the support of Artaxerxes the First. Ezra must leave with the support of Artaxerxes the Second."

"How?

IT was late, but they were still talking.

The clouds scurried beneath the moon. The rain had ceased, but a cold, strong wind had risen and was whistling between the wooden shutters. Antinoes had covered himself and Lilah with a huge bearskin from the Zagros Mountains. They were whispering in the shadows as they had so often whispered during their childhood. But their words were no longer childish words.

"You think Ezra hates you," Lilah was saying. "He doesn't, he only hates the life we lead here while Yahweh is waiting for us over there. You alone can teach the cupbearers and eunuchs of the king's table Ezra's true worth, and that there will be thousands who will follow him if he sets off for Jerusalem."

"It will be many days before the king lends an ear to my request," Antinoes replied.

"What does that matter? We can wait."

"Do you think Parysatis will wait?"

At that they fell silent, for these words were like ice in their bellies, and they did not yet dare confront them.

To dismiss them, Antinoes resumed in a lighter tone, like a true warrior and a hero of the King of Kings, "Artaxerxes might be interested in the idea of bringing order to Jerusalem, rebuilding its walls and making it a fortified town. Jerusalem is the weakest point on our western borders. They say Pharaoh has his eyes on it. If Jerusalem fell to the Egyptians, it would be a godsend to the Greeks. It would give them the coast and the ports of Tyre and Sidon. From there they could trade, and they could also launch armies toward the Euphrates. Yes . . . I'm sure that's how I need to present things. Some of the generals will be happy to hear it. Tribazes will listen to me, I'm sure. And he'll be better able to persuade the king than I would."

Lilah smiled in the shadows, searched for the warmth of her lover's body, in order to melt into it and inspire him with her strength.

But then Antinoes murmured, "Parysatis wants me to marry one of her nieces. She won't budge, I know." He hesitated. "She claims you've already agreed to break our promise."

Lilah's words were dry and contemptuous. "Parysatis knows nothing about real life. She knows only her own desires."

"She'll kill you if you don't obey. She'll humiliate you more than she already has, and then kill you in the cruelest way she can find."

"Would she kill you, too?"

"Without hesitation. And no one in the Apadana would protest. Not even Tribazes, who wishes me nothing but good. Parysatis hates him more than the others, if that's possible, because he led the army that defeated Cyrus the Younger. Parysatis's hate is stronger than Artaxerxes' trust. But I don't think she would. There'd be no point. She'd kill you and say, 'Now, Antinoes, you no longer have a promise to keep.'"

They listened to the wind. The red glow of the braziers danced on the walls.

"We no longer have a promise," Antinoes whispered. "We'll never be man and wife."

Lilah rolled on her side and embraced him, wrapping him with her body. She kissed his neck, chin, and temples. She made him tremble with desire again, drew him out of the shadows where he left his thoughts and pride. She made their young bodies dance, skin to skin, as free and untroubled as they had ever been. And when he was again inside her, she whispered, "I have only one word, my beloved. And I shall keep it. We will be man and wife."

"Lilah!" Antinoes breathed.

"Who will know it? If you're brave enough, who will know it? Not even Ezra!"

Master Baruch's Smile

ith Lilah's help, Antinoes wrote a tablet in his fine handwriting, asking for an audience with the King of Kings. Ezra's name was mentioned, as well as the reason for the request. The tablet spoke of Artaxerxes I, Nehemiah, and peace and order on the western borders of the kingdoms, which were still threatened by the Egyptians and the mercenaries of the Upper Sea.

Antinoes, unfortunately, had spoken the truth. It would take a long time before the tablet, addressed to Tribazes, the head of the armies, was passed to the scribes of the Apadana. There, as custom demanded, it would have to be copied in duplicate, according to the rules of the Citadel, in the Persian language as well as that of ancient Assyria.

Then the tablets would be handed over to the cupbearers of the Council of a Thousand, which, when it had time among all its many tasks, would judge their contents together with the chiliarch, the great lord Tithraustes. The chiliarch himself would then take time for wise reflection, after which he would pass his judgment to the counselors of the king's table. Under their supervision, a new, more appropriate request would be written on the huge royal scroll, without beginning or end, known as the Book of Days.

Finally there would come the time when Artaxerxes II, King of Kings, made his appearance to deal with the affairs of his kingdoms. The scribe of the Book of Days would read the request, Tithraustes would then give his opinion, and the king would decide. He would make his will known: what should and should not be written in response to the petition of Ezra, son of Serayah, an exiled son of Israel living in the lower town of Susa.

At this pace, the first snow fell before the king's answer had arrived, and the wait was getting on everyone's nerves.

More than anything, Antinoes feared Parysatis's spies. Realizing that their kisses were no longer enough to cheer them, Lilah decided it would be more sensible if they stayed away from each other until they knew the king's answer. Antinoes would also avoid Mordecai's house.

"It seems Parysatis has already succeeded in separating us," Antinoes sighed as they said good-bye.

"Never!" Lilah said, kissing his lips one last time. "She'll never separate us. Besides, you're nearer to me now than when you go off to war . . ."

Days passed, and still there was no news.

Ezra, whose resolve had been weakened for a time by Lilah's conviction, and to an extent by Master Baruch's words, was the first to mock.

"So, the Everlasting doesn't seem to be taking any notice of my sister's opinions!" he said sarcastically to Lilah and Axtraia, who had come bearing their basket of fruits and barley. "Artaxerxes hasn't sent for me. He has his god Ahura Mazda who, supposedly, supports him in everything. Why should he care about the Jews, or Jerusalem, or the Law of Moses? I was right not to listen to your daydreams, sister! My studies with Master Baruch

are sure to bring me closer to the will of Yahweh than your imagination."

"You're not very patient," Lilah replied, dismissing his criticism. "Not very patient, not very trusting, and not very provident.
You should be taking advantage of this time to gather those who
will go with you. You should be telling people about your hopes
for Jerusalem."

"My hopes for Jerusalem?" He shook with laughter. "Lilah,
those who want to go with me can come and sit in this courtyard
as much as they like—provided they respect my studies. Then
their journey will be like mine: It is sure to lead them to the Word
of Yahweh and the Scriptures of Moses!"

Lilah had expected Master Baruch to support her, but the old
man refused to intervene on one side or the other. He seemed to
huddle behind his beard, overcome by age and fatigue, incapable
of one of those phrases with which he loved to surprise and infuri-
ate others. But when Lilah bowed to him to bid him good-bye, he
took her face between his soft old palms and smiled at her, a big,
silent smile that made his eyes sparkle as much as if he were
laughing. He did not say a word, merely continued to smile. And
his palms held Lilah's face, as if he were lifting it free of the
weight of the earth. She realized that he was encouraging her, in a
way that was typically his, and she felt her anxieties slip away.

During their following visit, Ezra again mocked Lilah, with a
harshness in which she thought she detected a touch of jealousy.
She decided she would not go back to the lower town until she
was able to take the King of Kings' answer with her.

Axatria rolled her eyes in horror. "What if it doesn't come?
What if there is no answer? What if—?"

"There's no 'what if,' Axatria! There'll be an answer, and it will
be the answer we're expecting. Ezra will appear before Artaxerxes."

Axatria looked at her as if she had lost her reason.

The month of Tebet arrived. Cold struck the Susa region in

one fell swoop. For three days, the sky was hazy with snow. Big flakes covered Mordecai's house, wrapping it in silence. Lilah seemed as cold and white as the snow, as if the length of the wait were draining her of blood.

DAWN was breaking, slowly and silently. The weavers were not yet at work, nor were Mordecai's workers. Lilah stood looking out at the daylight, trying to summon the strength not to let her impatience get the better of her. Sarah's voice made her jump more than the hand on the back of her neck. Before she could say a word, her aunt hugged her. "I had to be close to you for a moment. I want to tell you that I've thought it over. You're right, about Ezra. I told Mordecai: Lilah's right. I don't know if it will happen, if the king will give him an audience, or if he will set off for Jerusalem. We'll see. But you're right. Ezra is Ezra. Yahweh's hand is on him. It's been so for a long time."

They embraced with a little laugh that sounded like a moan.

"You aren't getting much sleep," Sarah said gently, stroking her niece's cheek.

"No one has been getting much sleep lately," Lilah replied. "Neither you, nor Uncle Mordecai. Oh, my poor aunt! Ezra and I have given you more worry than pleasure."

Sarah hugged her a little harder. "Dreams, that's what you've given me, Lilah—dreams. And I haven't always been very clever." She hesitated, then laughed, with a laugh that sounded like a sob. "Sarah—that's the right name for me. Sarah with a barren womb. Just like Abraham's Sarah. Except that the angels of the Everlasting won't be paying me a visit when I'm really old!"

"Aunt!"

Sarah placed her fingers on Lilah's mouth to silence her. Her

eyes were shining, and her low voice was hoarse with the harshness of the words that came from her mouth. "You can't imagine
the shame! The shame of not having given Mordecai a child. The
shame of being so happy when the two of you arrived in this
house. It was terrible. Your mother and father had just died, and
because of that I was finally able to live like a woman. Children in
my house! Oh, you can't imagine! Mordecai was transformed by
it, too. I became a real mother. In my eyes, at least. Even though
you always call me 'aunt,' for so long I wanted to hear you call me
'mother'! Then you grew up, and another dream came true. You
were becoming a woman, a beautiful woman, the lover of a handsome man. Your belly would swell as mine never would. I used to
wake up at night thinking I heard your sons and daughters crying.
Yes, that was my greatest wish. To have grandchildren running
and yelling in this house. To forget about the carpets, the weaving, the customers! For years I had that dream: Lilah's children
would soon come and throw themselves into my arms. If I hadn't
been a mother, I would at least be a grandmother."

She fell silent, her whole body trembling. Lilah remained motionless, with a lump in her throat. Sarah breathed deeply, and
smiled an ironic smile. "Sometimes I dreamed of the children
Ezra might have, but that didn't last, I must admit."

Lilah smiled, too. Tears welled in Sarah's eyes and rolled down
her cheeks, and she said very quickly, in one breath, as if fearing
she would not be able to finish everything she had to say, "Now I
have to get used to it. I shan't see children running in this house,
I won't be awoken by their cries. To the end of my days, I'll be
Sarah with the barren womb. Do you understand?"

"Aunt," Lilah murmured.

Sarah shook her head, stubbornly and bravely. "No, don't say
anything. There's no need. I know. That terrible mad queen will
never allow you to marry Antinoes. And I know you. You won't

yield either. If you can't marry him, you won't marry anyone else. You won't be anyone else's lover, and then you'll be like me: a barren womb." Sarah was looking her niece straight in the eyes. In her voice, there was perhaps a faint tinge of hope, a desire to be contradicted. Lilah could not find anything to say in reply and lowered her eyes.

Sarah nodded gently. "I suppose you're right to do this," she whispered. "But you may change your mind later. We never know what the Everlasting expects of us. You're so young! It's not so long since you were a child."

A door slammed in the courtyard, then silence returned. They separated, as if their bodies were suddenly too heavy, turned in again on their own sadness.

"Perhaps you could . . ." Sarah hesitated. What she had to say was difficult, and she no longer dared look at Sarah. "I know that you take herbs," she breathed at last. "When you see Antinoes. You could be pregnant, then he'd have to—"

"But to what end?" Lilah interrupted, without raising her voice. "To have a child and give it a life of shame? Antinoes could never make it his son or daughter without the wrath of Parysatis falling on the child. She wouldn't rest until she destroyed it."

Sarah frowned, and said nothing. They were both silent.

There was more noise in the house now. Mordecai's voice rang out, then the cries of handmaids answering him. Soon they would hear the first clattering of the weaving frames.

"It's so cruel," Sarah muttered. "If there's anyone who doesn't deserve this, it's certainly you."

"No one deserves to suffer Parysatis's madness."

Sarah turned abruptly and gripped Lilah's hands. "What I'd like to know is whether or not you're going to follow him." Her eyes were intense, her mouth harder, as if she were getting ready to receive a blow. "If you also leave for Jerusalem, Mordecai and I will be alone again. He'll never want to leave Susa."

Lilah shook her head. "Oh, Aunt Sarah! I don't know! I don't know!"

A FEW mornings later, Axatria returned from the lower town, her cheeks red.

Alone, as before, she had gone to take clean washing and food to Ezra and Master Baruch. She had found Sogdiam in a state of great excitement, although deeply unhappy that he no longer saw Lilah. For the past few days, Zacharias and some twenty members of his family—brothers, uncles, and nephews— had been coming to listen to Ezra reading from the great scroll of the laws of Moses.

"Sogdiam says that each time the reading is over, this Zacharias and his family crowd around Ezra and ask him, 'When will you lead us to Jerusalem? What are we doing here, wasting our time?' Ezra loses his patience, having constantly to explain to them that they can set out for Jerusalem without his help. 'The road is there,' he says. 'You only have to take it!' He says that he isn't Nehemiah, that he can't go back to Jerusalem before his studies are over and without the agreement of the Citadel . . . Anyway, you know all that."

"And what does Master Baruch say?" Lilah asked.

"Ah, Master Baruch!" There was a gleam in Axatria's eyes. "Master Baruch, apparently, doesn't say a word while Zacharias's family are talking to Ezra. Not a word, not even a sign of life. But look!" Amused, she drew a small papyrus scroll from her tunic. "Just as I was about to leave, he asked me to arrange his bed. I'd already done it a little earlier, but you know Master Baruch's whims. While I was plumping the pillows, he slipped this into the sleeve of my tunic. Ezra was reading in his corner, and didn't see a thing. 'Give this to Lilah,' Master Baruch whispered. 'Only to Lilah.'"

Lilah had unrolled the papyrus while Axatria was speaking. A few lines were written on it, the letters so fine and the ink so translucent that she had to go outside into the daylight to decipher them.

My dove. Don't lose confidence. Ezra loses his temper, but Ezra listens to you as much as he listens to Yahweh. Have no fear. The hand of Yahweh is upon you. Have no doubts. Think of the sea that Yahweh opened before Moses. Have no fear, my dove. Go to the most powerful and make yourself heard, and all will go well.

"What did he write?" Axatria asked impatiently.

She had to repeat her question twice before Lilah read Master Baruch's words to her.

Axatria was disappointed. "That's not very helpful, is it?" she said, exasperated. "He may be going off his head a little. Sogdiam says he hardly ever gets out of bed. When he slipped me this scroll, his eyes were laughing like a child's. That happens with the very old. They become like children again."

Lilah did not reply.

What Master Baruch had not written, she could hear, as clearly as if he were whispering in her ear.

THIS time, it was not the third cupbearer who came to fetch Lilah, but a eunuch from Parysatis's guards. He had short hair and hairless cheeks, and wore a bearskin cloak and a large red turban. Lilah was taken to the queen in the same costume with which she left Mordecai's house. Over a tunic of yellow wool, drawn in at the waist by a blue belt, she had put on a big woolen veil woven with silver threads and embroidered with green and purple silk. Her hair was held in place by an ivory comb carved with five-branched stars. Opalescent amber earrings hung from her ears, and a matching necklace wound twice around her neck.

She held herself very erect as she walked, her chin high, her mouth full and firm. She was not only beautiful; one glance at her was enough to convince anyone of the strength and intensity of her will. Even the handmaids and the eunuchs noticed it as they led her through the maze of corridors and halls.

She was not kept waiting long.

The queen received her in a bedchamber as round as the inside of a tent. The walls and floor were covered with dozens of carpets and tapestries. A large fire was burning in a bronze hearth that took up the middle of the room. The smoke was taken out through the ceiling along a brass conduit. Lying on a bed suspended from the beams and covered with animal skins, Parysatis was playing with some Egyptian kittens. They all had black fur and green eyes. She chuckled happily, tickling them in a thousand ways, cursing whenever one of them scratched her wrists. Her thin white tunic, identical to the one Lilah had seen her wear during her previous visit, was spattered with tiny bloodstains. She did not seem to hear the announcement the eunuch made as Lilah walked in through the tapestry that served as a door.

Lilah advanced to within some ten paces of Parysatis and bowed low, eyes closed.

When she stood up again, Parysatis's eyes were on her. The queen looked at her for what seemed an interminable length of time, while the kittens, impatient and eager to play, sought her hands, gripped her tunic, scratched her thighs and stomach.

For a moment, their steps muffled by the carpets, the handmaids and eunuchs moved about the room, stoking the fire and the perfume burners. Then they vanished, all except two eunuchs who stood guarding the door. Lilah did not dare make a movement, even though she was starting to feel numb.

Parysatis was still looking her up and down, unconcerned about the kittens who had now snuggled between her thighs. Her eyes were so fixed, the pupils so enlarged, that Lilah wondered if she might not have taken a drug. Then, without warning, Parysatis threw the kittens across the room. They mewed angrily, while the queen, taking her eyes off Lilah, turned on her side.

She pulled a leopard skin around her shoulders. "Well," she said, in a flat tone, "I knew you didn't lack nerve. But to address a request to me, Parysatis, that's something I've never had inflicted on me before."

"Thank you, my queen, for replying."

"Who said I'm replying, you conceited girl?"

Lilah fell silent and lowered her eyes. Beads of sweat formed on the back of her neck.

"No one, ever, asks anything of Parysatis."

"No, my queen."

"So why did you send me that tablet, you fool? Are you so determined to make me angry?"

"No, my queen."

Confident and determined as she was, and bolstered by Master Baruch's words, fear still gripped Lilah's chest like a vise. She had to take a deep breath.

The most foolhardy of the kittens was climbing up an animal skin toward Parysatis's hand. She caught it by the tail, and it mewed.

"I'm waiting," she muttered.

"My queen, I thought you were the only person who could help me."

Parysatis gave a cry, which turned into a laugh. "Me, help you? Are you mad? Help you? Why should I help you?"

The laugh ceased as it has started. There was a silence.

Parysatis pressed the kitten between her breasts and stroked it. She turned slowly toward Lilah. "Help you in what?"

"My queen, my brother, Ezra, wants to ask the King of Kings for permission to take our people out of exile here in Susa and in Babylon and lead them to Jerusalem."

With her short index finger, Parysatis was forcing the kitten to open its mouth wide. It bit the finger, energetically at first, then with increasing anger. Parysatis chuckled, took it by the neck, and pushed it out of sight under the leopard skin, against her hip. She looked at Lilah, and raised her eyebrow in surprise.

"Why? Aren't they happy here?"

"Zion is the land marked out for our people by Yahweh our God, my queen. Today, Jerusalem, our city, is in ruins, for we are here instead of there. Chaos reigns there, decay is gathering pace. Nothing is respected, neither our laws nor those of our great king Artaxerxes. If the fall of Jerusalem is not good for us Jews, it is not good for the King of Kings either. Soon, the Greeks and the Egyptians will be able to seize the city. That would weaken all the western borders."

Parysatis's eyes had become sharper as Lilah spoke. "Politics! Look at that! You appear before Parysatis, acting like a queen, and talk to me about politics! What business is it of yours? Such things are not for women—let alone little girls like you."

"My queen, that is why I would like my brother, Ezra, to appear before the King of Kings."

Parysatis groaned and shook her head. "So obstinate, and always ready with an answer! Why your brother and not someone else?"

"Because he alone can do it, my queen. He and no one else."

"'He and no one else,'" Parysatis mocked, aping Lilah's voice. "And, of course, you're the one who decides that! A Jew from the lower town, wallowing in dirt and poverty, listening to the stale whining of an old man who ought to have died long ago. And he's supposed to be the leader of the Jews?"

Parysatis's laugh was as sharp as a rattle. Lilah shuddered. She felt as though thousands of needles were pinching her lower back.

"Ah, you see! I surprise you. Parysatis knows more than you think. I know everything, Lilah my girl, I know everything. Never forget that."

A long silence followed. A distant look had come into the queen's eyes, as though she were thinking of something else. Lilah thought she could hear the kitten mewing beneath the leopard skin. The other kittens were playing noiselessly under the bed.

"You ask," Parysatis said abruptly, "but what are you offering in return?"

Lilah said nothing, and lowered her head.

"This is what you offer," Parysatis said. "Your brother leaves for Jerusalem, and you follow him."

Lilah did not look up.

"I want to hear your answer, my girl!" Parysatis demanded.

"Yes, my queen."

"You go to Jerusalem and forget Antinoes."

On Lilah's back, the needles had become fangs. "Yes, my queen."

"Forget about promises, forget about weddings. Forget about Antinoes between your thighs. Do you understand?"

"Yes, my queen."

Parysatis's cooing laugh burst out in the thick air, as sinuous as a snake. "That's what you came to tell me, isn't it? That you're afraid of me and you're begging me to let you go a long way away from your great love. Farewell promise, farewell promise! But you're too proud to admit it. Not brave, really, just proud. A proud little girl who plays at being a lady, that's what you are. Now you can thank me."

Lilah looked up. Ashamed as she was, she could not prevent tears from streaming down her cheeks. "Thank you, my queen," she murmured.

Parysatis smiled and screwed up her eyes. Her upper lip was curled over her small teeth, and the folds around her mouth spread to her cheeks, making her look ten years older.

She took her right hand out from beneath the leopard skin, still holding the kitten. She threw it at Lilah's feet, where it rolled over and then lay motionless. It was dead, its neck broken.

"If you want Parysatis's advice, Lilah, my girl, make sure I forget you."

⬤

HER eyes were wide open in the darkness of the bedchamber. Parysatis's words kept going through her head. The kitten's mews, its dead body, everything merged together, confused and terrifying.

What had the queen said? What had she said herself? She could not remember. Was she to understand that Parysatis would help her, would talk to the King of Kings, advise him to send for Ezra?

How could she know?

Had she merely humiliated herself more, and in vain?

What had she agreed to?

Never to see Antinoes again.

Never to love Antinoes again. Never to kiss him or caress him. And perhaps get nothing in return.

Again and again, the queen's words, the whole scene, twisted through her thoughts, like a top endlessly spinning.

"Lilah . . ."

She was so absorbed in constantly turning these terrible things over in her mind that she did not hear the whispering.

"Lilah!"

She made out a shadowy figure. She was no longer alone in the room.

"Lilah . . ."

For a split second, she thought it was Antinoes. Antinoes taking advantage of the darkness to join her, in spite of Parysatis's spies.

But it was a woman's scent she smelled. At last she recognized the voice. "Axatria!"

"Not so loud. There's no point in waking the whole house!"

"What's happening? Why have you come up here without a lamp?"

Axatria was thrusting a shawl into her hands. Lilah resisted, ready to protest.

"Shhh, don't make a noise . . . Sogdiam is downstairs."

"Sogdiam? What's he doing here?"

"He'll tell you himself. Hurry up."

Axatria was already pulling her toward the door and the shadowy corridors.

A few moments later, Lilah found Sogdiam in the kitchen, huddled in front of the last embers of the hearth. In spite of the blanket Axatria had put around him, his teeth were chattering, his hands held tight around a steaming cup of herb tea.

He tried to get up when they came in, but his deformed legs were so numb, they could hardly carry him. Lilah and Axatria rushed to him to stop him falling.

"He's been wandering around the city since sunset," Axatria said.

"I had to hide before I came here," Sogdiam grunted, pulling the blanket over his head. "If not, the guards would have caught me. No chance of passing unnoticed with my bad legs."

"Has something happened to Ezra?" Lilah asked.

"No, no. Ezra's fine. I've come because of Master Baruch. He's the one who's not well."

"What's the matter?"

"Let him drink his herb tea and get a bit warm, or else he'll be ill," Axatria said. "I'll go and find him a dry tunic. His own tunic is like a block of ice."

◉

"AT first," Sogdiam said, regaining his strength, "I didn't notice anything. Master Baruch kept complimenting me a lot on my cooking, and asking for a little more of this, a little more of that. And I was happy to give. 'Look,' I thought, 'Master Baruch has a good appetite and really likes my dishes!' I cooked him fish, millet balls, barley biscuits filled with stuffed pigeons, olives, and dates—all good food, I can assure you! I didn't know the recipes, but they were so tasty! One recipe leads on to another, then another . . . Master Baruch ate everything, left nothing. And if Ezra didn't like it or wasn't hungry, he'd eat Ezra's portion, too! Of course I found it strange, but you know how Master Baruch is. He's the strangest character I've ever met. One day he's laughing, another day he doesn't open his mouth or his eyes. One day he's grumpy, the next day he talks all day. Four nights ago, I woke up and heard him moaning. This time, he was really ill. I waited for Ezra to call me to help him tend to him, boil him herbs, as you taught me. But no, they didn't ask for anything. Master Baruch didn't want it. I stayed there in the dark like an idiot, listening to them argue. 'You're making yourself ill, master,' Ezra was saying. 'And I know why. You're going against Yahweh's will. I know.' 'Don't boast, my boy,' Master Baruch answered, moaning. 'You know nothing at all. Apart from your pride, you know nothing. I'm old, and the old are so ill they die, that's all.' 'You can't make yourself ill like this, master,' Ezra said again. 'The Law forbids it. Sogdiam will look after you!' To which Master Baruch retorted, 'Go back to your studies, then! You're wasting time, Ezra. You shouldn't be here, losing your sleep, dealing with an old man.

Only an ignorant fool would bother with such things!' Anyway, they argued like that for hours. In the morning, when I went to see Master Baruch, he was exhausted. To tell the truth, I thought he was dead. Ezra was quite shaken. He couldn't study. Zacharias and the others were out in the courtyard, like almost every morning, but he sent them away. All the same, I made an herb tea for Master Baruch's stomach. When I put the cup down beside him, he refused to drink, and you'll never guess what he said!"

Sogdiam, his eyes bright with excitement, looked from Lilah to Axatria, then back to Lilah.

"'Sogdiam, my boy,' he said, 'if you want to be a good Jew, make me a nice loaf of barley bread filled with pigeon's eyes, fish sperm, offal from a lamb killed according to Yahweh's rules, onions, a lot of garlic, and curdled milk.' That's what he said. After a night like that!"

"And did you make it?" Axatria asked, after a pause.

"No. Impossible. Where could I find a lamb killed according to the rules in the lower town? And in any case, Ezra forbade it. He claims Master Baruch is trying to kill himself even though the Everlasting has not demanded it of him."

"Well?" Axatria prompted.

The excitement drained from Sogdiam's eyes. He rubbed his cracked lips and turned to Lilah. "That's why I'm here. Master Baruch has decided he won't eat or drink until I've baked him his filled bread. What can I do? Where can I find the offal? I couldn't stay in the lower town, fretting. Who could help me if not you? But with my legs, it's not easy to get about in the snow, especially at night. I lost my way. Ezra had told me where the house was, but how to find it in the dark, with all these streets and all these houses?"

Lilah was speechless. She drew Sogdiam to her, and kissed him on the temples.

"It's all right, my boy, it's all right," Axatria said. "As soon as it's light, we'll leave in the chariot. We'll hide you under a blanket. As for the offal, there must be some in the house. Do you think Master Baruch really wants it? The one thing certain is that he mustn't die of starvation."

BY the time they got to Ezra's house, there were so many people in the street that Sogdiam had to reveal himself and speak before they were allowed through. How had the news that Master Baruch was dying spread through the lower city? Lilah had no idea. It was if the air itself had spread the rumor.

They went through the gate. The courtyard, although also overrun with people, was strangely silent. Lilah recognized Zacharias. She ran to the study.

Ezra, dark rings under his eyes from exhaustion and sadness, was sitting on his stool beside Master Baruch's bed. He stood up when she came in, and took her in his arms with a sigh of relief.

"He's still breathing," he whispered, before she could ask.

Lilah knelt by the old man's bed. His eyes were closed, his features were still, his face framed by his soft, abundant beard and hair, looked at peace. For a moment, Lilah was unable to move. She was numb with tenderness, fear, and sadness. She stared at the old man's lips and nostrils: They were pallid, without the slightest sign of life. Shyly, she touched his brow. It was barely warm. Nor were his cheeks much warmer. It was too late, it seemed to her. Ezra was wrong: Master Baruch had stopped breathing.

Without realizing it, a cry escaped her lips. She looked up at Ezra. Without a word, he shook his head and kneeled beside her.

Delicately, he placed a thin sheet of silver in front of Master Baruch's nostrils.

It misted over.

Sogdiam and Axatria had been watching their every gesture from the doorway. "Is he still breathing?" Sogdiam asked, in a barely audible voice.

Lilah nodded.

"In that case, we mustn't waste any more time," Axatria said in a low voice. "Come to the kitchen."

She pulled the boy by the sleeve. Lilah heard Sogdiam protesting, "To do what?"

"To make his filled barley bread."

"You're mad! He won't eat anything now, in the state he's in."

"How do you know? He's alive, he asked for barley bread, that's all that matters. Come on, hurry up and light the stove."

Axatria was right. She was speaking the very words that Master Baruch would have wanted to hear.

Lilah tried to smile, but did not have the strength. She sat down on the edge of the bed. Her shoulders began to heave under the wave of sobs that overwhelmed her. Ezra put his arm around her and drew her to him. She sought out his hands, intertwined her fingers with his. She bit her lip to stop herself shaking too much. For the first time in years, Lilah saw tears glistening in Ezra's red-rimmed eyes. She yielded against him a little more. Their temples touched. Through their clothes, Lilah could feel the warmth of his body. She had almost forgotten that Ezra had a body as young as hers. It had been such a long time . . .

Brother and sister. Ezra and Lilah!

It had been such a long time!

IT was just before dusk that Master Baruch awoke.

His eyelids opened suddenly and there was his gaze, quite bright and alive. He immediately recognized the faces bending over him, and smiled. "My dove," he whispered. "I knew you would come."

"Sogdiam came to fetch me, Master Baruch," Lilah said.

"A good boy, a good boy."

His eyes closed. Lilah thought he had fallen asleep again. But the fingers of his right hand were moving slightly.

"Both of you," he whispered in an almost inaudible voice, without opening his eyes.

Lilah and Ezra did not understand immediately. His old fingers moved more nervously. Finally, Ezra placed his hand on Master Baruch's right hand and Lilah took hold of the other. The old man smiled slightly.

They remained like this for a while.

The murmur of voices could be heard in the courtyard. From the kitchen, where Axatria and Sogdiam were performing a miracle, there came a delicious aroma.

Again Master Baruch's eyes opened wide. Clear and lucid, they came to rest on Lilah.

"It will come to pass," he breathed. "You did what you had to do, I know. Have no doubts. It is Yahweh's wish."

For the first time since Lilah had left Parysatis, the shame that had clung to her like an extra skin was dissolving. It was as if Master Baruch's simple words were purifying her. Her eyes filled with tears.

Now he was looking at Ezra. "Everything has an end, Ezra," he said.

"Master . . ."

"Listen to me. Everything has a beginning and an end." He paused for breath, and to recover a little strength. "Remember Isaiah's words: 'At dawn, you will be born again, you will grow quickly, and justice will walk before you . . . and Yahweh will bring up the rear with all His weight!'"

He fell silent again after this great effort, but his will remained strong in his eyes.

"A time for study and a time to rebuild the walls of Jerusalem," he murmured. "A time for Baruch Ben Neriah to thank Yahweh."

Ezra was about to speak, but the old man's eyes closed again.

Lilah thought that it was over. But after a moment of total silence, Master Baruch's fingers squeezed hers. "I can smell barley bread, filled barley bread! What a delight . . ."

Lilah sought Ezra's eyes. He nodded. "Sogdiam has just baked it for you, master."

Master Baruch's eyelids and lips quivered. "Bring it in, bring it in."

Ezra ran to find Sogdiam and Axatria. The bread was placed right in front of Master Baruch's face. Old as he was, the smile that lit up his features was as radiant and carefree as that of a young man greedy for life and brimming with hope.

A moment later, he stopped breathing.

ALL night long, candles burned in the house. Although no one person made the decision, tallow, wicks, and oil were found. By the time the clouds had cleared to reveal the stars, the courtyard and the streets around Ezra's house were also illuminated by hundreds of candles.

Zacharias and his people sang, and Ezra read some words from the scroll of Isaiah, which Master Baruch had known by heart:

Rejoice with Jerusalem, be glad for her, all you who love her,
Rejoice with her, all you who have mourned for her,

You will drink your fill at her comforting breasts,
You will drink with delight at her overflowing breasts . . .

In the morning, the sky over Susa was filled with mist. It made the sun white and the snowy ground dazzling. When the white disk of the sun reached its zenith, which, at this season, was lower than the Citadel, they came.

On foot, without a chariot, but armed. Ten soldiers with felt helmets and fur capes, javelins in their hands. They cut through the silent crowd. When they reached the gate, their officer asked for Ezra, son of Serayah.

When Ezra appeared, the officer handed him a wax tablet. "By order of our king, Artaxerxes the Second, king of the peoples from east to west by the will of Ahura Mazda, the great god. You, Ezra, son of Serayah, are ordered to appear by the statue of Darius the father, at the foot of the southern steps to the Apadana, the day after tomorrow. Present this tablet before midday and you will be taken to him. That is the will of the great king Artaxerxes."

The soldiers turned back the way they had come, and the crowed stood aside to let them pass.

The visitors were dumbstruck with amazement. They repeated the officer's words to themselves without grasping their meaning.

Ezra held the tablet in his hands, incredulous, and as nervous as if the wax concealed a magic spell or a poisonous animal.

Lilah felt her legs shaking. If Axatria had not been behind her, she would have collapsed.

The king had summoned Ezra!

Parysatis had spoken!

Master Baruch had been right!

Zacharias was the first to cry, "Praise be to God! Praise be to the Everlasting!"

The cry was echoed among the onlookers, and spread through the courtyard. The men raised their hands to heaven, snapping their fingers, applauding. Their hats and turbans and caps moved up and down. Tears of mourning were transformed in a moment into cries of celebration. The joy was so intense that the inhabitants of the lower town were taken aback, and even shocked.

By the time evening came, Sogdiam had had to explain a hundred times why there had been so much laughter. This, he said, was perhaps the true miracle of Master Baruch's death, and the reason for the beautiful smile with which he had savored the final moments of his earthly life.

But as they were about to place the old sage's body in the earth, Ezra suddenly stood up and looked fixedly at Zacharias and Lilah.

"It's impossible."

He went to find the wax tablet from the Citadel, written with all the skill of the Apadana's scribes, and waved it above his head. "It's impossible!" he said again. "I can't appear before the king!"

All those who heard these words froze in amazement. They repeated them to each other as they had earlier repeated the good news. And this time, a curious silence spread from the courtyard to the surrounding streets.

"Why is it impossible?" Zacharias asked at last, his voice timid.

"Whoever appears before the king must bow down. He must bend his knees and even blow a kiss on his palm toward Artaxerxes."

"Yes," Zacharias said, with a frown. "We know."

"Whoever does not bow down," Ezra went on, waving the tablet, "is seized by the eunuchs, and the audience is canceled."

"May the Everlasting protect you!" Zacharias said, rolling his eyes. "You'll bow down and everything will be fine."

Ezra roared with anger and started walking up and down in front of the astonished crowd.

"How can someone who must lead Yahweh's people to their land bow down?" he cried, looking at Lilah.

But it was again Zacharias who replied. He went up to Ezra and tried to calm him. "Come! What harm is there in bowing to the King of Kings? It's the rule. Even the lords of the Citadel, even the envoys of the Greeks, have done it. There's nothing shameful in it."

"Zacharias!" Ezra roared.

In his anger, he let go of the tablet. For a moment, it flew between earth and sky, as the crowd cried out in horror. Sogdiam shifted his weight and leaped toward it. Because of his legs, he had to twist his body, but he managed to catch the tablet before it could reach the ground and break. Sogdiam came down heavily on his back, but his grimace of pain was mingled with a look of relief.

Ezra barely glanced at him. He pointed at Zacharias, then at those around him. "What is not shameful for the Gentiles is shameful for us!" His voice swelled, and he opened his arms wide. "This is how it starts! You want me to lead you to Jerusalem. You want to carry the stones to rebuild the walls of the Temple. You want to be the hands that will purify it, that will open its doors, and you don't even know what it means to bow down! Artaxerxes walks hand in hand with his god Ahura Mazda as if he were the master of the universe! He demands that we bow down before him as if he were a god of heaven and earth!" Ezra's voice was less furious now. It contained more sorrow than anger. "Zacharias! And all of you, sons of Levi, sons of Jacob, sons of the Kohanim, including the first of them, Moses' brother Aaron! You who ought to carry them within you as the blood carries your steps, have you forgotten the words of Yahweh? 'You shall not bow down before any idol. You shall not bow down before any false god, or before any man who claims to be a god!'"

Ezra's voice fell silent.

Heads bowed.

Lilah, who had bent to help Sogdiam, felt her body grow cold. Had so much effort been in vain? She hoped for a moment that Master Baruch would raise his voice and suggest a solution to Ezra. But Master Baruch's voice was silent forever.

"There is something you could do," Axatria said unexpectedly. All eyes turned to her.

She was looking at Ezra with a shy smile. "If the king isn't a god, then he doesn't know how to separate true from false."

Taken aback, Ezra frowned. "What do you mean?"

"That you can look as if you're bowing down without actually doing it. Watch."

She stepped forward and bent her body in a graceful movement, and as she did so the thin bracelet she wore around her wrist slipped off. She bowed deeply and picked it up from the melted snow on the ground, and at last stood up, blowing hard on her frozen palm in what might have been a kiss of great tenderness.

There was a silence. Sogdiam burst out laughing. Others laughed, too, and as Ezra blushed to the roots of his hair, the laughter spread through the courtyard.

Axatria, just as scarlet as Ezra but with a gleam in her eyes, murmured, "Yahweh will know you did nothing shameful. But Artaxerxes won't know, because he's only a man."

Lilah saw Ezra reach out his hand toward Axatria. Now he, too, was laughing heartily. Lilah closed her eyes and thought she could see Master Baruch's smile.

The Book of Days

Before opening the ironclad door of the tower, Lilah stopped and held her breath. There was nothing around her but the immense silence of the city. It was too cold, the night too dark, for Parysatis's spies to think of venturing out.

The street was empty. Not even a stray dog.

She closed the door noiselessly behind her, crossed the ground floor, and slipped into the garden. She walked forward rapidly, hands in front of her for protection. She brushed against trunks and bushes. The darkness was so dense that she bumped into the wall of the house when she reached it, grazing her fingers on the icy edges of the bricks.

She had to go around the columns at the entrance. By the time she knocked softly on the shutter, she was soaked to the bone.

"Who is it?" he asked, almost immediately.

"Lilah."

These were the last words they spoke for a long time.

He undressed her close to the braziers. His breath burned every inch of her skin as he made love to her with an intense, almost painful slowness.

Later, when she was asleep, the fine hairs on her temples damp with sweat, he began to caress her again. He took her with the gentleness of a dream. She barely woke, breathing in his kisses.

Outside, the night of Susa was still profoundly silent. The snow was falling again.

When Lilah rolled again onto Antinoes' chest, the pleasure did not prevent her tears from flowing. Nevertheless, these tears were like a gentle, comforting rain for her eyes. Antinoes' caresses had washed her clean, calmed her. She clung to his neck. He held her tightly against him. For a brief but indelible moment, they were as indestructible as the night and the stars.

Before morning, Antinoes woke her so that she could take advantage of the darkness to leave the house. He had made ready for her a fur cloak lined with silk.

She would have liked to tell him that nothing had changed, either in her heart or in her will, that he was already her husband for all eternity, that Parysatis's threats did not frighten her. But at that moment, Antinoes whispered in her ear, "I'll be with Ezra in the Apadana." He kissed her once again. "Have no fear. Everything will be all right."

No, she had no fear, not anymore.

EZRA presented himself at the gate of Darius just before sunrise.

He was dressed in a new purple and blue tunic that went all the way down to his feet. It had been given to him the day before by Zacharias and the men who had been occupying his courtyard for days. Their wives had colored and woven the wool with such skill that it had the suppleness and brilliance of Oriental silk. On his head he wore a stiff felt hat, on which they had embroidered, in blue wool run through with silver thread, the seven-branched candlestick described by Yahweh to Moses. A cylindrical leather case hung on his chest, attached around his neck by a solid strap. Inside, Ezra had slipped the precious scroll of Moses' Scriptures, which his father's fathers had transmitted to him across the centuries.

Accompanied by Zacharias and a handful of companions, he climbed the long flight of steps that, rising from the royal city, ran alongside the enormous wall of the Citadel for one *stadion* in length. Standing out in relief from the brightly colored bricks were images of the battles of Darius, the first and greatest of the King of Kings, drawn with such realism that it was possible to identify every one of the soldiers.

Above and below, to a height of fifty cubits, there were other images, of wild beasts, fabulous monsters, and the men of the peoples Darius had conquered and who now paid tribute to Artaxerxes II.

The gate of Darius was at the top of the steps. No one, not even the king, could reach the square of the Apadana, then the Citadel, without going through it.

Its two leaves were so massive that it took a train of four mules attached to a winch to move them. It was framed by the defensive wall and by two towers, a hundred cubits high and just as wide, crenellated at the top. The bricks of the towers were colored light blue and yellow. Ahura Mazda spread his gold and bronze protecting wings there, over twenty-seven cubits in width. It was said that the wings reflected the sun so strongly that at certain hours of the day, they could burn the eyes of those who stared too long at them.

Two huge identical statues of Darius, five times life size, faced each other on either side of the bronze and cedar leaves of the gate. Real hair, from thousands of heads, had been used to make their wigs and beards. The necklaces and bracelets, each the diameter of a chariot wheel, were of real gold, cast from the spoils of battles fought in Hyrcania and against the Parthians. The Egyptian sculptors who had made these colossal statues had used precious stones for the eyes. At dawn and dusk, when the sun's rays struck the stones, a blue and purple ray was formed that forbade entry to all living creatures and purified the entrance to the Apadana.

Three times every morning, horns would sound, the gate would half open, and the courtiers of the royal city and the lords of the Citadel would then crowd through it and bow down before the statues of Artaxerxes on the Apadana. Each would present to the guards a bronze and gold disk, as big as a man's palm, carrying the effigy of the King of Kings. This medal was handed down from father to son. If they lost it, it was never replaced. If they committed a sin, it was destroyed, and their family and descendents were forever banished from the Apadana.

Strangers from all parts of the world, some from the lands ruled by the King of Kings, some from barbarous and unknown nations, mingled with this crowd. All kinds of faces could be seen, all kinds of eye and skin color, as well as the strangest clothes. The most disconcerting languages were spoken. But few among these people were allowed to pass between the breathtaking eyes of the immense statues of Darius.

To get through the gate and enter beneath the icy shade of the towers, these strangers had to present a wax tablet written by the scribes of the Apadana ordering them to appear.

When Ezra showed his, a guard looked at it carefully before handing it to some scribes, who studied it attentively in their turn. He was allowed to pass, but, in spite of his protests, Zacharias and his companions were rejected unceremoniously. They barely had time to shout a few words of encouragement before they disappeared into the crowd being held back by the guards' spears.

Ezra was directed toward a narrow gallery, where he was searched. With a care that was quite humiliating, the guards made sure that he was not concealing any weapons, any vials, any ointments. To his great terror, and in spite of his violent opposition, they pulled Moses' scroll from its leather case and unrolled it.

While Ezra looked on angrily, two young eunuchs slid the tips of their index fingers over the scroll, then held them out to be licked by a puppy in a cage. They waited until it was clear that the animal showed no signs of poisoning, and at last Ezra was able to go through the gate of Darius. Blinded by the daylight, he entered a world that few men had been able to see with their own eyes.

Everything inside was so inordinately large, Ezra had the fleeting impression that he had been reduced in the flash of an eye to the size of a child. On the left, beyond the parapets, the Shaour, tiny from this distance, shimmered as it meandered through the snow-covered fields like a thread winding its way across the pattern in a carpet. On the right, the houses of the upper town were like a child's building blocks, and the gardens dark strips where green peeked through here and there beneath the snow. The sky was so pure and so close, it seemed as if you only needed to lift your hand to be able to touch the clouds.

Before him lay the courtyard of the Apadana. The floor was of marble, stretching as far as the eye could see, as far as the walls of the palace itself, which was smooth, without a single opening, like a perfect cliff of brick. Each flagstone on the floor was so well joined to its neighbors that it would have been impossible to slide a fish bone between them.

Everywhere there were statues: figures of Artaxerxes II, effigies of Ahura Mazda with his bearded head and eagle wings, granite lions, steel and silver snakes, sensual porphyry nudes of the goddess Anahita, the raging horses and bulls of the god Mithras, clad in leather and gilded furs. Offerings burned in bronze bowls. Large numbers of people bowed before them, singing or crying praises. Some lay on the icy flagstones, others danced and bared their chests to the cold. Still others simply stood motionless, bent in two as if the frost had turned them to stone.

A large number of guards were strolling about, dressed in green and yellow tunics, the sleeves and necks embroidered with stones and gold rings. Taller than most men, they were made to seem taller still by the cabled hats that held their curly hair and were tied beneath their oiled beards. From their leather and silver baldrics, the ivory handles of curved daggers emerged. They carried javelins from which hung globes of silver or gold, according to their rank.

Two of them came straight up to Ezra and demanded to see his tablet. Then, without comment, they led him to the other side of the Apadana, where there was a roof supported by twelve columns covered in thick gold leaf. These columns, which could be seen from all sides, were so imposing that it had taken a thousand men to transport them and raise them.

Pressing the leather case containing Moses' scroll against his stomach, Ezra hurried behind the guards. They entered the area beneath the roof, which was alive with activity. Amid a crowd of scribes and aides, lords came and went. These were the men who ruled the kingdoms in the name of the king. The guards did not linger. They led Ezra to one of the many doors leading into the palace, then through the maze of corridors and courtyards.

They stopped on the threshold of a vast hall with a carpeted floor, and stepped aside to let him pass. The hall was divided into two halves by a veil. The visible half, where tables and cushions had been laid out, was brightly lit. Behind the veil, the shade looked soothing.

A host of servants bustled between the low tables and the seats, on which sat, in all their finery, those to whom Artaxerxes had granted the glory of being present today.

Curious, puzzled faces turned to Ezra as he entered, and the buzz of conversation diminished for a moment. A man stood up and signaled to him to come closer. Ezra recognized Antinoes, in spite of his sumptuous costume and the round hat that covered his hair.

As he stood there frozen in surprise, Antinoes came up to him and held out his hand. "Come and sit with me," he said by way of greeting. "The king isn't here yet, and the meal hasn't started."

Ezra hesitated, then replied abruptly, "I haven't come here to eat."

Antinoes smiled. "I suppose not," he admitted. "But the king won't receive you before he's had his meal."

He explained the way the audiences were held. The king ate alone or in the company of the great chiliarch and a few concubines. Then he would send for whomever he wished from among those whose audience had been written by the scribes in the Book of Days.

Antinoes pointed to the veil. "Until then, you won't see him. He stays in the other part of the room, behind that veil. The light is arranged in such a way that Artaxerxes can see us clearly, while we can't see him or even be sure where he's sitting. He changes his position at every meal."

"Are you telling me it's not even certain that Artaxerxes will receive me?" Ezra asked, his voice harsh.

Antinoes indicated the dozens of courtiers around them. "Almost every one of the people here has received a tablet for the audience, like you. As you can see, there are almost a hundred of them. Not even ten will be called before the king."

Ezra's eyes grew wide in astonishment, and his mouth tightened with anger.

Antinoes placed a calming hand on his wrist. "Don't worry. You'll be received."

"Why are you so sure?"

Without replying, Antinoes smiled again, with a sad, affectionate smile that surprised Ezra as much as the contact of his hand on his wrist. "Come on," he said. "There's no point in standing. When you enter this hall, the greatest virtue is patience."

EZRA let himself be led to a table reluctantly. As soon as they were seated, eunuchs placed food and drink on the great platter in front of them. Before they walked away, they casually tasted from each of the goblets in order to demonstrate that they contained no poison.

"Why are you so sure the king will receive me?" Ezra asked again.

"Because he must."

Ezra frowned. "Do you, a Persian, also think the hand of Yahweh is upon me?" he asked ironically.

"That may be so, since Lilah believes it. But what is certain is that Artaxerxes will give you an audience soon because, like your god, his mother, Queen Parysatis, wants it."

"I don't understand," Ezra said, his face becoming harder.

Antinoes then explained how Lilah had decided to make her brother's true worth known to Artaxerxes, and how she had gone to Parysatis to plead her cause.

When he stopped, Ezra looked away, then asked after a moment, "Would Parysatis dare throw Lilah to the lions?"

"Without hesitation."

Ezra was silent again before continuing. "So you won't be able to marry her?"

Antinoes looked at him in silence.

"And what are you doing here?" Ezra asked.

"I was summoned, because I'm the one who wrote to request an audience for you."

Ezra's expression softened for the first time. "You wrote the request?"

"We used to be brothers, Ezra," Antinoes said, with a touch of anger. "I haven't forgotten that, even if you claim not to remember. In your determination to respect your God's laws and rules, you've become harder than a brick wall!"

Ezra again avoided his eyes. His hands kneaded the leather case containing Moses' scroll.

"Don't misunderstand me," Antinoes went on, in the same tone. "You truly owe your presence here today to Lilah. She's the one who believes that the hand of your God is upon you. She's the one who thinks you have a future that I don't understand. But I love Lilah as a man can love only one woman. And my love is not like yours! All it asks is her happiness!"

Ezra had turned pale. He sat there, stony-faced, indifferent to everything around him. "No, it's to Yahweh that I owe my presence here."

Antinoes nodded. "I suppose that's how you see things. But I'd say that your God has placed his will in Lilah's hands. His will, added to your sister's courage. Because nothing is more dangerous in this city than to let Parysatis decide things. There's always a price to pay."

There was a slight movement at the other end of the room. The last courtiers still standing sat down. "What do you mean?" Ezra asked, uneasily. "What price has Lilah paid to get me this audience?"

Suddenly, silence descended on the hall like a wave.

"The king has just sat down behind the curtain," Antinoes whispered without moving his lips. "You mustn't speak now until you're ordered to. Eat, or if you don't want to eat, keep still. Remember he can see you, and you can be sure he'll be looking at you."

⬡

AS Antinoes had predicted, patience was the greatest virtue anyone waiting for an audience could possess. The king's meal was interminable, and the silence that hung heavy over the hall made it seem even longer.

From time to time, the courtiers would hear a few murmurs emerging from the semidarkness beyond the curtain. Female voices, a short burst of laughter. They themselves ate in silence. The only sounds came from the dishes and the bowls of lemon water that the servants brought them so that they could rinse their fingers. They all ate slowly and diligently, their heads bowed over the brass platters. But no one ate until the eunuchs had first tasted each of the dishes placed before them.

Ezra sat stiffly on his cushion. In spite of Antinoes' warning, he could barely conceal his irritation at such a long wait. Like the others, he felt the silence weigh on him, and was a touch edgy at the thought that the king could see them but that there was no way of knowing exactly who he was looking at. Clearly, Artaxerxes liked to be thought of as a deity. To the courtiers, he probably was. Ezra felt his mood darkening.

Nervously, he fidgeted with the ring Axatria had given him, which he was wearing on his forefinger. It was a red stone set in silver, which Sarah had taken from Mordecai's chest. His uncle's fingers were much broader than his own. All he had to do was

separate the index finger and middle finger a little and the ring
would slip off as if by accident. He hoped he would soon get a
chance to use it, but was starting to doubt it. Beside him, Antinoes had applied himself conscientiously to his food, which indicated that he was not really hungry and took little pleasure in the
meal.

Suddenly, harps, flutes, and drum struck up a melody behind
the veil, and a youthful but powerful voice—Ezra guessed it be-
longed to a young eunuch—started singing. The words glorified
the manliness and warlike power of Artaxerxes and his ancestors.
Then, with the same suddenness with which it had begun, the
music stopped, and at that moment the veil opened.

The crowd of courtiers stood up. Antinoes pulled Ezra by the
tail of his tunic to get him to stand up, too, and bow like the others.

But hardly had they stood than two guards came up to them.

"Ezra, son of Serayah," one of them said. "Artaxerxes, master
of nations, King of Kings, wants to see you."

WHILE the eunuchs and servants wore sumptuous clothes, and
the tunic of the chiliarch Tithraustes glittered with gold and precious stones, Artaxerxes was dressed in a simple white tunic. His
long beard was threaded with gold braid, and over his wig he
wore a tall hat woven with gold and stones. The wig itself was so
voluminous that it made his face seem unusually long and thin.
Ointments had been applied to his eyelids to make them black,
and his gray eyes given color with a touch of kohl. Between the
shadows of his beard, his lips had been painted to emphasize the
way they curled voluptuously. He was sitting on a huge chair
strewn with stars made from emeralds and pearls, and his feet
rested on a stool of gold and ivory—it was said that he carried it

himself as he moved about the palace, and even when he rode in a chariot.

On his right stood the chiliarch, and behind, the three scribes of the Book of Days, helped by some twenty young eunuchs, crouching quietly until they were needed. To his left, the musicians waited for a gesture from the king. All around, fifty guards, among the tallest ever seen, formed a circle.

Reaching the boundary previously marked by the veil, Antinoes bowed. He went no farther, but Ezra continued walking straight toward the king.

A murmur went through the courtiers.

The king's face remained impassive.

Ezra took a few more steps, then put his head down and made a little bow, his right hand dangling toward the floor. The ring slipped from his fingers, and he bent as if following it in its fall. He stayed down for a brief moment, then straightened up again, and blew on his palm just as Axatria had done in the courtyard of his house.

Unfortunately, he lacked Axatria's grace and enthusiasm. The movement he had made was so unlike a bow that the chiliarch Tithraustes signaled to the guards. Artaxerxes raised his hand from the armrest of the seat and smiled with amusement.

Taken aback, Tithraustes made sure that his master was still in a good mood, before doing his duty. "Ezra, son of Serayah, Jew of Zion," he announced. "My king, he has come to ask you for help and support in leading to Jerusalem those of his people who have been living among us, in the Susa region and in Babylon, since their father's exile. That goes back, my king, to the days when Darius was not yet King of Kings."

Like all the people in the hall, Ezra remained completely still until the king, who was no longer smiling, spoke for the first time.

"Your greeting, Ezra, is not that of a man who loves me. And yet you have come to ask me for help."

Antinoes saw Ezra's shoulders and neck stiffen. Then he heard his clear voice declare, "Do not see it as an offense on my part, my king. I give you all the respect I owe you. But it is true, my love goes to Yahweh, my God. As for bowing down, I obey the Law that Yahweh gave my people."

The answer was so unexpected that the scribes and the chiliarch turned to Artaxerxes, waiting for his anger to explode. Instead, the king looked at Ezra more attentively. "That is not a pleasing answer," he said. "Unless you can explain it to me."

"My king, as the chiliarch said, my people are the people of Jerusalem and Judaea, the land that Yahweh, master of the universe, apportioned to us at the birth of time—provided that we follow his laws and decrees. Your father, your father's father, and the great Cyrus, King of Kings, recognized the greatness of Yahweh's laws. They considered them good and useful. That's why the great Cyrus, after conquering Babylon, made a decree in Ecbatana, giving us the right to live according to these laws and to establish them in Jerusalem and throughout Judaea."

Artaxerxes appeared to reflect for a moment, then turned to the scribes. "Is this true?" he asked. "Is it written in the Book of Days?"

There then began a strange ballet. The scribes and their aides began rummaging through the chests with which they were surrounded. From these, they took out hundreds of papyrus scrolls, checking their contents on the wooden handles. They performed this task swiftly, unconcerned about the dozens of eyes watching them. At last, after what seemed quite a short time, given the scale of the work, one of them unrolled one of the scrolls, which was some five or six cubits in length. With an expert eye, he looked all through it, and finally smiled, stood up, and bowed.

"Yes, my king," he said. "Cyrus the Great spoke in favor of the Jews of Jerusalem."

Artaxerxes, who now seemed to be taking pleasure in this

battle of wits, turned to Ezra. "And you, do you know the words he spoke?"

"Yes, my king," Ezra replied, without flinching. "Cyrus, king of Persia, declared, 'Yahweh, God of heaven, gave me all the kingdoms of the earth and entrusted me with the task of building him a Temple in Jerusalem, in Judaea. Whoever among you is part of his people, may his God be with him! May he go up to Jerusalem and build the Temple of the God of Israel, the God who is in Jerusalem.'"

There was a moment of stunned silence, followed by murmuring among the onlookers. Artaxerxes pursed his lips, and ran his fingers through his golden beard.

"Are you claiming that Cyrus knew your God but knew nothing of Ahura Mazda, Anahita, and Mithras?"

"Those were the words he spoke, my king."

Artaxerxes grunted, and pointed a finger at the scribes. "What does the Book of Days say?"

This time, the answer was not long in coming. "O my king, what Ezra has just said is written word for word."

There were more murmurs around Antinoes. Artaxerxes looked at Ezra, thoughtfully. "These laws of your God of heaven," he asked at last, "who knows them?"

"I do, my king."

"All of them?"

"All of them."

"How can this be?"

"Because I've studied them every day for years."

"Where?"

Ezra raised the leather case and took out Moses' scroll. "They are written here, my king."

"And who wrote them?"

Ezra recounted how Moses had led Yahweh's people out of Pharaoh's Egypt, how he had led them to the mountain of Horeb,

where Yahweh had dictated his commandments to him: laws and
rules that concerned all things and all occasions in life, so that
then, through the children of his brother, Aaron, they could be
transmitted from generation to generation.

"And you claim to know each and every one of them?" Artaxerxes asked.

"Yes," Ezra replied.

Artaxerxes smiled and pointed to Ezra's hat. "If everything
proceeds from a law, why did you have that candlestick embroidered on your hat?"

"Because Yahweh commanded Moses: 'You will make a candlestick of pure gold. Its base and its shaft will be of hammered
gold. Its flowers, buds and branches will form one piece with it.
Six branches will extend from its sides . . . '"

When he fell silent, Artaxerxes made a sign. One of the
guards came up to Ezra, took the scroll from his hands, and
handed it over to the scribes, who proceeded to search in it for
the commandment that had just been quoted.

"My king," they said at last, "what Ezra has just said is written
word for word."

Now there was only astonishment and silence around Antinoes. And Ezra's audience lasted so long that no one else was received that day. Artaxerxes asked a thousand more questions, and
each time he had the answers checked in the Book of Days. Then
he asked Ezra what help he expected from him.

Ezra explained what Nehemiah's task had been and why it
had remained unfinished. He recounted how King Darius had in-
stituted a search of his archives and cellars for the objects stolen
by Nebuchadnezzar during the sack of Jerusalem, as well as the
measurements of the Temple that had to be rebuilt. That, too, Artaxerxes commanded to be checked in the Book of Days. Once
again, the answer was that Ezra was telling the truth, word for
word.

"Ask me what you want," he said at last, "and you will have it."

"It can only be to your advantage for law and order to prevail in Jerusalem, my king," Ezra declared. "Today, the walls of Jerusalem are again cracked and broken. Disorder enters in like the wind and profits your enemies. Day after day, the whole of Jerusalem is a more and more open breach in the frontier of your kingdoms. And through this breach the chaos of war, the chaos of nations without laws, can reach even you. Give me the power to leave Susa with those of my people who wish to follow me. Give me what I need to rebuild the Temple and make it worthy of Yahweh, and I will give you calm and peace and stability. Jerusalem, made strong again by the Law of Yahweh, will protect you from the Egyptians and the Greeks."

"May Ezra's words be written in the Book of Days," Artaxerxes replied. "May it also be written that I, Artaxerxes, King of Kings, grant him what he asks."

"EZRA came back to the lower town a hero," Lilah said. "It was already dark. Zacharias and his family escorted him with candles and torches from the royal city to his house. They sang and danced all night long, and then, as soon as dawn rose, they ran to the Jewish houses to spread the good news. By now, there isn't a single child of Israel in the upper town who doesn't know that Ezra, son of Serayah, is going to leave for Jerusalem with the agreement of Artaxerxes in order to rebuild the Temple."

There was a touch of mockery in Lilah's voice, but mostly it was calm and gentle.

They were in Antinoes' bedchamber. The shutters had been carefully lined with blankets so that no light could be seen from outside. "It's when you think Parysatis's spies are dozing that they're most alert," Antinoes had said.

"Ezra is the only one who doesn't seem enthusiastic," Lilah continued. "As soon as anyone tries to congratulate him for impressing Artaxerxes with his answers during the audience, he cries, 'I know very little! You think it's a lot because you're ignorant.' Or else, 'Until I have a letter from Artaxerxes in front of my eyes, it's pointless for you to sing my praises. It isn't yet certain that Yahweh's hand is upon me. I'm carrying on with my studies!' Zacharias protests, of course. Then Ezra loses his temper: 'Where are the Levites who are supposed to be going with me? You promised me hundreds. But when I count you, I can't even see ten who are capable of reading Moses' scroll! There are thousands of exiles in Susa, yet I don't see them crowding into the lower town, ready to set off for Jerusalem! They say they're impatient, but where are they?'"

Antinoes laughed, so accurate was Lilah's imitation of Ezra's voice. Lilah rolled onto her back, stretched out on the bed, and gazed up at the dark ceiling.

"My uncle Mordecai is very impressed, too," she went on, her tone no longer mocking. "He knows he won't go to Jerusalem. His workshop and my aunt's workshop mean too much to him. But he has a bit of a bad conscience. He's going to give my brother some chariots so that he can travel comfortably. When I told Ezra, he replied, 'They're all like our uncle, my sister. All these fat children of Israel are ready to give me their gold, provided they're not obliged to get up from their cushions. They have no desire to see Jerusalem again. They're so content here, in the arms of Artaxerxes! Do they imagine Yahweh isn't judging them?'"

Antinoes had stopped laughing. They were both silent. The silence weighed on them, but the words that remained to be said weighed even heavier on their hearts.

Antinoes' face crumpled like a piece of cloth. "But you're not like your uncle," he whispered. "You're Ezra's sister, and you'll go with him to Jerusalem."

Lilah did not reply at once. She closed her eyes. Antinoes looked closely at her mouth, her chest swelling as her breath came faster.

"Yesterday," she said at last, "Ezra asked me, 'And what of you, my sister? Will you follow me or will you stay with your Persian?' That made me angry. I replied that my Persian had a name. And that I shan't give him an answer until he has spoken it."

She fell silent, her eyes still closed. Antinoes did not dare move, hardly dared to breathe. He had no doubt about Lilah's decision. But he could not help himself: His hands shook as if he expected something different to emerge as if by a miracle from that beloved mouth.

"I went to the lower town," Lilah resumed, softly. "He greeted me more tenderly than he has for a long time. 'Antinoes told me,' he said. 'He told me you went to see Queen Parysatis for me.'"

Lilah's voice broke. She bit her lip and tears formed beneath her closed eyelids.

"He said, 'I know it was Antinoes, your lover, who wrote the letter seeking an audience from Artaxerxes in my name. I've been unfair and harsh toward him. I can speak well of Antinoes now. But that changes nothing. You must understand me. All I'm doing is following the Law of Yahweh. There's no other choice. How could my sister live her whole life with a man who's not a child of Israel? At the foot of the mountain of the Commandments, Yahweh said to Moses and Aaron, "How dare you let the women who have slept with Midianites live? They are unclean. The bitter water of my curse will flow over them."'"

Antinoes had seized Lilah's hand. She clung to him, holding him so tight she seemed suspended in the air. "He keeps saying he needs his sister. And it's true. I know it. I've always known it. Just as I know that what he's doing is great."

"I know it, too," Antinoes replied at last. "And so does Parysatis. There will be no miracle for us. You must go with Ezra to Jerusalem."

Lilah opened her eyes, and her tears flowed. She looked closely at Antinoes' face. "I could hide. Only go as far as Babylon. Wait there until Parysatis forgets me. Then we can meet again in a year. Yes, in a year, Parysatis will have forgotten me. She might even be dead!"

"Parysatis will never forget you. Wherever you are, if you're with me, her cruelty will reach you. And don't count on her dying. Demons go on for a long time. In any case, Ezra will never leave you in Babylon either."

Lilah raised Antinoes' hand to her lips. "Will you forget me, then?"

"No. I'll carry you within me all the days of my life."

Gently, he forced her to stand, and took off her tunic. He took a candle in each hand, the better to see her naked body, and walked around her.

"Every inch of your skin will be stamped on my eyes," he promised. "I will see your face in my dreams. I will kiss your breasts and your belly in my dreams. I will be inside you, night after night, and in the morning I will have the scent of your kisses on my lips. In the morning, my penis will grow hard at the memory of your hips."

Lilah realized that Antinoes was weeping, too. She smiled. "You came back to Susa to make me your wife . . . ," she said in an almost inaudible voice.

"There are too many people who don't want it."

"I made a promise, I must keep it."

She took the sheet from their bed and held it above her, like a canopy. Then she, too, began moving around Antinoes with a light, dancing step.

"I am Lilah, daughter of Serayah," she whispered. "I choose my husband according to my heart and before the Everlasting, Yahweh, my God."

A radiant smile lit her face, while her hips danced the

wedding dance and her arms moved the sheet so that it was over her lover's head.

"I choose Antinoes, he who has chosen me since the first day of love."

Antinoes started to laugh and raised his arms to hold up the sheet. They both turned and turned, looking each other in the eyes, their hips in the same swaying motion.

"I am Lilah, daughter of Serayah. As long as Yahweh gives me breath, I will have no other husband."

"I am Antinoes, lord of the Citadel of Susa. May Ahura Mazda and Anahita protect my love for Lilah. May they give strength and loyalty to time."

They laughed, tears glistening on their cheeks, their joy as intense as their despair.

"I am Lilah, daughter of Serayah, and before the Everlasting I keep my promise. I am Lilah, wife of Antinoes. That is written in the Book of Days, to the end of time."

"I am Antinoes, husband of Lilah. May Ahura Mazda bring me Lilah's kisses, to the end of time."

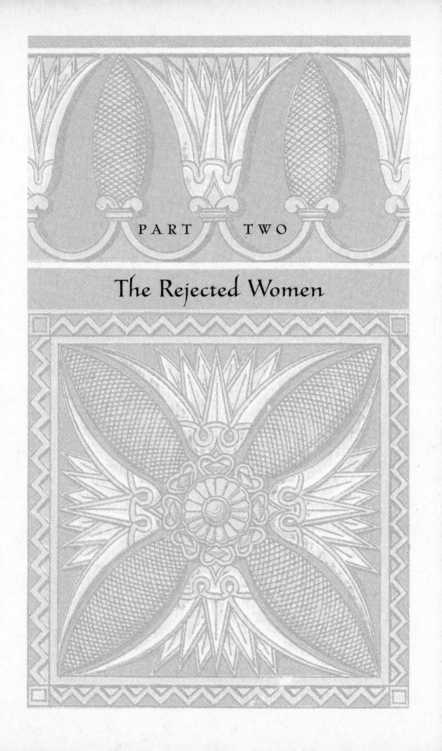

PART TWO

The Rejected Women

ntinoes, my husband.

Almost a year has passed since we turned beneath the wedding canopy. A year since your lips last touched mine, and your hands last caressed my breasts and hips.

A year that has been so long, I no longer have any yardstick by which to measure it.

But not a day or a night has passed that I have not whispered your name, that the desire to hear your voice and feel your breath on the back of my neck has not wrenched my stomach and crushed the few joys I still have left.

Yet I have been patient.

On our wedding night, I made a promise that one day we would meet again. In Susa or in Babylon, perhaps in Jerusalem, perhaps somewhere else in the world. I made a promise that Yahweh would not keep us apart for the rest of our lives. Yes, I made you that promise: A day will come when Lilah, your wife, will be by your side, will bear your children and watch them grow. Antinoes and Lilah will be a real husband and a real wife, not just ghosts and memories.

Today, however, I fear I cannot keep that promise.

It is not of my own free will that I say this. Not at all.

But something so terrible has happened that I no longer know what tomorrow will bring. I no longer know what I can and cannot do. I am writing to you because I am afraid. Because I no longer know what is just and what is unjust. It is like being swept away by a swollen river, struggling in the current while the banks recede. And yet, as I write, I tell myself it is madness to blacken this papyrus with words! For I know absolutely nothing about your present life. I know nothing about you, my beloved husband.

In truth, I am not even sure you are still alive!

But I cannot think about your death. That is impossible, Antinoes, my love.

Have you been in many hard battles? Have you sustained wounds, have you known victory? Sometimes, during the hours of despair, when solitude becomes as cold and clinging as winter mud, when the color has gone from the trees and the sky, and the beating of my own heart frightens me, I think that another woman may have become your wife and taken the place I left empty. Then I reproach myself for my obstinacy. Yes, I reproach myself, I punish myself by dreaming about the things I chose to reject: going away with you, far from Parysatis, far from Ezra. Far from Susa. Being by your side, seeing your eyes and your mouth, watching each dawn, each twilight with you.

I am aware that a man as handsome and strong as Antinoes, my husband, cannot remain alone. How could he live without a woman's body against his? Without love or caresses? With nothing but memories, memories that by now may be nothing more than smoke scattered on the wind? For that is our truth, my husband. We are no more to each other than the ghosts of our memory.

These thoughts torture me endlessly.

But they torture me less if I talk to you like this, putting words down on the yellow fibers of the papyrus. I am writing this letter to you, but I have nowhere to send it. No country, no city, no camp, no house to address it to. This is just my madness, my dream of keeping you alive and by my side.

Antinoes, my beloved, my husband before the Everlasting, the only man who has placed his lips on me.

TO make you understand—if that is possible—the madness all around me today, I must begin with our departure from Susa.

The order that separated us came the day after our wedding night. That very day, you had to leave Susa for Carchemish on the Upper Euphrates. Parysatis had done her work. She was separating us with an expert hand. You and I were both paying the price for the letter with the seal of Artaxerxes, which the guards from the Citadel came and placed in Ezra's hands.

Zacharias climbed onto a strong basket that Sogdiam brought him and read the papyrus scroll, in such a powerful voice that even those who were in the street outside the house could hear the words distinctly. Since then, I have heard them repeated so often that today I can write them without thinking.

Artaxerxes, King of Kings, to Ezra, scribe of the Law of the God of heaven:

I give this order to those in my kingdom who belong to the people of Israel, the priests and the Levites, and who have volunteered to leave with you for Jerusalem. May they go there, for you are sent by the king and his seven counselors to bring order to Judaea and Jerusalem according to the Law of your God . . .

Everyone listened, openmouthed. In spite of the cold, their hearts were warmed by these words, which upheld the will of Ezra.

> I, Artaxerxes, order all the treasurers beyond the river to do as Ezra asks, to give him a hundred talents of silver, a hundred kors of grain, a hundred packsaddles of wine, a hundred pack-saddles of oil, and salt without limit . . .

When the letter had been read in its entirety, there was no explosion of joy such as there had been after Ezra's audience in the Apadana. There was no singing or dancing. The faces around me were solemn, serious, and full of respect.

Artaxerxes' letter was not only an order, not only an expression of power. It bore witness to the fact that the hand of God was now upon Ezra. I had been sure of it for months, and Master Baruch was equally convinced, but now everyone knew.

It took several more days to prepare for our departure. Now that it was certain, volunteers started arriving in their hundreds and their thousands. Many came from the villages around Susa. Soon, the lower town was overrun, and the inhabitants started complaining. Zacharias obtained permission to use an area of waste ground on the banks of the Shaour, near the lower town, and pitched his tents there.

But in spite of the large number of people who had chosen to follow him, Ezra was not content. "Yahweh demanded the return of all our people to Jerusalem!" he stormed. "Not just a few!"

He sent enthusiastic young men to every Jewish house. In response, my uncle Mordecai and others came to visit him. They explained that not every family could leave Susa and just abandon, with a flick of the wrist, the work of a lifetime: the factories, the workshops, even the posts in the Citadel that had often been obtained in the first years of exile.

"The exile is over," Ezra replied, without listening to their complaints. "You have no good reason to remain among the Persians, except for your gold and your comfortable cushions."

And so, for five days and five nights, the Jewish houses of Susa were full of as much weeping as joy. There were those who were leaving and those who were staying. Fathers sent their sons, sons refused to follow their fathers. Lovers, wives, and sisters were separated, or torn as I myself was.

Contrary to what I had feared, Aunt Sarah did not beg me to stay. She locked herself in her bedchamber, her eyes red with tears, for the first time indifferent to what was happening in the workshop. In truth, it was those who were staying behind who had to bear all the sadness. The sadness of separation and the sadness of shame, for Ezra's harsh words had done their work.

In order to assuage his anger—and perhaps Yahweh's, too—those who chose to remain offered all the wealth they could. We were given wagons, food, clothes, carpets, and tents in profusion, as well as livestock of all kinds and hundreds of mules. Some even offered slaves and servants.

These were strange days.

And the way I lived through them was even stranger.

To tell the truth, I felt no joy.

I reproached myself for not being happy. Hadn't I wanted what was happening more than anything? But, however much I reproached myself, nothing brought me peace or satisfaction.

I had already started to miss you, Antinoes. I had imagined that I had hugged you in my arms tightly enough to keep the imprint of what I had lost, but the burden was heavier to bear than I had imagined it would be. I began to doubt that I could manage it. I was no longer the confident woman who had mustered the courage and determination to confront Parysatis.

I was only a young woman of twenty-two and a wife of a few days. I was terrified. My whole life stretched before me, a life I could not even imagine.

Fortunately, Ezra guessed nothing of my doubts, for I did not see him before the departure, or even during our journey to Babylon. Zacharias and his family were always around him, as well as a band of young zealots who had come from all parts of the Susa region. They drank in his words and his rages like morning milk.

It was not that anything disagreeable had happened! No one had spoken an unpleasant word or made an unpleasant gesture. But it soon became clear to me that I was no longer welcome near my brother while serious decisions were being made concerning our departure. These were men's decisions, about things only men knew about.

I was not hurt by this. I had my own preparations to make, and many tears to wipe away. Axatria was as nervous as a she-cat who has lost her little ones. She lived in dread of not being able to come with us, because of the rumors that were circulating: Ezra's young zealots were asserting that my brother wanted only Jews with him. Only the children of Israel, men, women, and children, could take to the road and return to populate Jerusalem, they claimed. The servants, and even, in some cases, the wives and husbands who were not Jews could not join the travelers.

However, this rumor was never confirmed, and it died down. Instead, it was announced that Ezra was ordering a two-day fast on the banks of the Shaour before our departure.

OH, Antinoes, my beloved, if only I could lay my head on your shoulders!

I had to interrupt this letter to bury a child.

At the moment, that is the most terrible of my tasks, though not the least frequent. It is difficult for me to take up my stylus again without my hands shaking.

I am sure you can imagine our departure from Susa. There is no need for me to waste any words on it. Mordecai had made a chariot specially for Axatria and me. Aunt Sarah had decorated the benches with the most beautiful rugs from her workshops. Beautiful and strong: I still sit on them, although the chariot itself has been pressed into other uses.

There were at least ten thousand of us. In the evening, when the front of the column reached the place where we were to pitch our camp, the rear was still far out of sight! Ezra was at the head, of course, followed by Zacharias and his family and the young zealots. There were no women among them. Then came the families, in order of tribe, according to the old lists Moses and Aaron had drawn up beneath the mountain of the commandments.

On the morning of the first day, we found Sogdiam standing at the side of the road, with his weight on one hip. As we helped him into our chariot, I felt happy for the first time in a long time.

We laughed as he told us how he had tried every means to stay at the front, with Ezra. It was hopeless: He was still a long way, he moaned, from being a good enough Jew to have that right.

He had also not greatly appreciated the previous two days of fasting, and devoured the meal we gave him with a tiger's appetite.

We were lucky to have him with us during that long journey. I am lucky to still have him with me today. He has performed a thousand miracles, and not only in cooking soup and filled bread loaves.

That day, it was through him that he learned our first destination. We were heading for the banks of the Euphrates, in order to get to Babylon.

"Ezra is very unhappy," Sogdiam told us. "According to him, there aren't enough of us. He thinks the Jews of Babylon will be more receptive to him than those of Susa."

It took us nearly a moon to reach Babylon. We had to go

down as far as Larsa before we found a bridge across the river, which was then in full spate.

Each day was hotter than the previous one, but slightly less oppressive. We grew accustomed to raising the tents and taking them down again, to walking long distances, to our backs growing stiff on the benches of the wagons and chariots. For many it was difficult to sleep surrounded by the noises of the night, the cries of wild animals, the rustling of insects and snakes.

The light of the stars, the play of the moon and the clouds, brought back to me the memory of our nights in the tower of your house. And these memories would make the next day easier. After a while, I became indifferent to the thousand discomforts of the journey.

Ezra had sent Zacharias ahead of us. When we reached Babylon, we were greeted with songs and flowers. An area of land had been prepared for us to pitch camp. It was so far from the city that the great ziggurat, with its gardens, looked more like a mountain than a building.

It was the next day that I saw Ezra again for the first time. Axatria and I had just made our beds in the tent when he lifted the flap.

I barely recognized him. His tunic was gray with dust, his hair long. He told me later that he had lost the ivory ring I had given him, which usually held it in place. His thinness and his grim expression were frightening to behold. His eyes shone with fever. The leather case containing Moses' scroll never left him, day or night. He held it so tightly in his hand that the bones could be seen through the skin of his fingers.

Clearly, he had fasted harder than anyone.

Axatria was unable to hide her distress, and reproached him for his pitiful appearance. He silenced her unceremoniously and ordered her to leave us alone. She obeyed with total submissiveness, and without showing the least anger.

A little later, Sogdiam brought him an herb tea. Ezra barely noticed his presence.

"Why is your tent so far from mine?" he asked me. "Why haven't I seen you since we left Susa? I wasn't even sure you were in the caravan."

I replied that there was no reason for him to be unsure that I had left, since we had agreed on it. "And this is my place," I added. "You chose those you wanted around you, and I don't think I would be welcome among them. It doesn't seem to be a woman's place."

He avoided my eyes. For a moment, Antinoes, you would have recognized the young Ezra, whom you sometimes teased. As handsome and fragile as a gazelle, full of fire, and yet all at once lost in the midst of his enthusiasm.

I was about to smile and tease him when he said, "I miss Master Baruch. Not a day goes by that I don't miss his counsels. And I miss you, too. There's no reason for you to be so far from me."

I asked him what he was finding so difficult. Everything, he replied bitterly. Nothing was going as he had foreseen. He was trying to follow the Law of Moses in everything he did, but as soon as he took one step forward, a thousand obstacles arose.

"It's ignorance more than anything else!" he cried, suddenly impassioned. "You have no idea how ignorant these people are, Lilah. For instance, I can't find any Levites capable of assuming responsibility for the sacred objects of the Temple. And yet, according to the Law, it is they who must take care of them until we get to Jerusalem and place them in the Temple. God of heaven, how is this possible? It seems there's no longer a single priest, in all of Babylonia, descended from the families inscribed in David's register! And the few I can find who still know even a few of their duties can't perform them."

"Why not?" I asked in surprise.

"Because they don't have thumbs!"

It was true. It had become a tradition among the Levites to cut off their thumbs. The reason went back to the early days of the exile. Since the priests, following King David's instructions, were excellent players of the ten-stringed lyre as part of their sacred duties, Nebuchadnezzar had decided they would become his musicians. So the Levites had cut off their thumbs in order not to be forced into such humiliation. Succeeding generations had followed suit.

"Ezra," I asked, "why do you let yourself become so discouraged, as if you were on your own?" And once again, I calmly repeated what I had said so often before his audience with Artaxerxes. "Trust in Yahweh. If he wants you to go to Jerusalem, if it is his will that you rebuild the Temple, his desire that the Law that is so dear to you be respected, why would he put obstacles in your way?"

"Because we're so unclean, so imperfect," he replied, "that we're unable to please him."

"Isn't that why we're going to Jerusalem? To better ourselves? To learn to live according to the Law? To get back on the path of justice and the covenant?"

"We're a long way from it, Lilah! Such a long way!"

I laughed. "Yes, we've only got as far as Babylon! We haven't yet crossed the desert. But it may be that Yahweh is less impatient than you. Fortunately for us."

We talked for another moment, defending our particular points of view.

"Take down your tent," Ezra said at last, "and come and pitch it close to mine this evening."

I agreed, on two conditions: that Sogdiam and Axatria could remain with me, and that the wives, sisters, and daughters of those with whom he had surrounded himself at the head of the column could do the same. He granted my demands.

The next day, I at least succeeded, to Sogdiam's great relief, in convincing Ezra not to order a new fast of purification. Many of us were already weakened by the journey. We didn't need more hunger; we needed more strength. Ezra accepted reluctantly. His young zealots had not looked kindly on my arrival, or that of the other women. That I should convince Ezra to put off a fast was even less to their liking. From that moment, they looked at me with mistrust, a mistrust that has been growing ever since.

Be that as it may, that day Ezra had an altar erected, and, instead of the fast, for three days he made a huge number of offerings. More than a thousand rams were sacrificed, I think, almost as many lambs, more than ten bulls, and a number of goats. Smoke hung over the camp, and the smell clung to the canvas of the tents for a whole moon.

That was also the time it took Zacharias to return with about a hundred young Levites who all still had their thumbs, even if they knew very little.

So we spent four Sabbaths in Babylon. Ezra recovered his strength and confidence. Finally, from among the two great families descended from the princes appointed by David, he was able to name the twelve priests who would be in charge of the Temple: Sherevyah, Hashabaya, and their brothers.

It was an opportunity for an evening of feasting and chanting, an opportunity for everyone to cheer up and be carefree. Once again, it was clear to everyone that the hand of Yahweh was now firmly upon Ezra.

Not that this prevented petty squabbles: As soon as they were named, those who found themselves in charge of the sacred utensils in the Temple starting worrying about the journey ahead.

"Ezra, we have two or three months of wandering before us. We're going to cross the desert, and we know it's swarming with Amalekites and all kinds of brigands. Our wealth will attract them like flies!"

Ezra replied that there were a great many of us now. We

would be like a whole city on the move; anyone would think twice before attacking us.

"That's what you think, Ezra! May the Everlasting bless you, but you've spent your life studying; you're not accustomed to these things. Crossing the desert is quite another matter! Many—too many to count—have disappeared, many have been robbed. Many wives, mothers, sisters, and daughters have been raped . . ."

And so on, until the reason for all this uproar finally emerged from the mouth of one of them.

"Why didn't you ask Artaxerxes for an armed escort? He would have granted you one. Why don't you ask the satrap of Babylon? Artaxerxes' letter entitles you to one."

Annoyed by this, Ezra replied that Abraham and Moses had not needed an armed escort when they had crossed the desert.

Sherevyah and one of his brothers, Gershom, had already proved their knowledge of the Scriptures. Now they stated that Moses himself had had an army, and that Joshua was a great soldier, as was Aaron's son, their ancestor as well as Ezra's.

That night, Ezra came to see me, trembling with rage. Since that business with the fast, he had not sought any counsel of me. Nor did he ask any of me now. All he wanted, although he did not realize it, was for me to caress him with my words—perhaps even with my hands, because his neck was tense with anger. I asked him to share my meal, but he refused to eat.

"There is nothing new in this," I said to him, trying to calm him. "You must simply keep telling them how things are, until they start to trust you. How many times did Zipporah ask her husband, Moses, to return to Egypt and take on Pharaoh before he agreed? He was afraid. He did not feel that he was capable of doing it. And yet he was Moses."

Ezra understood what I meant. Lit by torches, he climbed onto a wagon. His voice was so loud, most of the vast camp could hear him.

"I know what you're all afraid of: that we'll be cut to pieces during our journey. You want to know why I didn't ask Artaxerxes for an escort to protect us. My answer is simple: I would have been ashamed. I would have felt such shame, for myself as well as for you, I wouldn't even have dared move so much as my big toe. Is it to the King of Kings, the master of the Persians, that you will turn when you are afraid? Is that the trust you will need, if you want to follow me? If that is the case, I say to you clearly: You can stay here, and I'll go alone. An armed escort? When we are marching toward the Lord Yahweh? When we are marching toward his Temple and want to live according to his Law? Who are you? Where are the children of Israel? Where are those to whom Yahweh one day said, 'I am making a covenant with you'? Tomorrow, we will fold our tents and move forward with our wagons and chariots full of food and gold for the Temple, with our women and children and cattle, and we will go to Judaea under the protection of Yahweh. What you must tell yourself before anything else, what you must take into your hearts, is that the hand of our God protects us, whereas on those who abandon him, the full force of his anger falls. If you must fear something, fear the Everlasting! For one thing is sure: You are not yet worthy of his justice."

And so, when the next day dawned, our noisy company of twenty thousand set off again, leaving the ramparts of Babylon behind.

Strangely, the farther we got from them, the more the walls of the city seemed to glitter. In the milky light before the sun had fully risen, the staircases and gardens of the ziggurat appeared to rise far into the sky, so high that the top of it melted into the clouds.

Then the city disappeared behind a hill of gray dust.

And because everything reminds me of you, Antinoes, seeing Babylon vanish like that, so simply and so utterly, was like losing you all over again.

Antinoes, my beloved.

I had never imagined that murmuring these words would help me to get from one day to the next. I murmured them as I'm sure Ezra would have liked me to murmur the laws he taught us sometimes in one of our temporary camps, whenever he granted us a few hours' rest.

It was about this time, too, that a curious dream came to me, several nights in a row, a dream that would have amused you. I saw myself in our caravan, exactly as it really was. It was evening, and Sogdiam came to see me, with a mysterious expression on his face. He took me aside from the column, and led me to a place from which there was nothing to be seen but the immensity of the desert, its gorges and ridges of sand.

Suddenly, Sogdiam disappeared. I looked around, turning and turning, and at first there was only desert, only stones and sand. Then, far in the distance, some figures appeared. Within a moment, these figures were climbing the nearby dunes. I couldn't make out their faces, but I could see clearly the horses, the camels, the weapons hanging from the saddles. I was afraid that these were the bandits we dreaded so much. I ran back to the caravan and took shelter in my tent. To my own surprise, I warned no one of the danger, especially not Ezra. I fell asleep, just as I usually fell asleep in reality: murmuring the name of Antinoes.

After a very short sleep, I was suddenly woken by a hand on my mouth. Not for a moment, however, did I feel afraid. I immediately recognized my husband's soft skin, and his smell.

Then you carried me to your horse. At dizzying speed, we rode toward Jerusalem. We were surprised to find it a peaceful city, with none of the horrors that had been described to us. We were able to settle there, and we threw a great wedding banquet, at which you gave me gifts. In public we were man and wife, which was exactly right for the city as it was, a city pleased with the love that lived within its walls. Ezra, when he arrived, simply had to resume his studies.

I woke from this dream torn between the happiness of having had it and the bitterness around me. But the dream came back over many nights, and one day, at dusk, I decided to leave the column. Just as in the dream, I walked until I could see nothing but desert.

And there I waited, stupidly, until late in the night for you to appear.

Sogdiam and Axatria made a great fuss when I returned. They had assumed I was lost and could not find my way back to the caravan in the dark. Not a likely occurrence: It was hard to miss the thousand fires glowing in the night. The following night, my dream did not come back, and I have never dreamed it since.

THE more we advanced, though, the more I began to feel at peace again. I even felt a certain pleasure in our undertaking. It has to be said that we were a prodigious sight.

My Antinoes, you who have seen great armies, you may be able to imagine our river of men and women!

The wheels raised clouds of dust as they turned and made an almighty din. There was never a moment's silence. There was always shouting, weeping, the braying of mules, the groaning of camels. Even at night. At night, in fact, the camp, with all the hearths lit, was like a river of fire. Occasionally, I was reminded of the river of stars that crosses the sky, which people in Susa have called, since ancient times, the way of Gilgamesh.

Some claimed that to walk from the front to the rear of our column while it was resting would take all night, from dusk to dawn!

And, of course, it was alive with incidents—some tragic, some funny. Dozens of wagons overturned, and hundreds of men and animals were injured. There were disputes, love affairs—some open, some secret—weddings, births, and deaths. There were even two murders, and a few thefts, on which Ezra had to pass judgment, just like Moses.

One night, Sogdiam saved my life by surprising a snake slithering silently two paces from my bed. Although he is not the nimblest of men, he managed to shoo it away, then killed it with his kitchen chopper. These snakes were the thing we feared the most. Small but extremely poisonous, constantly thirsting after the milk in our pitchers, they killed more than a hundred women and children during the two months our journey lasted.

My most beautiful memory is of what I learned during those days. I acquired the most wonderful of skills: that of helping women in childbirth. I learned to support a woman during delivery, to control the rhythm of her labor, to welcome the baby's head and sometimes its limbs, to draw it out into the light so that it can take its first breath, to make sure that first breath is sweet.

Yes, that was the beauty of those days.

Then, one afternoon, we crossed the Jordan, and the next day we saw the hills of white stones surrounding Jerusalem.

I HAD to interrupt this letter because night fell. We don't have enough candles or lamp oil. There's no point in my wasting them on writing a letter in the dark, a letter I don't even know where to address.

The night was quieter than many others, with no attacks, no screaming, no wounded people. We were all able to get a little rest, and are now starting a new day with renewed strength. It is a strange thing to be surprised every morning by the rising of the sun and to wonder if we will live long enough to see dusk again.

It is all over for the beautiful, elegant Lilah. My tunic is no more than a long strip of cloth I've worn and washed too many times. The one thing I still have left that is at all becoming is my shawl, although the colors are so faded they can barely be told apart. My hands have carried so many sacks, so many stones, so much firewood, my palms have been torn on so many thorns, they look like those of the workers in my uncle Mordecai's workshop.

And my face!

We have no mirrors but, whenever I happen to glimpse my reflection in a pail of water, I scare myself. Almost nothing remains of the beauty that so impressed Parysatis and stoked her jealousy. Now, the queen would not even look at me.

I don't suppose you would either.

My skin is dry and weather-beaten. Every day there are longer, deeper lines in my brow. There are lines at the corners of my eyes and lips, too—fine, dense lines, like cracks in glazed pottery that has been roughly handled. My face seems to have aged ten years.

Blazing sun, wind, rain, scorching heat, hail, and frost: These are the ointments that have produced such fine results—that, and the fact that I grimace more than I smile.

The soles of my feet are covered with calluses because of the rope sandals I wear. But I'm happy to wear them. Without them, I would have to walk barefoot, like many, over the hot, sharp stones.

A week ago, for the first time, I lost a tooth. I'm still able to hide it, because the gap is at the back of my mouth. But I can write it here, because there is little chance you will read these horrors.

That was something I thought about for a long time last night, as I waited for sleep. There are very few ways to get this letter to you. Perhaps I could persuade Sogdiam to leave me and go back to Susa? But even then . . . Brave as he is, it would be a long and dangerous journey for him. Although it is hardly less dangerous staying here and ruining our bodies and our hearts.

Yes, our hearts. For among all the injustices that punctuate our days, nothing could be more unjust than the fact that both our bodies and our minds are becoming ugly, in the middle of this country that is so beautiful, in this land of milk and honey the Everlasting granted to Abraham and Jacob, Moses and Joshua, Sarah and Leah and Rachel and Hannah and all those who preceded us!

I can assure you, Antinoes, that when I first set eyes on Jerusalem, I really saw the land of milk and honey, the good, vast land, inexhaustible in its sweetness and riches, that had so often held our imagination spellbound as children in Babylon, Jewish children exiled and far from home.

It was the end of spring, and the earth had come back to life. The fruit trees—cherry, peach, plum—were in blossom. Olive trees swayed, gray and silky, on the hillsides. Cliffs of very pale rock rose on the ridges like languid hands. Great cedars and ageless oaks lent their vast shade to the flocks. Lambs leaped between the bushes of sage, thyme, and myrtle, arousing the smell of the earth like a lover's caress drawing the fragrance from the body of an indifferent woman. And where plowshares had passed over it, the earth was almost as red as blood, like real flesh.

And there amid the hills, like a jewel in its casket, Jerusalem lay waiting. The walls, built from the smooth, pale stone of the cliffs, gleamed with whiteness. There are no bricks here. Everything is of stone, as if those who built Jerusalem had imitated the Everlasting making mountains.

Everything was very calm, very peaceful. As we approached,

we made out more clearly the cracks in the outer walls. But there was nothing disturbing about that. Swarms of swallows sang above these ruins, where they had built their nests. Stumps of stone that had once been the bases of defense towers were held entwined by opulent shrubs with little yellow flowers. Agave, tamarisk, and even olive trees had long been growing between the cracked blocks, from which the mortar had oozed like sap.

Water gushed from invisible springs beneath the walls. We discovered pools of water so pure and so blue that they did not seem real.

No, there was nothing threatening about all this. It seemed as if the city, with an almost maternal gentleness, was welcoming the fields and the surrounding hills in a perfect, unbroken dialogue.

Alas, this feeling of serenity was merely due to the joy of finding what we had so long desired! It was a fantasy, the lingering breath of a dream that would soon fade. I know now how hard those stones are, and that the ruins were brought about by violence and hate. I have learned that the sense of calm was nothing but the result of defeat and destruction.

And now, when I close my eyes and dream of beauty, of the milk and honey I thought I saw when we arrived, I cannot help weeping. Why is it that the most magnificent flowers conceal the deadliest of poisons?

◉

ALTHOUGH Ezra had sent Zacharias and some of the young zealots ahead to inform the inhabitants of our arrival, we were not greeted with much enthusiasm. After all, Nehemiah had left behind him the memory of a huge effort that had ended in terrible failure.

In addition, the city is not large, and there were not many more people living there than there were in our caravan.

You can imagine, Antinoes, what it must have been like for the inhabitants of Jerusalem to discover this multitude on the ridges of the hills. Twenty thousand men and women, ten thousand wagons raising dust and scattering the flocks, a whole noisy nation on the march. And now this impatient, disorganized rabble was coming to a halt outside their walls!

We sang and sounded horns to proclaim our joy and our relief that we had arrived. A whole night spent dancing, the most joyful I was ever to know. Our hearts relaxed like a bow after the arrow has been released. Without drinking a single cup of wine or beer, we were intoxicated because we had at last seen our Jerusalem!

When the next day dawned, it was raining. We were exhausted, our minds still dizzy with joy. But we only had to go through the Water Gate, as it was called, to become aware of the scale of the task awaiting us.

Inside, Jerusalem was just as ruined as its outer walls. Half the houses were no longer inhabited. Many were roofless, half burned, the walls torn open. A terrible stench rose from disused wells. Occasionally, one house had collapsed on top of another. Entire streets were filled with rubble.

Ezra howled with distress when the old men of the city led him to the Temple. The building that Nehemiah had barely managed to finish was already devastated. Where once there had been doors, there were now fragments of charred wood. The altar for burned offerings had long since been profaned. Its cracked basin had become home to ten cats as wild as tigers and a playground to their offspring. A tamarisk had overrun the great staircase at the entrance. In the open hall, more tamarisks and a medlar tree rose higher than the walls, the crenellated tops of which had collapsed. In places, signs of fighting could be seen. Carved stones and columns had been broken with sledgehammers. Thick grass grew between the marble flagstones, pulling free the steps of the sanctuary. The right-hand wall gaped open, as if a monster had

walked right through it. As for the great courtyard around the
outside of the Temple, the inner walls were no more than rem-
nants, and the flagstones were piled high with refuse.

The following night, there was no singing or dancing. The
darkness was filled with the cries of Ezra, the Levites, and the
young zealots. They tore their tunics, covered their heads with
ashes, and prayed until dawn.

And so here we were, as distraught and helpless as the inhabitants of Jerusalem. A few old men gathered around Ezra and
joined their passionate lamentations to his.

But after the tears, the rage, and the despair, there were decisions that needed to be made.

Ezra wanted to proceed with the purification of the Temple
immediately. Many of the priests and the Levites—Sherevyah,
Hashabaya, and their brothers—shared his opinion.

It was then that Yahezya spoke for the first time. He had always lived in Jerusalem. Thin and gentle in face and body, he had
welcomed us with unreserved kindness. As Ezra and his people
debated, he spoke up in his polite manner.

"I understand your impatience, Ezra. You came here to rebuild the Temple. You find it in this terrible state, and no task
seems more urgent. But look around you. There are thousands
and thousands of you here, at the gates of Jerusalem. You don't
know where to pitch your tents. I daresay a great many of you will
have to settle in the valley that leads to Hebron. Unfortunately,
the land there is disputed. Do you think the Moabites and
Horonites, Gershem and Toviyyah and all the other kings and
chiefs around Jerusalem, are simply going to accept you? Don't
forget, Ezra, it was their brute force, their wickedness, that reduced Jerusalem to this ruin that so distresses you. It's because of
them that every time a stone is put up, it is immediately torn
down. Nehemiah suffered because of them. He confronted them.
Nehemiah is dead. They are still here—or their sons are. Do you

think they'll leave you in peace in your tents when it would be so easy for them to make you suffer?"

Yahezya's gray-green eyes looked at us calmly. In spite of the gravity of his words, his voice was gentle and patient.

"It might be more sensible to build solid roofs," he went on. "Considering how many of you there are, it won't take you too long to rebuild those houses that are not so badly ruined. You have wives, mothers, and children to shelter. The Temple is unclean, but it's been unclean for a long time. The only thing Yahweh is impatient for is your success, Ezra. If Toviyyah brings war and bloodshed to your tents, you will only be slowed down even more."

One of Ezra's young zealots laughed sharply. "Obviously, you've been living in Jerusalem for a long time, Yahezya! Listening to you, it's clear why the Temple of Yahweh is in such an unspeakable state. Who are you to say what the Everlasting is impatient for? He led us here, holding his hand firmly over Ezra. What are you afraid of? It's this Toviyyah of yours who ought to be afraid of us, because we're here through the power and will of Yahweh!"

Many heads nodded. I knew that Yahezya had spoken the truth, but I did not protest. Wasn't it largely my doing that people thought like this? Hadn't I said endlessly that we must fear nothing, but on the contrary trust to Yahweh's protection in all things?

I kept silent. Not that Ezra would have listened to me anyway. He had not cared about my opinion for a long time, since well before we arrived in Jerusalem. He simply wanted me near him. Doing the sensible thing no longer mattered to him. Nor to those who crowded around him, their mouths full of praises.

Although the meeting went on for quite a while, the final decision came as no surprise.

Ezra declared that the most urgent thing for us to do was to proceed with the purification of the Temple.

As Yahezya had predicted, we had to pitch our tents as far as the valley of Hebron. Then Ezra asked all those—Levites, priests, and others—who would be working in the Temple to fast for two days, living on nothing but prayers, in order to be in a state of purity to undertake the task awaiting them.

But the way things came to pass was, alas, quite different.

AXATRIA and I were washing linen when Sogdiam came to find us, all excited, and urged us to go with him to the Water Gate.

Ezra had been there since morning, leading the fast with the help of the priests who would be involved in the purification. The most fervent of the men in our caravan were there, praying with the priests and the Levites, so tightly packed together that it was impossible to get through. The women had climbed the little hill opposite the entrance to the city, on the other side of the pools. By the time we joined them, rumors of an unusual event had already spread.

From our vantage point, we were able to see the white she-camels, the white mules, and the magnificent costumes that had just emerged as if by magic from the city. A murmur swept through the crowd like a wave. Somebody whispered, with a respect that did not conceal fear, "It's Toviyyah, the great servant of Ammon!"

I recognized the name as one of those mentioned by Yahezya. Some around us thought that these white mules and camels, which seemed to have sprung up in the city overnight, were some kind of miracle, but Sogdiam kindly explained that he had seen them arrive an hour earlier by the north road and enter Jerusalem through the Jericho gate.

Toviyyah is a fat man, not totally unlike one of Parysatis's eunuchs. I suppose he is younger than his corpulent frame and perpetually dissatisfied air suggest. He is a child of Israel, but, from father to son, his family have refused to recognize Yahweh as their god and submit to him. On the contrary, they took advantage of the abandoned state of Jerusalem after the exile to pillage what wealth remained, to suck out its strength and turn it to their advantage. And it was that wealth that he was proudly displaying before us that morning.

But while it was easy enough to dazzle those who had always lived in the poverty and decay of Jerusalem, all this pomp and ceremony left us indifferent. We were from Susa and Babylon, the treasure houses of the world.

We may have eaten dust during our journey, and we may have looked like beggars, but our memories of the palaces of Babylon and the Citadel of Susa were still vivid.

A silver ladder was brought to help Toviyyah down off his she-camel. He asked to see Ezra, in a sharp voice that echoed between the pools.

His hair covered in ashes, his tunic open, the precious leather case containing Moses' scroll beating against his bare chest, Ezra stepped forward. "Do you want me?" he asked, in a voice that surprised us with its composure.

Toviyyah's lower lip curled in disgust. He circled around Ezra, and looked with disdain at the priests, Levites, and zealots. Dressed as they were, identically to Ezra, they made an impressive sight, like some strange half-men who lived in the ruins. They took their places beside Ezra, forcing Toviyyah and his guards to step back.

"It seems you have a letter from the King of Kings in Chaldea!" he cried. "It seems you've entered the city of Jerusalem brandishing this letter and proclaiming that this is your home! It seems you're saying the Temple belongs to you and your priests, and that everyone here has to submit to you and your throng because you have that papyrus scroll in your possession!"

From where we were, we heard angry voices raised in protest. But Ezra put up his thin hand and demanded silence. He pulled Artaxerxes' letter from the case where he kept it, along with the scroll of the Laws, and brandished it under Toviyyah's nose, although taking care not to let him touch it.

"You're right about one thing," he said. "This is indeed a letter from Artaxerxes, King of Kings, master of the kingdom of Judaea. But you're wrong about the rest. Jerusalem isn't mine, any more than it's yours. The Temple doesn't belong to the priests. Every word that comes out of your mouth is a blemish. This is the city set aside for the children of Israel by Yahweh. This is the Temple, this is the altar where the people of the covenant offer burned offerings to God. This is the land of Canaan where the Laws and the Justice Yahweh taught to Moses must hold sway. And I am Ezra, son of Serayah, son of the sons of Aaron. The reason I'm here to bring this about is that the hand of Yahweh is upon me and on those who follow me."

This long speech seemed to glide off Toviyyah like water off a bird's feathers. He looked at the huge crowd and smiled. "And just because you're supported by Yawheh," he mocked, "you think that all you have to do is come here with a letter from the Persian king and your dreams will come true?"

Ezra said nothing.

Toviyyah's smile grew wider. "You're a young hothead. This letter you brandish under my nose is worthless. I, Toviyyah the Ammonite, rule here, and I decide what's good and what's bad. And don't count on the armies of the Persian to support you. They haven't appeared here for many moons."

These words were greeted with an icy silence. Pleased with this reaction, Toviyyah opened his arms wide and addressed us all in a shrill voice, which was even shriller when he spoke loudly.

"Look at you, all of you! You arrive in a country your fathers' fathers left because they couldn't defend it. Your God abandoned them, just as he had abandoned Jerusalem. Your fathers' fathers went off to the rich fields of Babylon and forgot all about Jerusalem and their God. And now you've come back, singing, knowing nothing about the land of Judaea! You've come back, proclaiming, 'This is my home, it belongs to me, I'm the one who should burn incense in the Temple!' I say, 'No!'"

The priests and the zealots around Ezra muttered angrily, but my brother again ordered them to be silent.

Toviyyah's fat cheeks shook with anger. He pointed at the men covered with ashes. "It's Toviyyah who decides if the walls of Jerusalem can heal or not. It's Toviyyah, the great servant of Ammon, who decides what's good and what's bad for the Temple of Jerusalem. And it's Toviyyah who receives taxes."

Again, his words met with an icy silence.

We were all too stunned to protest. The words he spoke were worse than anything we had expected. They were humiliating words, which clothed truth in lies and trampled on our most cherished hopes.

But Toviyyah was enjoying himself. "Ammon bids you all welcome," he said, smiling contemptuously. "He'll be happy to receive his share when you start working in the fields. For these fields you see beneath your feet, where you've pitched your tents, don't belong to you and will never belong to you. Here, the Persians are of no importance. The soldiers of Egypt and Greece chased them away long ago. The only person who can protect you is me! I have two thousand armed men for that."

At that moment, a stone struck his thigh.

It had been thrown by Ezra.

This plunged the gathering into disarray. Toviyyah's guards moved to seize my brother. The young zealots rushed forward, yelling, and pushed them back. The guards looked as if they were ready for a fight, but a gesture from Toviyyah stopped them in their tracks. He knew it was pointless: There were ten of them and twenty thousand of us. But he also knew that he had other means to strike at us.

Carried away by their anger, the young zealots jostled Toviyyah, and even lifted him onto his she-camel, which brayed with fear and got up so abruptly that it almost knocked him off. Toviyyah clung to the saddle, comically. Waving his arms in all directions, and squealing like a frightened bird, he finally regained his balance, only to find that he was back to front: He was facing his camel's hindquarters. The whole crowd exploded with laughter.

Just imagine, Antinoes, my love, ten thousand, fifteen thousand, twenty thousand people laughing! An immense laugh of relief that must have echoed as far as the Jordan.

Only when the laughter had died down did Ezra speak.

"You're wrong again, Toviyyah. Since the day Nebuchadnezzar entered Jerusalem, your father and your father's father have been wrong and have passed their error on to you. Now, a man may deceive himself, but a child of Israel cannot deceive Yahweh. You think the letter that brought me here was written by Artaxerxes. No! It was the will of Yawheh, his desire to return to his Temple, that dictated this letter. You're wrong again if you think we fear you. You're wrong, because all we need is the help and strength of Yahweh. But you did right in coming here today. As you see, we've torn our tunics and covered our hair with ashes. Today is the day of purification. Today, we're preparing to wash the soil of Judaea clean of the refuse that covers it. And you are part of that refuse."

Deathly pale, Toviyyah, with the help of his guards, turned as well as he could in his saddle. Back in the right position, he looked once again at the vast crowd. And all at once, he burst out laughing. He whipped the neck of the she-camel and disappeared into the city, still laughing. A little later, we saw him trotting along the road to Jericho.

We had mocked him, but as we watched him riding away, his laughter seemed more threatening than all his poisonous words.

Not without reason.

That night, the fourth or fifth after our arrival, the war began.

The tents farthest from the walls of Jerusalem were laid waste. Blood flowed, and screams and laments tore the air. The men, women, and children in them were cut down without pity. Wagons burned, lighting the darkness so that it appeared to be broad daylight and we could see clearly the misfortune that was only just beginning.

IT feels strange to be describing these events. They only go back about ten months, but to me they already seem very distant.

Perhaps it is because I have seen so many hacked bodies since then, so many women running through the night, clutching their dead children to their breasts or screaming with pain.

Not that I've become hardened. Don't think that, Antinoes, please don't think that! But there comes a moment when you become like a grave that has been filled to the brim and cannot take any more bodies. And I who have only ever really learned one skill, that of helping to give birth, am caught up in the fever of supporting those who open their legs so that the blood of life can flow once more, while our memory is red with the blood of death.

I HAD to stop writing, because I was sent for.

Sometimes, the absurdity of what I am writing paralyzes my wrist, and my stylus is unable to move forward across the papyrus. If only I could be like a gourd or a jar, from which the contents pour out until at last it is empty! I am speaking to you, Antinoes, my husband, yet all the things I have told you remain inside me!

Perhaps that is one of the ways Yahweh is taking his revenge?

You try to remember, to extract the words from your mind to stop it from exploding with pain. But then you suffer all over again because you remember . . .

But who knows? Perhaps you will read these words, my distant husband, and they will rekindle in you your love for Lilah.

⬤

THAT first disaster lent weight to Yahezya's words and gave him the courage to go back to Ezra and the priests and put forward his ideas again. Still as calm and gentle as ever, he explained that the night's attackers were not Toviyyah's men.

"However wicked he is, however much he may hate us, Toviyyah wouldn't have the courage to strike us. He claims he knows nothing about Yahweh, but he fears him! Yesterday, Toviyyah tried to obtain your submission in return for his protection. You refused both. It didn't take him long to tell everyone that your wealth was for the taking, like ripe fruit on a tree. And that he wouldn't defend you."

"Who attacked us, then?" people demanded.

"Either the Moabites, or Gershem's men. To judge by the arrows and the other traces we found, I'd say Gershem's men. Gershem's kingdom adjoins the territory of Judaea along the Jordan. In the last few years, he's attacked Jerusalem many times, just as he did during the time of Nehemiah. Not lately, though—Jerusalem was too poor and empty for him."

"How can we be at war with them? We don't even know them!"

"You *are* at war," Yahezya assured us sadly. "Here you are, defenseless, unarmed, with thousands of women and children. You have wagons full of clothes, furniture, carpets, even gold. Pardon my frankness, Ezra, but your weakness is as obvious as your wealth! What a godsend for those whose only law is plunder and war!"

These words left everyone dumbfounded. I am quite sure Ezra had never thought about this. To be honest, neither had any of us, including me.

Zacharias was the first to object that no one had come to Jerusalem to make war, and that Yahweh could not have been waiting for us on the soil of Judaea merely to see it soaked with our blood.

"That may be so," Yahezya replied. "But you're talking like this because you don't know how things used to be here in Jerusalem. The walls you see were rebuilt by Nehemiah. And Nehemiah never hesitated to fight. 'We're rebuilding Jerusalem,' he used to say, 'with a trowel in one hand and a sword in the other.'"

There were cries of protest, but Ezra agreed with Yehazya.

"He's right. Master Baruch, who taught me everything I know, showed me letters that Nehemiah wrote to Babylon and the King of Kings. Those were indeed his words: 'with a trowel in one hand and a sword in the other.'"

And he declared that from this day on, these words would also be ours.

Thus began our new life in Jerusalem.

The purification of the Temple was postponed. Some set to work building permanent houses inside the city, while others repaired the most gaping holes in the outer walls. Yahezya led Zacharias and his people to a place near Jericho, where the blacksmiths worked, in order to buy swords and spears, anything that could be used for killing. It was a risky undertaking: Toviyyah's soldiers could easily have slaughtered them on the road, before they had even acquired weapons. In fact, they did not encounter the slightest difficulty. Yahezya was almost certainly right: Tovvi-yah refused to recognize the power of Yahweh, but he feared it all the same.

As soon as they returned, groups of men were formed and trained to defend us.

And so, before the great heat of summer made the work harder still, the city was repopulated, the streets cleared, and hundreds of fields plowed and sown.

This was also a time when true bonds of friendship were formed between people. The work varied a great deal from one house to another. Ezra and I were given a narrow building near the Temple. It only required about ten days of work, since its roof had not been demolished. Others took much longer. But we all helped each other unhesitatingly, as the need arose.

Meanwhile, Sogdiam transformed a lean-to into a communal kitchen, which was indispensable while people only had the poorest of hearths to work with. Every morning and every evening, old women who had become fond of Sogdiam came to help him bake hundreds of loaves. He made them weep with laughter by telling lots of stories I had no idea he knew. Day after day, they supplied food for a starving people, a people exhausted from cutting stone and wood, carrying and mixing mortar.

Those who went to the hills to cut down the trees we needed or to pull blocks of stone from cliffs known to the old men of Jerusalem were accompanied by armed men. But apart from a few fights with thieves, there were no more attacks.

And so, in a short time, the city came back to life. Children ran in the streets. Gardens sprang up here and there. Workshops opened. Those who had had trades in Susa began practicing them again. People smiled at one another. Couples came to see the priests, and sometimes even Ezra, to ask for their marriages to be blessed. Hundreds of children were born. As the building work was coming to an end, I went back to working with the midwives who had taught me the skills of childbirth. Every day, I had the great joy of welcoming one or two new lives into my hands.

To everyone's surprise, even Yahezya's, Toviyyah did not reappear. He made no attempt to approach Jerusalem and check on the progress of the rebuilding.

Merchants came, to buy and sell. They told us that the neighboring peoples were talking a lot about us, with respect and a degree of fear. We concluded that our determination intimidated them. The priests sang Ezra's praises, for Yahweh's hand was still firmly over him.

Thus, for a brief while, one moon perhaps, we were carefree again, drunk with the pleasure of our self-imposed mission.

One morning, we awoke to the sound of lamentation in the city. Sogdiam told me that the time had come, and that Ezra was beginning the fast of the purification of the Temple.

The priests, the Levites, and all those who answered Ezra's call gathered before the ruins of the sacrificial altar. There, with much wailing, they again tore their garments and covered themselves with ashes.

After another day of prayer, Ezra gave the order to clear the refuse from the courtyard around the Temple.

They lifted the soiled stones one by one. It was a colossal task. For nine days, from dawn to dusk, they carried them outside the city, and dumped them in an unclean place that the old priests had designated for the purpose.

They demolished the sacrificial altar with sledgehammers and built a new one according to the Law, with raw stones from the hills.

After this, the old men who had been there in Nehemiah's time came to see Ezra. "We need the *naphta* fire!"

They led Ezra to a well that no one had noticed, hidden as it was beneath a heap of irreparable ruins. Once the rubble had been cleared, the lid of the well was discovered to be in good condition. At the bottom, instead of water, there was a stinking black substance, like pitch. The old men explained to Ezra that he had to coat the floor of the Temple with this pitch before it could be rebuilt.

"But how can I rebuild it cleanly once this stuff is everywhere?" Ezra objected.

The old men laughed. "Let Yahweh do his work," they said. "Let the sun do its work!"

They did as the old men said. They spread buckets full of this foul-smelling substance on what remained of the old wood and on the loose marble flagstones. The air stank for leagues around the Temple, and many of us worried that soon we would not be able to breathe it. But when the sun struck the Temple in the morning, the pitch melted, smoked a little, and finally turned as glossy as black gold. For a moment, everything shone. Then, with a deafening bark, a blue flame sprung up.

"*Naphta!*" the old men cried with joy, dancing and singing. "*Naphta*, the barking of Yahweh!"

A moment later, the fire had vanished, and the marble flagstones were dry and no hotter than if the sun alone had burned them.

It was such a wonderful and surprising spectacle that for days on end children ran in the streets of the city imitating the barking of God!

Ezra and his people resumed their labor. They made new sacred objects to replace those they had not brought. The Levites put the seven-branched candlestick in the holy of holies, set up a new table on which they burned incense, and made new lamps to light the Temple. The carpenters working under their orders finished the doors, the porticoes, the gilded coronas, and the escutcheons that decorated the front of the building. At last, one day in the month of Av, Ezra declared that the Temple was clean and ready to welcome our chants.

For three days and three nights, we sang at the tops of our

voices, tears streaming down the most hardened cheeks. The streets rang with the sound of lyres, kitharas, and cymbals.

There was a huge offering, like the one that had preceded our departure from Babylon. The smoke rose and covered the newly built roofs of Jerusalem.

The fire still glowed so brightly in the night that when other cries and other flames sprang up on the other side of the city, we did not immediately realize what was happening.

Outside the walls, a troop of Gershem's men were galloping toward the city, screaming at the tops of their voices. There were five or six hundred of them, and they formed a snake of fire in the fields and hills. All at once, they launched a rain of burning arrows into the sky.

At first, it was strangely beautiful, like a sky full of shooting stars. But their orbit brought them down onto our thatched roofs.

New flames rose. New cries, new screams rang out.

By the morning, more than half the houses that had been restored were in ashes.

YAHEZYA was right.

Blood, fire, tears. That, for us, was Jerusalem.

Ezra wet my tunic with his tears. He had too many tears, too much anger, to show them in public. After the previous night's disaster, he came running to me like a lost child.

I was astonished by the body I held in my arms. Ezra had become so frail, I could have lifted him. Did he think that his mind and his passionate love for Yahweh were enough to keep him alive?

Perhaps.

But he was equally angry with his mind, and even—although he would not have dared admit it—with Yahweh. He hit his brow with the leather case containing Moses' scroll, and asked until he was breathless, "Why is Yahweh inflicting this misfortune on us, Lilah? Where is our sin? Hasn't the Temple been purified? Don't we respect every rule, to the letter? Why has He left us so defenseless? Lilah, what is our sin?"

What was I to answer? The whole city was weeping, as he was, but no one understood. Some put out the fires, others tended the wounded. Everywhere, the dead were mourned.

I was in no mood to look for an explanation.

While everyone wondered what sin we had committed, I was beginning to fear that I had made a mistake in urging Ezra to come to Judaea. It seemed to me that of the two of us, I was the one who had to bear the responsibility for what had happened.

It was a terrible thought, and I dismissed it.

Like everyone there, anger made me defiant. I still hoped to find in Ezra the strength and the justice we lacked, so that Yahweh might finally reward us.

All I could do now was support Ezra to the best of my ability.

He was exhausted by constant fasting. His hands were scarred and bloody from endlessly pulling and carrying stones. His skin was infected, due to a combination of splinters of wood and the ash with which he had covered himself during the fast. There were purulent swellings on his shoulders, and his feet were torn and bloody.

But the wounds on his body were nothing compared with the agitation in his mind. He had been under enormous pressure during the purification of the Temple. The new priests, those who had come with us, the Levites, and the zealots were all trying to win him over and influence his decisions. They all had strong but divergent opinions, and could argue from dusk to dawn, tangling you in a labyrinth of words until you no longer had any idea what they were talking about.

They all considered themselves scholars, and cleverer than

other people. They constantly cited the lessons of the patriarchs or the prophets. Some time before the purification of the Temple, the old priests who had stayed in Jerusalem after the death of Nehemiah had reluctantly but proudly revealed a hidden cellar on the other side of the city.

There, in spite of all the pillaging, they had preserved hundreds of papyrus scrolls, and even a few tablets from long ago. According to them, no decision could be taken without consulting the opinions of the wise men of the past. So the exhausting debates began again, more convoluted than ever.

No one person was any longer in a position to impose decisions that could guide and regulate our lives. On that day of mourning, there was only one thing I was sure of: We had come to Jerusalem looking for the light, and now we were groping in the dark. And the darkness would only increase unless Ezra recovered the power of his mind and was once again in a state to decide things undisturbed.

I ordered Axatria and Sogdiam to bolt the door of our house, and to prepare herb teas and food.

It took a great deal of persuasion before Ezra agreed to eat. Axatria's herb teas worked miracles. He fell asleep, and did not wake again for two days.

While he slept, I had to defend myself against the anger of the zealots and the priests. They could not bear the fact that I had taken Ezra away from them. They screamed and shouted, rousing anyone who would lend them a willing ear.

The priests wanted to pray continuously in the purified Temple, and for some obscure reason they could not do it without Ezra. The Levites wanted my brother to give them specific tasks and appoint them to particular positions and ranks, according to the Law and the writings of David. Our house was surrounded, but fortunately Ezra did not wake up.

Since I would not yield, they concluded that I was plotting

against them. I let them talk. But their anger had reached fever pitch, and the fear that Gershem's warriors would return merely increased it.

"Just wait until tomorrow," I said to them. "Let him rest a little! You're killing him with work. Do you want to march behind his coffin? Can't you understand how patient Yahweh is?"

My words aroused protests, like the wind raising sparks from a fire.

"What business is it of yours, girl?" they replied. "Ezra should be in the Temple assuaging the wrath of Yahweh, and you stand in our way? Who has given you that right? It isn't our demands that exhaust Ezra, it's the stupidity of those like you who cannot fear the wrath of Yahweh. Don't you realize you're playing Toviyyah's game, and Gershem's? You're paving the way for all those who hate Israel! You're going to kill Ezra, and us with him!"

The stronger their words, the more aggressive they became. Sogdiam was powerless to protect me. Those he had fed devotedly for weeks now jostled him and called him a cripple, a good for nothing, a *nokhri*—a stranger. It was not until Yahezya and some of his friends came and stood in front of my door, armed, that we were left in peace for another night.

At last, after his long sleep and a good meal, after Axatria had rubbed his pitiful body with ointments and oils and massaged his tired shoulders, Ezra seemed in better condition.

But when I told him how we had had to defend his sleep tooth and nail, and had been insulted for our pains, he was not amused. At first, he wanted to rush out, as if he were at fault. I held him back: that could wait awhile. I begged him to reflect before getting caught up again in the clash of incompatible demands and desires.

He yielded with a discouraged sigh. "They're right to be angry. Lilah, something isn't right in the way I handle things. We've only just purified the Temple and already our houses are destroyed!

We've not long arrived in Jerusalem, and already the troubles are starting just as they did in the time of Nehemiah! Tomorrow we'll rebuild the houses destroyed yesterday, but the following night Gershem or the Horonites will attack the Temple. Or smash the ramparts, destroy our crops in the fields. They'll attack anything, as long as it is ours. They'll keep doing it, endlessly, because Yahweh is not with us. I thought he was, but he isn't! The covenant is still broken, and look at the consequences."

As he spoke, he kneaded the leather case that hung around his neck. His eyes sought mine, trying to find consolation in them, and a sense of confidence that I was incapable of giving him. His heart was heavy with sadness, and I was quite powerless to assuage it.

The words he had just spoken expressed exactly what I was thinking.

"Lilah, Lilah, my beloved sister," he said, with tears in his eyes. "What must I do so that Yahweh will judge us to be pure enough and good enough and again grant us his strength?"

I could find nothing to say.

He grimaced strangely, and looked at me without seeing me. I saw the muscles of his neck tense. I expected to see him run from one room to the next, as he did when he was angry or excited. Violently, he tore the leather case containing Moses' scroll from around his neck and pressed it roughly to my breast.

"Everything we need to know is here, in this scroll!" he roared, shaking like a tree in the wind. "What good are these walls? Yahweh doesn't care about our walls! We're wasting time building houses that disappear in fires or fall down on our heads! Yahweh is mocking us. He doesn't expect us to become masons! He's testing us, and he'll keep testing us, until we finally hear his word. We must obey his Laws and his rules; that is his will. And we go around complaining, Why? Why? It's a question I answered in

Susa, and my answer is still the same: Because we're not living according to the rules!"

I smiled. I understood.

I took hold of his wrists and said calmly, "Master Baruch used to say, 'The word of Yahweh is in the Word of Yahweh. Nowhere else.' He loved to repeat Isaiah's words. 'Hear the Word of Yahweh! What is the point of these offerings of rams, these fatted calves? I want no more of the blood of bulls and goats. Stop bringing me these hollow offerings.' You're right. Building the walls was Nehemiah's task. Establishing justice, teaching the Word of Yahweh, that is Ezra's task."

He smiled. His frail body shook with joy as it had shaken with fever not long before. "Yes, yes! What is the point of these walls of gold, this incense, if the Word of Yahweh falls on deaf ears and blind eyes?"

I tied the leather case back around his neck. "Teach everyone what is written in the scroll," I said. "You alone can do it. If Ezra commands it, everyone will agree."

His dark mood returned as quickly as it had previously vanished. "How can I? More than half of those who've come with us from Susa and Babylon can't even read or write. As for those who were living in Jerusalem before we arrived, they're worse still."

"Anyone can learn to read and write."

"Don't dream, Lilah," he said, in a harsh, mocking tone. "In Jerusalem, dreams lead to bloodshed."

"I'm not dreaming. Let all who can read and write teach the others. Let them each copy part of Moses' scroll. They'll learn the Word of Yahweh by writing it."

For a while, he said nothing. He closed his eyes, with a radiant smile on his face that I could not remember seeing for a long time, a very long time.

"The Temple of the Word of Yahweh will enter their hearts,"

he said at last. "No one will be able to set fire to it, or reduce it to ruins. The joy of Yahweh will be a fortress for his people. And the people of Yahweh will be the people of the Book until the end of time."

And that is how things were done.

It was not easy, and there was a great deal of reluctance.

Many of the priests considered that it would be unclean to have Moses' scroll copied by hands not designated for the task in King David's tablets. The Levites also greeted the idea with horror. How could Ezra think of abandoning the Temple, even if only for a short time?

The idea soon gained ground that this was the proof of my malevolent influence. This was why I had taken advantage of Ezra's weakness and kept him away from the Temple. And when Ezra quoted Isaiah, they quoted Jeremiah: "Now the days are coming when I will make the cry of battle to be heard among the sons of Ammon, his cities and his daughters will be burned, and Israel will inherit the land from his heirs." According to them, we had to make war on Toviyyah. Such was the will of Yahweh.

But Ezra held firm. "Let us get to work," he said. "On the first day of the seventh month, the whole city, men and women, husbands and wives, will gather at the Water Gate. And everyone will read with one voice the laws that Yahweh taught Moses."

SOMETIMES, after you have had one calamity, and you are sure another one is coming, happiness can appear unexpectedly, at least for a time.

Happiness now came to Jerusalem, moving from alley to alley, from house to house, where people bowed their heads over letters, words, and sentences.

A song of happiness rippled through the city, as hands guided other hands to move a stylus over a scroll.

A song of happiness throbbed in the houses, when, after learning the alphabet, fathers and mothers amused themselves reciting it at night to their children so that it might feed their dreams.

There was no longer any distinction between the great and the small, the learned and the untutored. All that remained was the will of a whole people to be strong in its knowledge and its words, including the great Word the Everlasting had given it, a nation that had the whisper of memory always on its lips, as a lover has his beloved's name.

Oh, Antinoes, my husband, you would have liked that time!

A time of milk and honey, a time of abundance in the land of Judaea! We were together, united in a single cause. All of us, men and women, young and old, were deciphering the same letters, uttering the same words, each and every one of us with the same desire for justice.

There were no more complaints, no more quarrels.

And perhaps the hand of Yahweh was upon us, for we no longer heard anything about Toviyyah, Gershem, and the Horonites, or the harm they wished to do us.

I started to hope again. My doubts vanished. We had been right to urge Ezra to leave for Jerusalem. Our separation, Antinoes, was a good price to pay for his reward. In my heart, this was compensation for my humiliation at the hands of Parysatis.

For the very first time since my arrival in Jerusalem, I felt at peace. I gloried in this madness called happiness and hope.

Yes, I thought, I would be able to keep my promise after all. Soon, everyone would know Yahweh's rules, everyone would be able to live according to his justice. Soon, the Everlasting would renew his covenant with his people, and the houses of Jerusalem would ring with peace and joy as now they hummed with thousands of voices reading.

Then my duty would be done, and I could again set off for Susa or Carchemish or the other side of the world to rejoin you.

◎

ACCORDING to Ezra's wishes, on the first day of the seventh month of the year, rams' horns blew on the square in front of the Temple. Others echoed it across the land, from the Galilee to the Negev. Thirty or forty thousand people gathered by the Water Gate. There were so many of us, so tightly packed together, that the earth looked like a colorful carpet of human flowers.

Ezra and the priests climbed the steps that led to the ramparts. The sun was not yet high. There was a slight coolness in the air, and the swallows sang as they gorged themselves on morning insects.

And then there was silence. Real silence.

Over Jerusalem, and over the whole of Judaea. Those who were there will swear it, to the end of time. A silence such as belongs only to the Everlasting fell on his nation at that moment.

Ezra took Moses' scroll from its container. In the silence, everyone heard the rustle of the papyrus against the leather.

Ezra spread out the scroll, put one end between the fingers of one of the old priests, and unrolled it in its entirety. It stretched for perhaps five or six cubits.

In the silence, the forty thousand heard the crackling of the papyrus that had once been touched by the finger of Aaron, heard Ezra's sandals scraping against the stones of the rampart.

The swallows were gone. There was only the blue sky and the white stones of Jerusalem the beautiful.

Ezra placed his finger on the papyrus.

My throat was dry. Doubt made me close my mouth and took my breath from me.

What if this was madness?

What if Ezra's desire to turn a whole nation's heart into the heart of a word was again nothing but a mad dream?

Was it possible that these thousands of people could become the nation of the Book, the nation that makes the Word of Yahweh its Temple?

Then Ezra looked at us. His mouth opened, but no sound emerged. In its place, a single voice, made up of thousands of women's voices, thousands of men's voices, old mouths and young together launching the first words into the sky.

> *In the beginning,*
> > *Yahweh created the heavens and the earth,*
> > *The earth was empty and formless,*
> > *Darkness was above the deep,*
> > *The spirit of Yahweh*
> > *Moved over the seas.*

The voices trembled. Perhaps the blue sky trembled, too, and the white stone, and Ezra's finger.

Then his hand glided again over the papyrus, and pointed to the following words: *"Yahweh named the light."* And the forty thousand, with one voice, continued the reading.

All Jerusalem trembled. All Judaea trembled.

The reading became a chant. Until the middle of the day, until we were sitting in our own shadows, we read. And everyone knew the words of the text.

At the end, our joy overflowed. We danced and laughed and wept, all at the same time.

"Today is the day of Yahweh our God!" Ezra cried. "Not a day of tears! Go, eat your fill, drink sweet wine and eat meat, today is Yahweh's day! The joy of Yahweh is now on your fortress, and no one can drive you from it! Open your eyes, open the scrolls of the teaching, and there you will find your Temple, forever. Your

Temple will be the Word and the teaching of the Everlasting: the Book. Tomorrow, go to the hills and gather branches. Tomorrow, build tabernacles in your houses, and in the public squares. Build them everywhere. Sit down in your tabernacles and read the teaching of Yahweh. You will see that there is no need of walls to read the rules and laws of our covenant with the Everlasting. In the Book, you will be safer than anywhere else. And no one will drive you away. The Word of Yahweh is a fortress."

And like my forty thousand companions, I laughed and danced. In the evening, I danced in the arms of Yahezya, in the arms of Baruch and Gershom and Jonathan and Ackaz and Manasseh and Amos . . . There were so many names, so many arms in which a young girl, a young wife, a young widow named Lilah could dance!

We were no longer alone. We drank wine, ate meat, swayed our hips, and swelled our chests, we, the thousands of wives.

We had read like the men, all united. Wives, daughters of Israel, wives of the sons of Israel. All united, without distinction. All wives and mothers.

That was the last time.

Ezra is right: The joy of Yahweh is a fortress.

THIS is how it happened, three days after the reading and the celebration that ensued. Everyone was laughing, building their tabernacles and sitting in them, reading.

The priests and Levites, those who call themselves the princes of the Temple, appeared before Ezra. "You go about proclaiming that Yahweh is happy with us. You are wrong. We say to you that Yahweh is angry. We warn you that soon those who hate us will strike harder than ever. They are already here. They are in Jerusalem, they are in your tabernacles."

"What are you talking about?" my brother asked in surprise.

"How can you teach the Law if the Word of Yahweh is not respected? How can the children of Israel appease the wrath of Yahweh if the first of his rules is not respected? Open your eyes, Ezra. Look at the faces, listen to the words. The people who surround us and live in abomination have married their daughters to our sons! That is the truth of it."

"Ezra, beneath the roofs of Jerusalem," others cried, "the unclean mix indiscriminately with the children of Israel. The unclean are among us. Worse still, they multiply like clouds. The Jebusites, the Ammonites, the Moabites, and so many others around Jerusalem have given their daughters to the men of Jerusalem! Their babies have been filling our beds since Nehemiah left! And this rabble walk the streets of Jerusalem as if they were the children of Israel! Soon they, too, will be of an age to mix their unclean stock with that of the people of Yahweh. Our destruction is inevitable. And you, Ezra, would like Yahweh to renew his covenant with us? To reach out his hand over you?"

I was not present at the scene. A child was being born not far from our house, and I had been sent for. But I was later told all the details of what had happened.

Hearing these words, Ezra rushed onto the steps of the Temple. There, he tore his clothes to shreds. He ripped his tunic and his cloak, as if twenty hands had grabbed hold of him. He demanded a knife. Before the eyes of the priests, the Levites, and the zealots, he shaved.

Shaved his head, shaved his beard. Now he was bareheaded and bare-cheeked, and as pale as a leper.

After that, he sat down on the steps of the Temple and would not budge. He remained like that, prostrated, with his mouth closed, his eyes vacant, his hands motionless.

The priests and Levites roused the crowd. People came from

all over to see Ezra, and cried out at the sight of his leprous head. They begged him to speak, to utter a word.

But he remained silent. Instead, it was the priests who cried, "Ezra is naked before the Word of Yahweh! Ezra fears Yahweh! Ezra bears all the infidelity of the exiles on his shoulders!"

It was at that moment that I joined the crowd.

I saw him with my own eyes, huddled on the steps, his face haggard, his eyes hardened by sadness. His mouth was like two lines cut by a sword.

He no longer saw anything, no longer looked at anything. Or perhaps he was thinking of old times, old promises from the days of our childhood, which he was now preparing to break. Yes, that was my first thought.

My other thought was that I no longer recognized him. That he was no longer the man who had wept in my arms only a few days earlier.

My brother was gone. He had disappeared, and his beautiful mouth, his eyes full of hope had disappeared, too.

Or was it the pallor of his skull and cheeks that made me think that?

At the evening offering, he suddenly stood up in his rags. The crowd around the Temple fell silent.

A terrifying silence.

As I write this, I am afraid again. My hand is heavy with the words it is about to lay down on the papyrus.

Ezra approaches the altar. He walks up to the beautiful new basin, only recently purified. We hold our breaths. Even the priests and the zealots are silent. They, too, are overcome with fear. You can see it in their eyes, the way they clench their fists in front of their mouths.

Ezra falls to his knees. He reaches out his hands to Yahweh, palms upward. Sounds come from him, not words at first, only moans. Then he cries to heaven, "My God, I am ashamed as I lift my head to you, for our sins are endless, our offenses can be heard even in the vaults of heaven! We have been guilty since the days of our fathers, and today we are still hugely guilty. It is because of our sins that we have been delivered into the hands of foreign kings, have suffered violence and captivity, are humiliated, even now! We have abandoned your commandments, as decreed by your servants and your prophets. 'The land you are inheriting is unclean,' they said, 'soiled by the surrounding nations and the horrors with which they nourished it. Your daughters must not be given to their sons. Their daughters must not be married to your sons!' Those were your rules. After all that has happened to us because of our misconduct, are we still going to disobey your orders, Yahweh? Are we going to ally ourselves with these nations and their abominations? How could you not be angry, so angry that you would destroy what is left of us? Yahweh, God of Israel, here we are before you, in sin. And we will not be able to stand upright until that sin has been atoned for. Oh, Yahweh, it is impossible to stand upright before you until the clean have been separated from the unclean."

THAT day, that night, and the following day, the zealots ran through the streets knocking on the doors of the houses.

You are clean. You are unclean.

You are a daughter of Israel. You are not.

Your children are unclean; leave this house, leave Jerusalem! Go, you are no longer this man's wife.

Separate, separate!

Pack your bags and go! You have been soiling our streets and our land for too long!

They pulled and pushed. They took the little ones and threw them in the street. Even babies in their cradles they put in the street. The big ones they pulled by their hair. Go, go, we don't want to see you anymore!

The women cried that they were loving wives. Why chase me away, we have loved each other for years? I have always lived in Jerusalem! I read with the others before Ezra, at the Water Gate! What is my sin?

They wept that they had traveled all the way from Susa with Ezra. I led the fast, I rebuilt the walls of the houses of Jerusalem, with my own hands I built a tabernacle in my garden to read the teachings of Yahweh. What is my sin?

The mothers cried out, and tore their babies from the hands of the zealots. My child, my child, what will become of you without a father?

The boys and girls sobbed in terror.

Look at us, their mothers implored. We have no other house, no other roof, no other family. Where do you want us to go without a husband, without a father?

Why chase us away as if we were evil incarnate? they all asked. We have loved a son of Israel, we have cherished him and caressed him. Where is the evil? Is our love evil? Why trample on us?

The husbands and fathers were silent. A large number of them were silent.

Almost all of them bowed their heads in shame and hid their faces in their hands. They ran to the Temple and bowed down and begged forgiveness.

It was a late summer's day, the kind of hot day when the swallows only fly as dusk approaches, and yet an icy wind was blowing through the streets of Jerusalem.

And those husbands and fathers who wanted to defend those they loved were beaten until they fell silent and their shame grew as their blood flowed.

The wives, the betrothed, the widows, the sons and daughters were driven toward the outer walls. They were driven with sticks, street by street.

For two days.

At first, there were endless cries. Then the cries gave way to resignation.

Some took one direction, others left in the opposite direction. No one knew where to go. They worried over their meager bundles, the children clinging to their tunics, the older ones carrying the babies.

At the Water Gate, where a few days earlier we had formed a carpet of human flowers, the blood ran black, stinking of shame.

And we, the sons and daughters of Israel, stood on the walls, watching them move away. We stood there, terrified and incredulous.

We did not feel the pain yet. Only astonishment.

Was Yahweh going to be pleased, now that we had cast out the unclean?

Toward the evening of the second day, some boys and girls came running back along the Jericho road. They were running toward Jerusalem, crying out the names of their fathers. Children of eight, ten, or twelve. Some of them older. A hundred children, girls and boys. Running toward the gates of the city on the road white with dust.

Then, on the walls of Jerusalem, hands gathered stones. Hands lifted these stones and threw them.

Yes, I write the truth. They stoned these children, until they fell or turned and ran. Until their mothers seized them and dragged them away, far from us.

Then I knew I could not stay.

It was all over for Lilah, sister of Ezra.

"HOW can you order such horrors?" I asked my brother. "Don't you see the women and children on the roads? Don't you hear them?"

He replied that he had ordered nothing, that it was Yahweh who decided everything. "It is Yahweh who wants this, my sister, not Ezra. It was not I who received his laws and his instructions. All I did was read them and learn them. Who knows that better than you, my sister? You who urged me to cross the desert to Jerusalem, when all I wanted was to pursue my studies. It was you who went and begged Parysatis. It was you who slept with the Persian so that he would deliver my request to Artaxerxes. It was you who said to Ezra, 'Go! Your place is in Jerusalem, your destiny is in Jerusalem, that is the will of Yahweh. He is holding his hand firmly over you.' Those were your words, Lilah."

"Yes. Those were my words. Yet Master Baruch taught us the goodness of Yahweh. He chanted Isaiah's words: 'You will succor the oppressed, you will plead for the widow.'"

Ezra laughed. "Isaiah said all kinds of things, sister. Was it not also Isaiah who said, 'Put an end to mankind, it is a mere breath, of no importance'?"

The expression on Ezra's face was terrible to behold.

I could not recognize him without his hair, without his beard. A savage face, I thought, a face that reminded me of Parysatis's beasts. I was angry at myself for thinking such a thing, but it was what filled my heart.

I asked him where Yahweh's justice was.

"Here, my sister," he replied, "in Jerusalem. It is his justice that will protect us if we follow every one of His rules, to the letter."

"I don't see any justice in forcing thousands of women and children out into open country, without fire, without a roof, without food. That isn't why we came to Jerusalem."

He laughed. "But it is, Lilah, it is! We came so that the Law of

Yahweh would live among our people. We are making it live. Only what is written on Moses' scroll. That and nothing else!"

"I can't do it," I said to the man who had been my beloved brother. "I can't be with those who throw stones at women and children. I can't separate the clean and the unclean by separating the wife from the husband and the children from the father. That is beyond my strength. It is beyond my love for Ezra. Beyond my respect for our God. If I must choose, then I shall leave with them. With the rejected women. With the strangers. That is the only place for me. Did not Moses, our master, say, 'Welcome the stranger in your house as one of your own. Love him as yourself, for you, too, were strangers in the land of Egypt'?"

We looked at each other, our hearts closed, the light of our shattered love in our eyes.

"If you leave this house, my sister," Ezra replied at last, "if you leave Jerusalem, we shall never see each other again. I shall forget you. I will no longer have a sister. I will never have had a sister."

I nodded, but said nothing.

I was sick of words.

There was a stench in words, like the stench of the burned offerings of rams and oxen that were beginning again and spreading their funereal smoke over the roofs of Jerusalem the beautiful.

⊙

SOGDIAM put his hand in mine. "Don't cry," he said gently, "I won't leave you. I'm not from here either. I'm only from anywhere you go."

I tried to dissuade him. Where I was going there would be no house, no comfort, little joy, and many tragedies. And certainly no kitchen.

"I'll just have to build one. Wherever we are, we'll need a kitchen, otherwise we'll die of starvation!"

He was already laughing.

"Will you come with me?" I asked Axatria.

She looked at me, arching her back and lifting her chin. "I won't abandon Ezra!" she hissed.

"I'm not abandoning him, Axatria. Ezra is with his God, he's with his priests and his zealots. He hasn't been with me for a long time. How can I abandon a man who's already turned his back on me?"

"Sometimes he needs you, and you know it."

"No, he doesn't need me anymore. After the things he's ordered, he doesn't need his sister's opinions."

"You see, you don't love him! I've long suspected it. In the desert, you didn't love him. When we arrived in Jerusalem, you didn't love him. The greater he's become, the more you've hated him."

What was the point in protesting? "Do you want to abandon those women and children outside the walls, who have nowhere to find shelter except in their sorrow?"

"Ezra has said it many times: It is the Law."

"But not your law, Axatria! You're a daughter of the Zagros Mountains. You're just as much a stranger as they are!"

"Oh, you love to remind me of that, don't you? That just shows how much you despise me. I know you always have. The Law of Yahweh may not be my people's law, but Ezra is my law."

"You're talking nonsense, Axatria! Don't you see that Ezra has never looked at you with affection, let alone love? That you're only his handmaid, and will never be anything else? Don't you know that? Don't you understand that by staying in Jerusalem with Ezra, you're trampling on your own life, your own dignity? You'll serve Ezra until he rejects you, because there'll be a time

when he won't even allow strangers as handmaids. Don't you understand that by staying in Jerusalem with Ezra, you'll never know
love, never have a husband and children?"

In response, she slapped me.

She pushed me out of the house, screaming that I was only
saying these things because I was jealous.

With the rage of someone in whom vengeance, sorrow, and
self-disgust have been too long brewing, she threw my few be-
longings out of the house that for a time had been mine.

There! Now I am a rejected woman, like the others.

⬤

BUT I did not leave Jerusalem like the others.

While I was arguing with Axatria, Sogdiam had been busy
telling everyone in the houses still friendly toward me that I was
leaving.

With his limping gait, he had run from one house to another.

"Lilah is going to join the women and children outside. And
I'm going with her!"

It was like oil waiting for a flame. The sadness and shame that
had been simmering in people's hearts since the day of the ston-
ing now boiled over.

In less time than it takes to say it, twenty wagons were filled
and mules harnessed to them. The former husbands gave tents,
sheets, tent pegs . . . They wept as they gave, and if they could
have, they would have offered their tears as sweet wine.

The Jewish wives gave and gave.

The children offered their clothes and their toys in memory of
those who had been their playmates.

There were two men who gave even more: themselves. May
their names be written here, and may Yahweh, if he so wishes,
bless them.

They were Yahezya and Jonathan.

For when the wagons were lined up outside Jerusalem, it was quite obvious that I would find it hard to drive them with only Sogdiam to help me.

"I'll go with you," Yahezya said. "I wouldn't be able to stay here in Jerusalem and work in my carpenter's shop, knowing all you women were out there."

"My wife is out there, I don't know where," Jonathan added, his eyes drowning in tears. "She is three months gone with child. It's impossible for me not to see her again. Impossible not to know if my child is a boy or a girl. I'm following you, Lilah." He turned to the dozens of others who were like him, and cried, "You, too, follow us!"

They lowered their heads and wept.

But during the days that followed, many went out into the countryside, taking food and kisses to their former wives and their children.

Then Ezra decreed that this was forbidden. No clothes, no food, no wagons. Everything in Jerusalem was the fruit of the people of Yahweh, and this fruit could not become food and seed for strangers.

***

THE first thing to do was to gather the women and children together, for they were scattered throughout the land of Judaea.

Some had already knocked at the doors of their fathers' and brothers' houses. Now, they were weeping over their fate, cursing Jerusalem and cursing themselves and their offspring: Because they had married Jews, they were now considered unclean by their own fathers.

Until the first rains of autumn came, we had to scour the

countryside every day in search of women hiding in bushes and holes, protecting their young like gazelles.

We traveled south, where Jonathan knew an area of land that was vast enough and dry enough to set up camp. It took a lot of work: pitching tents, bandaging wounds, collecting herbs to cure the children of their many illnesses, helping pregnant women through labor, feeding the hungry . . . And already there were quarrels, there was jealousy and despair . . .

And then, one overcast day, Gershem's men came galloping toward us.

Oh, what a godsend for them, these women without husbands, unprotected!

They did not hold back. They took what they wanted. They forced open thighs, never mind if the girls were virgins.

They raped. They took it in turns to rape.

They killed those who resisted.

The old women who pulled their hair while they were raping the girls like goats were disembowelled.

The children who tried to defend their mothers had their throats cut.

So did Jonathan, who fought to defend his pregnant wife. His wife was disembowelled and her bloody offspring held up.

"The rejected women of Jerusalem!" the attackers laughed and screamed. "What a feast, and all for us!"

They put the youngest and prettiest in chains. They shackled them like a herd of she-camels and dragged them off to the desert where they lived.

It was bound to happen.

Not a day or a night had gone by without our dreading it would happen.

In Jerusalem, they knew this would happen. When they expelled the women, they knew.

And Yahweh, my God, also knew.

LAST night, just before dawn, Sogdiam died.

They say his cart overturned and he was crushed beneath the wheels. They say he didn't suffer too much.

Sogdiam, my Sogdiam, is dead.

So are many others, of course.

They say Sogdiam was bringing back a wagon full of grain. He had been coming at night from Jerusalem more and more frequently. There are still men there who are trying to give us a little food—grain or vegetables—to stop their former wives and children from starving to death. But at night the Bethany road is dangerous, furrowed by the autumn rains. Or perhaps it wasn't the rain, but Gershem's men, or Toviyyah's. Neither miss an opportunity to strip us bare or murder us.

I did not think to ask if the grain had been stolen, which would have meant that Sogdiam had died for nothing.

My Sogdiam is dead!

I would like to weep, but I can't. My hands are cold, my feet are icy. Perhaps my heart has frozen, too?

I am gripping my stylus and writing.

I must seem confused to you now, Antinoes, my husband. I mix past and present. It is because of Sogdiam's death. But it is also true that everything is confused in my mind, my heart, my body.

Yesterday, toward evening, Sogdiam sat beside me for a long time in silence. "You write and write!" he said, reproachfully. "You spend your time writing like a scribe. Who will read your secrets?"

"You," I replied.

He looked at me as if we were dancing under the wedding sheet. I felt his warmth next to me. His lopsided body. I had only to look at him once a day and I could breathe more easily. When he slept, his eyes smiled.

Oh, my Sogdiam, who fed me like a mother! A boy of barely

sixteen. A child who'd become a man. A child I'd swept up in the whirlwind of my confusion when I'd urged Ezra to leave for Jerusalem!

Sogdiam, my beloved child!

It isn't true that I am writing this letter for Antinoes. I know that, and it would be a lie to maintain otherwise. Antinoes, my husband, will never read it. Sogdiam, my handsome, crippled child, will never take him this papyrus scroll in a leather container hanging from his neck.

Antinoes is far away. He is nothing more than a thought that wrenches my stomach every time I write his name.

He is far away, as far as the life I did not want, did not choose, did not accept. He has forgotten me. He is clasping a woman in his arms at this moment, as the ink slips from the stylus and enters the skin of the papyrus!

That is the truth.

No husband, I have no husband now. I have no more Sogdiam now.

That is the truth.

I write this letter as I once wrote, one night a long time ago, in my bedchamber in Susa, begging Yahweh. Asking, "Oh, Yahweh, why do we stop being children?"

Oh, Yahweh, why couldn't Sogdiam stay a child? Why did he have to die? Why must I become cold, why must I be nothing more than a hand that writes so that you may hear another voice, different from the voices raised today in Jerusalem?

Why so many painful questions?

* * *

> Man is humiliated,
> man is brought low, do not lift him,
> hide in the stone,

> *take shelter in the dust,*
> *terrified as you are by Yahweh,*
> *by his dazzling greatness.*
> *Now at last the arrogant eye of man is brought low,*
> *man's pride will bend.*
> *Yahweh alone will be held on high that day.*

THESE words also are Isaiah's.

They often come to my lips, though I don't know if they are good for us or not. They come to me like the angry clouds that race above our heads, chased by the whistling north wind.

They are the words I sang over the grave of Sogdiam, my child.

All the women who were there repeated the words after me. It was not as beautiful as our chanting at the Water Gate, but it rang out in the desolate air around us.

We are tired, though, of chanting for those we bury.

Just as my fingers are worn and calloused by the stylus.

Among the older women, there is a great desire to lie down anywhere on the ground and go to sleep at last, seeking the eternal oblivion that will come to us all soon. I could see it in their eyes as the earth covered Sogdiam. And I was surprised to feel the same desire, I who am only twenty-five.

From time to time, I lift the back of my hand to my lips. It was there that Sogdiam touched me for the last time. But my skin no longer bears the memory.

⬤

YAHEZYA has been wounded in the stomach, but he can still speak, can still lead us. He asked me to gather those who are still alive. He told us we should go to the sea of Arabia: There were caves there, which are easier to defend than an open field. He knew the way. He led us there, struggling to keep breathing until the cliffs of Qumran and the many caves were within sight.

That is where we are now.

With no land to cultivate, but protected by the walls we have built in front of the caves.

That is where we are now, gone to earth like desert rabbits.

Sogdiam used to bring us grain from Jerusalem.

But Sogdiam died beneath his cart.

From time to time, former husbands have come at night to see their children and weep in their arms.

But many no longer had wives. They were either dead or in the arms of Gershem's men.

Sometimes, the former husbands came to see their rejected wives, caressing them in a way that recalled the time of their love.

Then they left.

In the minds and bodies of the women, these caresses, this love, disappeared, just as the memory of Antinoes has disappeared from the mind and body of Lilah.

For us, the rejected wives, I say and I write, "Time is dead."

Yahweh pushed us outside, and time, for us, is dead.

That is the truth as spoken by Lilah, daughter of Serayah.

What I, Lilah, am writing, no one will read. My words belong neither to the sages, nor the prophets, nor Ezra. They will vanish in the sand of the caves of Qumran.

But I write because this must be said: These women, these wives, were innocent.

Their children were not guilty.

This I write: The injustice of it will lie heavy on men until the end of time.

EPILOGUE

Just over a year after the foreign wives were expelled from Jerusalem, one of the inhabitants came looking for Ezra outside the Temple. It was after the evening offering.

"I have learned that your sister, Lilah, died yesterday," the man said.

Ezra stiffened, as if the only way he could grasp the man's words was to revive a memory he had long since dismissed from his mind.

Then he asked where she had died, and when he was told, he thanked the messenger and returned to his tasks. He had much to do at that time, for he was establishing one by one the names and responsibilities of the priests, the Levites, the Temple porters, the blowers of horns, and others still, as laid down since the reigns of David and Solomon.

But next morning, before dawn, he woke two of the young zealots.

"Come with me. My sister has died near the sea of Arabia.

She was no longer a woman of Jerusalem, but she was my sister. It is my duty to see that she is buried according to the Law. If I do not go, who will?"

They took mules and crossed the silent city. Trotting to gain time, so that they could be back before evening, they took the Bethany road and sped toward the plateau of red ash, salt, and stones that overlooks the vast, desolate valley surrounding the sea of Arabia.

As they approached the edge of the plateau, Ezra became aware of a strange buzzing. It was as if thousands and thousands of bees were moving over a field of flowers.

He frowned, anxiously, thinking perhaps that Yahweh was about to show him something unusual.

What he saw when he started on the path that descended toward the plain, what made him open his eyes and mouth wide, was a brightly colored carpet of human flowers, like that which he had seen, one day long ago, in front of the Water Gate in Jerusalem.

They were there, in their thousands. Not only the rejected wives and their children, but the men of the city. They were all there, chanting in unison as they buried his sister, Lilah, in the dust.

A vast multitude of men and women, children and old people, chanting in unison, without waiting for Ezra's permission, the words of Isaiah so beloved of Lilah:

> *Now I shall give her,*
> *like a river of peace,*
> *like a river in full spate,*
> *all the wealth of nations.*

Ezra's companions, surprised at the sight, came to a halt.

He continued alone along the path, his face impassive. Then he, too, stopped.

His hands shook. From the assembled crowd, the throb of the chant of Isaiah rose toward him. For a moment, it seemed to him as if his cheeks, hardened by fasting and the sun and wind of the desert, were being struck by the words. His eyes faltered as they swept over the throng.

In the chanting, so powerful that it made the stones of the cliff behind him vibrate, he thought he could hear Lilah's voice, her laughter, her explosions of anger.

He saw her place her palms on his as she used to do in the old days in Susa, a long, long time ago, when the three of them were together: Antinoes, Ezra, and Lilah.

He heard a voice whispering in his ear, "You are Ezra, my beloved brother. Go, lead your people back to Jerusalem! Rebuild the walls of the Temple!" And he caught himself replying, "Lilah! Are you trying to teach me wisdom?"

Tears he had never before wept ran down his cheeks. His tired body filled with shame. Without realizing it, he began running toward the crowd. Like the thousands assembled there, like the women expelled from Jerusalem, he chanted Isaiah's promise:

> *You will be like a child,*
> *Suckled at its mother's breast,*
> *Carried in her arms,*
> *Dandled on her knees.*
> *As a mother comforts her child,*
> *So I will comfort you . . .*

But no one paid him any heed.

About the Author

MAREK HALTER was born in Poland in 1936. During World War II, he and his parents narrowly escaped the Warsaw Ghetto. After a time in Russia and Uzbekistan, they emigrated to France in 1950. There Halter studied pantomime with Marcel Marceau and embarked on a career as a painter that led to several international exhibitions. In 1967 he founded the International Committee for a Negotiated Peace Agreement in the Near East and played a crucial role in the organization of the first official meetings between Palestinians and Israelis.

In the 1970s, Halter turned to writing. He first published *The Madman and the Kings*, which was awarded the Prix Aujourd'hui in 1976. He is also the author of several internationally acclaimed, bestselling historical novels, including *The Messiah*, *The Mysteries of Jerusalem*, and *The Book of Abraham*, which won the Prix du Livre Inter. His biblical novels, *Sarah*, *Zipporah*, and *Lilah*, have been published throughout the world. He lives in Paris.

LILAH

BY MAREK HALTER

A Reader's Group Guide

ABOUT THIS GUIDE

The Old Testament is brought to vivid life through the eyes of Lilah, a woman whose choice between loyalty to her brother and marriage to the man she loves will have a lasting impact on the fate of her people.

Living in exile in Susa, the ancient capital of the Persian Empire, Lilah is in love with Antinoes, a handsome Persian warrior. She wants to marry him but does not feel that she can do so without the blessing of her brother, Ezra, a high priest and a scholar of the laws of Moses. Such a blessing isn't likely to be forthcoming, because Lilah's brother does not want her to have a husband outside of their faith. Lilah believes it is her brother's destiny to lead the Jewish people back to the Promised Land after centuries in exile. Torn between her love for Antinoes and her belief in her brother, Lilah decides to delay her own happiness with Antinoes in order to help her brother lead their people back to Jerusalem—and in so doing, she comes face-to-face with a decision that will change her life forever.

Set in the magnificent ancient culture of the Middle East more than four thousand years ago, *Lilah* is a rich and emotionally resonant story of faith, love, and courage that raises questions of loyalty and tolerance that are more relevant today than ever.

The questions in this guide are intended as a framework for your group's discussion of *Lilah*.

QUESTIONS FOR DISCUSSION

1. Before you read this book, had you heard of Lilah? If so, what did you know about her? Why do you think Marek Halter chose to write the story of her life?

2. Why is Ezra's approval of Lilah's impending marriage so important to her? Why does she utterly refuse to marry without his blessing?

3. Why is Parysatis so cruel to Lilah? Do you think she targets her specifically for any reason, or is this behavior, as Lilah interprets it, just the game she plays? What do you see as driving her attacks?

4. Do you agree with Lilah's decision to give up her future with Antinoes? Would you have made the same choice, if faced with her dilemma? In the end, do you see her as a heroine or a martyr? Do you think, when all is said and done, her loyalty to Ezra and her people led her in the right direction, or did you question her choice to the very end?

5. Consider the characters of Axatria and Sogdiam. What roles do they play in the context of Lilah's story? How is each an influence on the life-changing decisions that she makes, and why do you think they make the choices that they do?

6. Discuss the ways that leadership and power are portrayed in this novel. We see many different approaches—from Parysatis's control that is held with intimidation and murder to the rule of Ezra in Jerusalem, and the leadership roles that Yahezya and Lilah finally take among the women and chil-

dren who are cast out. What do you think is the strongest and most effective leader we see, and why? To what degree does each of them serve the people beneath them well, and to what degree do they fall short?

7. What lasting impact on Ezra's life does Master Baruch have? And Lilah's? Why do you think that it is Lilah who seems to be a more willing recipient of the messages the teacher tries to impart to his pupil?

8. We see many forms of exclusion in this novel: the Jews are a people apart from the Persians, women are kept separate from men, servants exist on a different plane than those they live among and work for. Each group chooses to define itself with a different set of criteria. What do you think of the issues this raises? To what degree is this separateness integral to identity, both in Lilah's world and now, and what dangers does it create? Where is the line between guarding identity and exclusion?

9. From where does Lilah draw her strength and her conviction? Does this change throughout the course of the novel, or is it constant throughout?

10. Ezra's studies of the laws of Moses bring him to a strict interpretation of God's will, as defined in the writings that later became part of the Old Testament that we know. But Lilah, and many others, vehemently disagree with this kind of literalism. In what ways does this debate resonate today, and what do you think of the issue of the letter of the law versus the spirit of the law? If the holy writings Ezra studies are the only way he has of knowing his God and they lead him astray, where else can he turn?

11. What do you think is the gravest mistake that Ezra makes? What did you see as the turning point for him? Is there a moment that he could have gone another way and chooses not to?

12. One of the main themes in *Lilah* is that of home, of family, and of connectedness. Discuss the places you see this theme explored in the novel, and in the end, what the meaning of family is in this context.

13. At a certain point, Lilah stops writing to Antinoes and admits that she has given up hope that he will ever receive her letters. But she continues writing nonetheless. What is the significance of this shift for her, and why do you think she continues to write even though she admits that in all probability, no one will ever read her words?

14. Why does Ezra not waver in his conviction to cut off the women and children who have left the city, even after Lilah joins them? Why is love for his sister and the pain of the husbands and fathers that have been left behind not enough to show him the folly of his ways, and why does he seem to grow only more cruel to the outsiders as time goes on?

15. What do you make of Lilah's chilling final words in this novel: "The injustice of it will lie heavy on men until the end of time." (p. 233)? To what degree do you agree with this statement? Have we moved past the kind of thinking that caused the pain and bloodshed Lilah witnessed? What other events in history, if any, does her story remind you of?

16. Does Ezra's emotion at his sister's death ring true to you? Do you think the realization that he had wronged and forgotten

her, and with her, his own better nature, will have an impact on the way he governs in the future? From what you have seen of his character, is he capable of changing, or of ruling justly without the guidance of another?

17. Discuss the three epigraphs that Halter uses at the opening of *Lilah*. What do you think of each individually, and what is he saying by juxtaposing the three?

Read an excerpt from the book that started it all.

SARAH

THE STUNNING FIRST NOVEL IN MAREK HALTER'S
BESTSELLING CANAAN TRILOGY

Sarah, the daughter of a powerful Sumerian lord, balks at the arranged marriage her father has planned for her. She flees to the vast, empty marshes beyond the city walls. There she meets a young man, Abram, a member of a nomadic tribe of outsiders. Many years later, Sarah and Abram meet again. The rebellious girl from the marsh has been transformed into the high priestess of the goddess Ishtar. Abram is a leader of his people, and he follows an invisible deity who speaks only to him. Sarah gives up her exalted life to join Abram's tribe and follow his one true God. It is then that her true journey begins—a journey that leads to her destiny as the mother of nations.

From the towering gardens and immense wealth of the ancient Sumerians to the great ziggurat of Ishtar, from the fertile valleys of Canaan to the bedchamber of the mighty Pharaoh himself, *Sarah* is a dazzling novel that reveals an ancient world full of beauty, intrigue, and miracles.

The Bridal Blood

Sarai clumsily pushed aside the curtain that hung in the doorway and ran to the middle of the brick terrace that overlooked the women's courtyard. Dawn was breaking, and there was just enough light for her to see the blood on her hands. She closed her eyes to hold back the tears.

She did not need to look down to know that her tunic was stained. She could feel the fine woolen cloth sticking wetly to her thighs and knees.

Here it was again! A sharp pain, like a demon's claw moving between her hips! She stood frozen, her eyes half closed. The pain faded as suddenly as it had come.

Sarai held out her soiled hands in front of her. She should have implored Inanna, the almighty Lady of Heaven, but no word passed her lips. She was petrified. Fear, disgust, and denial mingled in her mind.

Only a moment ago, she had woken suddenly, her belly ringed

with pain, and put her hands between her thighs. Into this blood that was flowing out of her for the first time. The bridal blood. The blood that creates life.

It had not come as she had been promised it would. It was not like dew or honey. It flowed as if from an invisible wound. In a moment of panic, she had seen herself being emptied of blood like an ewe under the sacrificial knife.

She had reacted like a silly child, and now she felt ashamed. But her terror had been so great that she had sat up moaning on her bed and rushed outside.

Now, in the growing light of day, she looked at her blood-stained hands as if they did not belong to her. Something strange was happening in her body, something that had obliterated her happy childhood at a stroke.

Tomorrow, and the day after tomorrow, and all the days and years to come, would be different. She knew what awaited her. What awaited every girl in whom the bridal blood flowed. Her handmaid Sililli and all the other women in the household would laugh. They would dance and sing and give thanks to Nintu, the Midwife of the World.

But Sarai felt no joy. At that moment, she wished her body was someone else's.

She took a deep breath. The smell of the night fires floating in the cool air of early morning calmed her a little. The coolness of the bricks beneath her bare feet did her good. There was no noise in the house or the gardens. Not even the flight of a bird. The whole city seemed to be holding its breath, waiting for the sun to burst forth. For the moment it was still hidden on the other side of the world, but the ocher light that preceded it was spreading over the horizon like oil.

Abruptly Sarai turned and went back through the curtain into her bedchamber. In the dim light, it was just possible to make out the big bedstead where Nisaba and Lillu lay sleeping. Without moving, Sarai listened to her sisters' regular breathing. At least she had not woken them.

She advanced cautiously to her own bed. She wanted to sit down, but hesitated.

She thought of the advice Sililli had given her. Change your tunic, take off the sheet, roll the soiled straw in it, go to the door and take some balls of wool dipped in sweet oil, wash your thighs and genitals with them, then take some other balls, scented with essence of terebinth, and use them to absorb the blood. All she had to do was perform a few simple actions. But she couldn't. She didn't know why, but she couldn't bear even the thought of touching herself.

Anger was beginning to replace fear. What if Nisaba and Lillu discovered her and roused the whole household, crying out across the men's courtyard, "Sarai is bleeding, Sarai has the bridal blood!"

That would be the most disgusting thing of all.

Why did the blood running between her thighs make her more adult? Why, at the same time as she gained the freedom to speak, was she going to lose the freedom to act? For that was what was going to happen. Now, in exchange for a few silver shekels or a few measures of barley, her father could give her to a man. A stranger she might have to hate for the rest of her days. Why did things have to happen that way? Why not another way?

Sarai tried hard to dismiss this chaos of thoughts, this mixture of sadness and anger, but she couldn't. She couldn't even remember a single word of the prayers Sililli had taught her. It was as if a demon had banished them from her heart and mind. Lady Moon would be furious. She would send down a curse on her.

Anger and denial swept through her again. She couldn't stay here in the dark. But she didn't want to wake Sililli. Once Sililli took charge, things would really start.

She had to flee. To flee beyond the wall that enclosed the city, perhaps as far as the bend in the Euphrates, where the labyrinth of the lower city and the reedy lagoons stretched over dozens of *ùs*. That was another world, a fascinating but hostile world, and Sarai wasn't brave enough to go there. Instead, she took refuge in the huge garden, which was full of a hundred kinds of trees and flowers and vegetables and surrounded by a wall that in places was higher than the highest rooms. She hid in a tamarisk grove clinging to the oldest part of the wall, where sun, wind, and rain had, in places, dissolved the stack of bricks and reduced it to a hard ocher dust. When the tamarisks were in bloom, their huge pink flowers spread like luxuriant hair over the wall and could be seen clear across the city. They had become the distinguishing feature of the house of Ichbi Sum-Usur, son of Ella Dum-tu, Lord of Ur, merchant and high-ranking official in the service of King Amar-Sin, who ruled the empire of Ur by the will of almighty Ea.

ןׂ ןׂ ןׂ

"SARAI! Sarai!!"

She recognized the voices: Lillu's piercing shriek and Sililli's more muted and anxious tones. Some of the handmaids had already searched the garden, but finding nothing, had gone away again.

Silence returned, except for the murmur of the water flowing in the irrigation channels and the chirping of the birds.

From where she was, Sarai could see everything but could not be seen. Her father's house was one of the most beautiful in the royal city. It was shaped like a hand enclosing a huge rectangular central courtyard, which was reached through the main entrance. At either end, the courtyard was separated by two green-and-yellow brick buildings, open only for receptions and celebrations, and by two smaller courtyards, the women's and the men's. The men's quarters, with their white staircases, overhung the temple of the family's ancestors, the storehouses, and the room where her father's scribes worked, while the women's chambers were built above the kitchens, the handmaids' dormitories, and the chamber of blood. Both opened onto a broad terrace, shaded by bowers of vines and wisteria, with a view of the gardens. The terrace allowed the men to join the women at night without having to cross the courtyards.

From her grove, Sarai could also see a large part of the city, and, towering over it like a mountain, the ziggurat, the Sublime Platform. Not a day went by that she did not come here to admire the gardens of the ziggurat. They were a lake of foliage between earth and sky, full of every flower and every tree the gods had sown on the earth. From this riot of greenery emerged the steps, covered in black-and-white ceramics, that led up to the Sublime Bedchamber, with its lapis lazuli columns and walls. There, once a year, the king of Ur was united with the Lady of Heaven.

Today, though, she had eyes only for what was happening in the house. Everything seemed to have calmed down. Sarai had the impression they had stopped searching for her. When the handmaids had appeared earlier in the garden, she had been tempted to join them. But now it was too late for her to leave her hiding place. With every hour that passed, she was more at fault. If anyone saw her in this state, they would scream with fright and turn away, shielding their eyes as if they had seen a woman possessed by demons. It was unthinkable that she could show herself like this to the women. It would be a blemish on her father's house. She had to stay here and wait until nightfall. Only then could she perform her ablutions in the garden's irrigation basin. After that, she would go and ask Sililli for forgiveness. With enough tears, and enough terror in her voice, to mollify her.

Until then she had to forget her thirst and the heat that was gradually transforming the still air into a strange miasma of dry dust.

צצצ

SHE stiffened when she heard the shouts.

"Sarai! Answer me, Sarai! I know you're there! Do you want to die today, with the shame of the gods on you?"

She recognized the thick calves, the yellow-and-white tunic with its black border instantly.

"Sililli?"

"Who else were you expecting?" the handmaid retorted, in an angry whisper.

"How did you manage to find me?"

Sililli took a few steps back. "Stop your chattering," she said, lowering her voice even more, "and come out of there right now before anyone sees you."

"You mustn't look at me," Sarai warned.

She emerged from the copse, straightening up with difficulty, her muscles aching from her long immobility.

Sililli stifled a cry. "Forgive her, almighty Ea! Forgive her!"

Sarai did not dare look Sililli in the face. She stared down at her short, round shadow on the ground, and saw her raise her arms to heaven then hug them to her bosom.

"Almighty Lady of Heaven," Sililli muttered, in a choked voice, "forgive me for having seen her soiled face and hands! She is only a child, holy Inanna. Nintu will soon purify her."

Sarai restrained herself from rushing into the handmaid's arms. "I'm so sorry," she said, in a barely audible whisper. "I didn't do as you told me to. I couldn't."

She did not have time to say more. A linen sheet was flung over her, covering her from head to foot, and Sililli's hands clasped her waist. Now Sarai no longer needed to hold back, and she leaned against the firm, fleshy body of the woman who had not only been her nurse, but had also been like a mother to her.

"Yes, you silly little thing," Sililli whispered in her ear through the linen, the anger gone from her voice, the tremor of fear still there, "I've known about this hiding place for a long time. Since the first time you came here! Did you think you could escape your old Sililli? In the name of almighty Ea, what possessed you? Did you think you could hide from the sacred laws of Ur? To go where? To remain at fault your whole life? Oh, my little girl! Why didn't you come to see me? Do you think you're the first to be afraid of the bridal blood?"

Sarai wanted to say something to justify herself, but Sililli placed a hand on her mouth.

"No! You can tell me everything later. Nobody must see us here. Great Ea! Who knows what would happen if you were seen like this? Your aunts already know you've become a woman. They're waiting for you in the chamber of blood. Don't be afraid, they won't scold if you arrive before the sun goes down. I've brought you a pitcher of lemon water and terebinth bark so you can wash your hands and face. Now throw your soiled tunic under the tamarisk. I'll come back later to burn it. Wrap yourself in this linen veil. Make sure you avoid your sisters, or nobody will be able to stop those pests from going and telling your father everything."

Sarai felt Sililli's hand stroking her cheek through the cloth.

"Do what I ask of you. And hurry up about it. Your father must know nothing of your escapade."

"Sililli."

"What now?" Sililli said.

"Will you be there, too? In the chamber of blood, I mean."

"Of course. Where else should I be?"

יְיָיְ

WASHED and scented, her linen veil knotted over her left shoulder, Sarai reached the women's courtyard without meeting a soul.

She had gathered all her courage to approach the mysterious door she had never gone anywhere near.

From the outside, the chamber of blood was nothing but a long white wall with no windows that took up almost the entire space below the quarters reserved for the women: Ichbi's wife, sisters, daughters, female relatives, and handmaids. The door was cleverly concealed by a cane portico covered with a luxuriant ocher-flowered bignonia, so that it was possible to cross the women's courtyard in all directions without ever seeing it.

Sarai went through the portico. Before her was a small double door of thick cedarwood, the bottom half painted blue and the top half red: the door of the chamber of blood.

Sarai had only a few steps to take to open this door. But she did not move. Invisible threads were holding her back. Was it fear?

Like all girls her age, she had heard many stories about the chamber of blood. Like all girls her age, she knew that once a month women went and shut themselves in there for seven days. During full moons, they would gather there to make vows and petitions that could be said nowhere else. It was a place where women laughed, wept, ate honey and cakes and fruit, shared their dreams and secrets—and sometimes died in agony. Occasionally, through the thick walls, Sarai had heard the screams of a woman in labor. She had seen women go in there, happy with their big bellies, and not come out again. No men ever entered, or even tried to peer inside. Anyone curious or foolhardy enough to do so would carry the stain of their offense down with them to the hell of Ereshkigal.

But in truth, she knew very little of what went on there. She had heard the most absurd rumors, whispered by her sisters and cousins. *Unopened girls* did not know what happened to those who entered the chamber of blood for the first time, and none of the *munus,* the *opened women,* ever divulged the secret.

Her day had come. Who could go against the will of the gods?

Sililli was right. It was time. She could not remain at fault any longer. She must have the courage to open that door.

צ י י

HER eyes, dazzled by the bright daylight outside, took some time to accustom themselves to the darkness. A mixture of strong odors floated in the enclosed air. Some she recognized: the scent of almond and orange peel oils, the smell of sesame oil, which was used in lamps. After a moment, she noticed another smell— thicker, slightly nauseating—that she had never smelled before.

Shadows took shape within the shadows, figures moved. The chamber of blood was not completely dark. A dozen candles in brass disks diffused a yellow, flickering brightness. The chamber was both larger and higher than Sarai had imagined, with other, smaller rooms off to the sides. The brick floor was cooled by a narrow channel of clear water. At the far end, the gentle murmur of a fountain could be heard.

A handclap made Sarai jump. There before her were three of her aunts, and behind them, standing slightly to one side, Sililli and two young handmaids. They all wore white togas with broad black stripes, and their hair was held in place by dark-colored headscarfs. They were smiling affectionately.

Her aunt Egime, the eldest of her father's sisters, took a step forward. She clapped again, then folded her arms over her chest, keeping her palms open. Sililli handed her a pottery pitcher filled with scented water, and with a graceful gesture Egime plunged her hand in it and sprinkled Sarai.

> Nintu, mistress of the menstrual blood,
> Nintu, you who decide on life in the wombs of women,
> Nintu, beloved patroness of childbearing, welcome Sarai,
> daughter of Taram and Ichbi, Lord of Ur, into this chamber. She

*is here to purify herself, and to entrust her first blood to you. She
is here to become pure and clean again for the bed of childbirth!*

After this prayer of welcome, the other women clapped three
times, then took turns throwing the scented water over Sarai,
until her face and shoulders were streaming. The scent was
strong, so strong that it penetrated her nostrils and her throat,
making her feel slightly intoxicated.

When the pitcher was empty, the women surrounded Sarai,
took her hands, and pulled her into one of the alcoves, where a
high, round, narrow basin stood. Sililli untied her linen veil, and she
was pushed naked into the basin. It was deeper than she had supposed: The freezing water reached to just below her barely formed
breasts. Sarai shivered, and hugged herself in a childish gesture.
The women laughed. They emptied phials into the water, then
rubbed her vigorously with little linen bags filled with herbs. The
air was filled with new scents. This time, Sarai recognized mint and
terebinth, as well as the curious smell of weasel bile, sometimes
used for smearing the feet as a protection against demons.

The oil softened the water. Sarai became accustomed to its
coolness. She closed her eyes and relaxed, and soon, the tension
and the fear faded under all the rubbing and stroking.

No sooner was she used to it than Egime was already ordering her out of the bath. Without wiping her, or covering her with
even a small cloth, Egime led Sarai to another part of the room,
where a brightly colored carpet had been rolled out. She made
her stand with her legs apart and placed a wide-necked bronze
vase between her thighs. Sililli took Sarai's hand. Egime, her eyes
fixed on the vase, started speaking in a loud voice.

*Nintu, patroness of childbirth, you who received the sa-
cred brick of childbearing from the hands of almighty Enki,
you who hold the scissors to cut the birth cord,*

Nintu, you who received the green lazulite vase, the sila-garra, from almighty Enki, gather the blood of Sarai.

Make sure that it is fertile.

Nintu, gather the blood of Sarai like dew in a furrow. Make sure that it is making its honey. O, Nintu, sister of Enlil the First, make sure that Sarai's vulva is fertile and as soft as a Dilum date and that her future husband never tires of it!

A strange silence followed.

Sarai could feel her heart beating against her temples and in her throat. The skin on her legs, buttocks, shoulders, belly, and forehead was beginning to prickle with heat, as though it had been stung with nettles.

Then, in the same sharp, commanding voice, her old aunt repeated the prayer. This time, the other aunts recited it in unison with her.

Once finished, they started all over again.

Sarai realized that this would continue until her blood ran into the bronze vase.

The ceremony seemed to go on for ever. With each word that Egime uttered, Sililli's hand squeezed Sarai's fingers. All at once, a cold pain froze her back and thighs. She was ashamed of her own nakedness and the position she was in. Why was it taking so long? Why was the blood taking so much time to flow now, when only this morning it had been flowing so abundantly?

The prayer was repeated twenty times. Finally, the water was tinged with red. The women applauded. Egime seized Sarai's face between her rough fingers and planted her lips on her brow.

"Well done, child! Twenty prayers, that's a good number. Nintu likes you. You should be pleased and thank her." She took the bronze vase and placed it in Sarai's hands. "Follow me," she ordered.

At the far end of the chamber of blood, against a red-and-blue mud wall, stood a terra-cotta statue, taller than Sarai. It was

a statue of a woman with a round face and thick lips, her curly
hair held in place by a metal ring. In one of her hands she held a
tiny vase, identical to the one that Sarai was carrying. With the
other hand, she held high the scissors of birth. The altar below
the statue was covered with food, as if laid for a feast.

"Nintu, Midwife of the World," Egime whispered, her head
bowed, "Sarai, daughter of Taram and Ichbi, salutes you and
thanks you."

Sarai looked at her, uncomprehending. With an irritated pout,
Egime seized her right hand, dipped her fingers in the blood, and
rubbed them over the belly of the statue.

"Now you do it," she ordered.

Pursing her lips in disgust, Sarai obeyed. Egime then took the
bronze vase and poured a few drops of menstrual blood into the
small dish held by the statue of Nintu. When she stood up again,
her face was wreathed with a big smile, quite a change from her
usual expression.

"Welcome to the chamber of blood, daughter of my brother.
Welcome among us, future *munus!* If I've understood Sililli's
muddled explanations correctly, it seems you haven't eaten since
this morning. You must be hungry."

There was a great burst of laughter behind Sarai. It was Sililli.
Sarai let herself be drawn into her arms, finding it surprisingly
comforting to lay her head on her handmaid's ample bosom.

"You see," Sililli whispered, with a touch of reproach in her
voice, "it wasn't so terrible. It wasn't worth making so much fuss
over."

THAT evening, before her meal—cakes and fruit and barley and
honey biscuits and fresh ewes' cheese—she was given a new tunic,
a fine linen tunic with black stripes, like the one worn by her aunts

and the handmaids, and a shawl for her hair. Then the women taught her what to do when her periods came: how to make little wool tampons dipped in a special oil, the one whose strong, slightly disagreeable odor had greeted her when she first opened the door.

"It's olive oil," Egime explained. "A rare and precious oil produced by the *mar.Tu,* the men with no city. You can thank your father for that: He has it brought for the king's wives and sets a few amphoras aside for us. When there's none left, we use flatfish oil. Believe me, that's much less sweet and really stinks. After we've used that, we have to soak our buttocks in cypress oil for a whole day. Otherwise, when our men come to our beds, they might think our vulvae have turned into fishing baskets!"

The joke was greeted with gales of laughter. Finally, Sililli explained to her how to fold the linen that she had to wrap around the area between her thighs.

"You must change it every night before going to bed and wash it the next day. I'll show you the sink, at the other end of the chamber."

In fact, the chamber of blood contained everything women might need during their seven days of confinement: comfortable beds, plenty of food—fruit, meat, cheese, cakes—supplied by women from outside, and lots to do. There were baskets overflowing with spun wool, and weaving frames full of work in progress.

As Sililli was only there because of Sarai's initiation, she could not spend the night. Before she returned to the women's courtyard, she prepared an herb tea, which she gave to Sarai in a steaming goblet.

"That way you won't have a stomachache tonight," she said, kissing Sarai gently on the head. "Now, I'm not allowed back in here until twilight tomorrow. If anything's the matter, just ask Aunt Egime. I know she's a bit abrupt, but you can see how much she loves you."

She must have put something else in the drink besides herbs

for the stomach, for not long after she had left, Sarai fell into a deep sleep untroubled by dreams.

When she woke, her aunts and the handmaids were already busy, weaving with just as much dexterity in the semidarkness as they would in broad daylight, chattering all the while like birds, and only breaking off to laugh or to swap good-natured jibes.

Egime ordered Sarai to thank Nintu and offer some food on her altar. Then Sarai washed herself in the basin, while a handmaid poured oils into the water and smeared her belly and thighs with a scented pomade.

When she was clean, Egime asked if she was still bleeding regularly. After that, Sarai had a breakfast of ewes' milk, slightly curdled cow's cheese mixed with honey, and barley bread soaked in meat juice and spread with crushed dates, apricots, and peaches.

But just as she was about to help with the weaving, and to learn how to pass the spindles between the thinnest threads, her young aunts approached, bearing a tall sheet of bronze.

Sarai, surprised, looked at them uncomprehendingly.

"Take off your tunic, we're going to tell you what you look like."

"What I look like?"

"Exactly. You're going to look at yourself naked in the mirror and we'll tell you what your future husband will see when he puts the marriage ointment on you."

These words sent a chill through Sarai far greater than the morning's bath. She glanced at Egime. Without interrupting her work, her old aunt nodded and smiled, with a smile as imposing as a command.

Sarai gave a disdainful shrug, though she was far from feeling as calm as she pretended. She regretted the fact that Sililli wasn't here. If she had been, her young aunts would never have dared to mock her.

With an abrupt movement, she took off her tunic. While the

women sat down around her, chuckling, she tried to appear as indifferent as she could.

"Turn around slowly," one of the aunts ordered, "so that we can see you properly."

Her moving figure was reflected in the bronze mirror, though she could hardly see herself in the dim light.

Egime was the first to comment on the spectacle. "The bridal blood may be flowing from her womb, but the fact is, she's still only a child. If her bridegroom wants to taste her honey cake as soon as he puts the ointment on her, he's going to be disappointed."

"I'm only twelve years and two seasons old," Sarai protested, feeling hot with anger. "Of course I'm a child."

"But her thighs are slim and well shaped," one of the handmaids said. "She's going to have beautiful legs, I'm sure of it."

"She'll always have small feet," another said, "and small hands, too. That should be quite graceful."

"Is a husband interested in his wife's feet and hands the day he puts the ointment on her?" Egime muttered.

"But look at her buttocks, sister. He'll have his money's worth there. See how high and hard they are. Like golden little gourds. What husband could resist taking a bite of those? And the dimple at the top. I tell you, sisters, in a year or two, her husband will get plenty of milk to drink there."

"Her belly's quite nice, too," the youngest of the aunts said, "and her skin as delicate as you could wish. A real pleasure to pass your palm over it."

"Lift your arms, Sarai!" another ordered. "What a pity, sisters! Our niece's arms are less graceful than her legs."

"She has elbows like a goose, but they'll do. The shoulders are pretty. I'd say they're going to be broad. What do you think, Egime?"

"Big shoulders, big breasts, that's what they say. I've seen that dozens of times."

They all burst out laughing.

"For now, though, the bridegroom won't have anything to get his teeth into!"

"But they're coming out, they're taking shape."

"Hardly! You can see her bones more clearly than her breasts."

"Yours weren't much bigger at her age," Egime said to her younger sister, "and look at them now: We have to weave you double-length tunics to cover them!"

They laughed again, not even noticing that tears were running down Sarai's cheeks into her mouth, she wiped them away with her wrist.

"What the groom definitely won't see, the day of the ointment, is the sweet forest. Not even a shadow! He'll have to be content with the furrow and, in my opinion, wait for the field to grow before he can plow it!"

"Enough!" cried Sarai, kicking over the bronze mirror and covering herself with her tunic.

"Sarai!" Egime roared.

"I won't listen to any more of your wicked comments! I don't need anyone to tell me I'm beautiful, and I'll be even more beautiful when I've grown up. I'll be more beautiful than all of you. You're all jealous, that's what you are!"

"Proud and snake-tongued, that's what *you* are!" Egime replied. "If your bridegroom doesn't pull a long face when he sees you, he will when he hears you. I hope my brother Ichbi has made careful plans. I wouldn't like him to get a rejection."

"My father hasn't decided to get me married. Why do you keep saying that? I have no bridegroom. You're all old and you're saying stupid things!"

She had almost screamed the last words. They echoed off the damp walls of the chamber of blood and subsided to the brick floor. The laughter ceased, and there was an embarrassed silence.

"How do you know you have no bridegroom?" Egime asked, with an even deeper frown.

A shiver ran through Sarai. The fear that had knotted her stomach the day before had returned.

"My father has told me nothing," she breathed. "He always tells me what he wants me to do."

Her aunts and the handmaids averted their eyes.

"Your father has no need to tell you about things that happen as they should," Egime retorted.

"Yes, my father tells me everything. I'm his favorite daughter—"

Sarai broke off. She had only to speak the words to realize what a lie they were.

Egime let out a brief sigh. "Childish nonsense! Don't invent something that isn't real! The laws of the city and the will of almighty Ea must be respected. You'll stay with us for four days, and on the seventh you'll leave the chamber of blood and be prepared for your wedding. The month of plowing is a good month for it. There will be meals and chanting. The man who is to be your husband must already be on his way to Ur. I'm sure your father has chosen someone rich and powerful. You'll have no cause for complaint. By the next moon, he will have put the ointment of cypress on you. That is what will happen. That is how it must be."

Also by Marek Halter

THE CANAAN TRILOGY BEGINS WITH TWO OF THE OLD TESTAMENT'S MOST UNFORGETTABLE WOMEN.

In the Sumerian city-state of Ur, Sarah, the daughter of a powerful lord, finds herself drawn to an exotic stranger named Abram. When she gives up her exalted life to join Abram's tribe and follow the one true God, it is then that her journey truly begins. From the great ziggurat of Ishtar to the fertile valleys of Canaan to the bedchamber of the mighty Pharaoh himself, Sarah's story reveals an ancient world full of beauty, intrigue, and miracles.

SARAH • $12.95 paper (Canada: $17.95) • 978-1-4000-5278-3

Although she is a Cushite by birth—one of the people of the lands to the south—Zipporah grew up among the Midianites. But the color of Zipporah's skin sets her apart, making her an outsider to the men of her adopted tribe, who do not want her as a wife. Then one day while drawing water from a well, she meets a handsome young stranger. A Hebrew raised in the house of the Egyptian Pharaoh, Moses is a fugitive, forced to flee his homeland. Zipporah realizes that this man will be the husband and partner she never thought she would have.

ZIPPORAH, WIFE OF MOSES • $13.95 paper (Canada: $18.95) 978-1-4000-5280-6

THREE RIVERS PRESS • NEW YORK

Available from Three Rivers Press wherever books are sold